the
JESUS COW

HARPER

An Imprint of HarperCollins*Publishers*

the JESUS COW

a novel

MICHAEL PERRY

THE JESUS COW. Copyright © 2015 by Michael Perry. All rights reserved. Printed in the United States of America. No part of this book may be used or reproduced in any manner whatsoever without written permission except in the case of brief quotations embodied in critical articles and reviews. For information, address HarperCollins Publishers, 195 Broadway, New York, NY 10007.

HarperCollins books may be purchased for educational, business, or sales promotional use. For information, please e-mail the Special Markets Department at SPsales@harpercollins.com.

Lyrical quotation in chapter 29 excerpted from the poem "On Listening to the Two-Headed Lady Blow Her Horn," from *The Gospel of Barbecue* by Honorée Fanonne Jeffers, the Kent State University Press. Copyright © 2000 by Honorée Fanonne Jeffers. Reprinted with permission.

"After the Fall" lyrics by Ray Wylie Hubbard (Snake Farm Publishing Administered by BMG/Chrysalis). Used with permission.

"There Are Some Days" (paraphrased) lyrics by Ray Wylie Hubbard (Snake Farm Publishing Administered by BMG/Chrysalis). Used with permission.

FIRST EDITION

Designed by Michael Correy

Library of Congress Cataloging-in-Publication Data is available upon request.

ISBN: 978-0-06-228991-9

15 16 17 18 19   OV/RRD   10 9 8 7 6 5 4 3 2 1

For the quiet ones.

After the fall
There is love after all

—RAY WYLIE HUBBARD

the
JESUS COW

PROLOGUE

O n Christmas Eve itself, the bachelor Harley Jackson stepped into his barn and beheld there illuminated in the straw a smallish newborn bull calf upon whose flank was borne the very image of Our Lord and Savior Jesus Christ.

"Well," said Harley, "that's trouble."

PART

ONE

CHAPTER 1

There is no better vantage point from which to survey the village of Swivel, Wisconsin, than from the tip-top of its historic water tower. Carolyn Sawchuck has made the climb every Christmas Eve for five years running. Right about the time Harley Jackson was discovering his surprising calf, Carolyn was reclining against the vent cap that crowned the tower. Reaching into her backpack, she withdrew a slender thermos and poured herself a steaming capful of EarthHug tea. Then she settled in for a look around.

The water tower—a classic witch-hatted four-legger—stands on an elevated patch of land tucked within the armpit angle formed by the interstate off-ramp and County Road M. The rare visitor who chooses to exit the freeway and follow the gentle decline of County Road M into the dwindled heart of Swivel itself will be greeted by an outdated and optimistic green-and-white population sign declaring 562 citizens, when in fact a real estate death spiral and lack of local industry has drained the census well below that. There was a time when the state two-lane ran smack through town and on holiday weekends the burg could muster up a bustle, but when the bulldozers pushed the new four-lane through they bypassed Swivel and left it to wither.

And yet, life persists. Across the road, the halogen-lit Kwik Pump is open 24 hours a day, 365 days a year. Even now, near midnight on Christmas Eve, its logo glows against the sky on a long-stemmed sign visible from the interstate, advertising the only local attraction capable of convincing tourists to switch off the cruise control and visit—and even then only for as long as it takes to top off the tank. Over the years the Kwik Pump had displaced all four of Swivel's gas stations, two of its three cafés, and the last lingering grocery. There had been a lot of grumbling, but these days the grumblers filled their tanks and stood in line with everyone else for lottery tickets, loss-leader milk, and heat-lamped breakfast burritos.

Just past the Kwik Pump was a small trailer court, then St. Jude's Catholic Church. Then came the railroad tracks, after which County Road M widened out into Main Street, which wore on its flanks the older, larger houses; the Solid Savings Bank; the Sunrise Café; the old Farmers Store (long since closed and converted to apartments); a former Laundromat now serving as Reverend Gary's Church of the Roaring Lamb; and, at the intersection of Center Street and Main, the Buck Rub Bar. The elementary and high schools stood in a field at the far dead end of Main (County Road M hung a left and continued into the country), and the northernmost and southernmost borders of Swivel were marked by the respective steeple-mounted and fluorescent-lit crosses of the Lutheran and Methodist churches.

The first time Carolyn Sawchuck climbed the water tower she hadn't been sightseeing—she'd been trying to solve a problem. To that end, her backpack contained bolt cutters, a headlamp, a can of WD-40, Vise-Grips, miscellaneous wire and pliers, a mini-crowbar, and a fat coil of oil-resistant hose. The weight was considerable, and halfway up the ladder she had to stop and catch her breath. Three-quarters of the way up, her quadriceps felt as if they'd been marinating in napalm. At the catwalk, she dared to look down and her breath departed with such force she feared she would be found frozen to the railing come dawn. But the problem had to be addressed. So she had pulled out the bolt cutters, snipped the padlock on the climbing guard, gone headfirst into the safety cage, and, rung by knuckle-whitening rung, climbed to the very summit.

Carolyn chose to make her initial climb on Christmas Eve for one primary reason: to avoid detection. Daylight hours were a nonstarter, obviously. An outsider might have chosen the dead-of-night wee hours, but Carolyn knew Constable Benson whiled away the night shift making slow passes through town with regular loops back to the Kwik Pump for coffee refills and chitchat with whoever was running the register. While he was no crack invigilator, there was still a chance he might sweep the old water tower with his spotlight out of habit (more than one drunken Buck Rub patron had tried to scale the tower after closing time, and spray-paint-toting high schoolers also, although this was most likely to occur during homecoming week) and catch Carolyn halfway up or down. In this regard, Christmas Eve just prior to midnight offered several advantages. Nearly everyone in town was either asleep, groggily eggnogged, or rushing to make midnight mass. And rather than making small talk at the Kwik Pump or cruising quiet streets, Constable Benson would be at the corner of Elm and Main with his vintage radar gun, picking off speeding Catholics.

She'd been terribly worried about getting caught that first time. Fearing a winking headlamp would betray her, she worked by feel, spritzing WD-40 over the rusted hinges of the vent cap before prying it open with the crowbar. Then she clipped the lamp to the rim of the vent opening so it illuminated the tank interior but was not visible from below. Next she pulled out the hose, one end of which was clamped to a short length of PVC pipe plumbed in the shape of a "T." The other end was duct-taped to a corn-cob size bolt of steel rebar, which she fed into the overflow tube that ran down the center column to ground level. The weight of the rebar drew the hose downward and kept it from kinking; when it hit bottom, Carolyn dropped the rest of the hose and the PVC "T" inside the tank. Then she extinguished the headlamp, replaced the cap, and—with great relief—turned to descend.

What she saw below surprised her.

Carolyn Sawchuck was not from this town. Never would be, by the standards of some locals. She had arrived out of the blue, and if not against her wishes then arguably against all she had hoped for. Certainly the trajectory of her first forty years—overachieving student, social activist, published author, and ensconced academic— had given no indication that she might land atop some podunk water tower. Her integration with Swivel's populace hadn't gone smoothly and remained incomplete. But on that first Christmas Eve, as she prepared to climb down, she had been caught off guard by what she saw spread before her: a modest grid of low-key streetlights casting a vaporous glow across the settlement as a whole—everything softened by drapings of snow, the stained-glass windows of St. Jude's illuminated from within, a twinkling sprinkle of Christmas lights salted throughout. There was something in the perspective that softened her view of Swivel. Carolyn Sawchuck was not pliable in any sense. But she sensed the value of this calibration.

And so it became tradition that her annual surreptitious Christmas Eve climb culminated with a cup of tea at midnight as Carolyn looked over the town that somehow, despite its bad luck, looked beautiful, and despite her best intentions, she had come to think of as home.

Sipping her tea, Carolyn considered the structure beneath her. It hadn't held water for years now, having been decommissioned in favor of a modern spheroidal model. By rotating ever so carefully upon her perch, Carolyn could see the new tower, well lit and shiny on the opposite side of the interstate where it stood on higher ground amidst a haphazard scatter of houses known as Clover Blossom Estates. At its very top a blue Christmas star glowed and an American flag waved. Unlike the old tower, which was silver and bore the name of Swivel in simple black block letters, the new tower was painted in the school colors of green and gold with blaze orange accents.

Carolyn shook her head. She far preferred the original tower. It had once been her dream to restore it, but these days it stood unadorned and unlit, and it was showing worrying wear. Her gloves had snagged on more than one rusty rung on the way up tonight, and she noted that when she lifted the vent cap, the hinges were stiffer than ever.

The first year Carolyn looked inside the tank, it was dead empty.

The second year, a small black puddle was visible within the bowl-shaped base. Now, five years later, the tower was far from full, but when she shone her carefully shielded headlamp inside she saw the black puddle had grown, rising to touch the sides of the tank.

That black puddle was Carolyn Sawchuck's greatest secret.

THE TEA WAS cooling quickly in the cold air. As water towers go, the old Swivel tower wasn't all that tall. Forty feet from base to vent. Because it stood at an elevation, there had been no need to place it atop longer legs, for which Carolyn was thankful. There were limits to her bravery. Still, there was no doubt the climb was much easier now than it was the first time. For one thing, on these annual maintenance trips her pack was a lot lighter—no coiled hose, no rebar, no plumbing supplies. And Carolyn Sawchuck herself was thirty pounds lighter than she was five years ago. You don't lose thirty pounds by climbing a water tower once a year. Carolyn Sawchuck had shed most of that weight by putting thousands of miles on her bicycle.

Thousands of miles, she thought, looking over the little town spread before her.

Going nowhere.

But she couldn't summon the old bitterness.

CAROLYN CONCLUDED HER survey of Swivel by studying Harley Jackson's barn. The lights were on, which gave her pause. She knew Harley worked twelve-hour shifts and often did his chores at a late hour, but this was later than usual, and she had also seen a yellow rectangle of light bloom and eclipse as someone—by the size of him, it appeared to be Harley's friend Billy Tripp—passed through the doorway. It was odd that the two men might be meeting in the barn at this hour. She was ready to climb down, but didn't want to get caught halfway if the pair reemerged and spotted her—a fair possibility, as Harley's barn was less than one hundred yards away.

In fact, the land beneath the old water tower was owned by Harley. His house and barn stood on a 15-acre remnant of his father's original 160-acre farm, which predated the interstate, predated the housing boom and bust, and predated the hectic present in every sense. Over time the farm was annexed into the village, sliced in two by the four-lane, shaved off lot by lot to meet property taxes and satisfy the bank and—just before Harley's father died—all but the residual patch sold off in one big chunk to Klute Sorensen, the developer of Clover Blossom Estates, who then—in exchange for a fat sheaf of tax breaks—donated land for the new water tower.

I'll wait a bit, thought Carolyn, studying the illuminated barn windows. She tipped back the last of the tea, which was threatening to freeze up, and recapped her thermos. It had begun to snow. She could hear the choir at St. Jude's.

Carolyn checked her watch: 12:05.

It was Christmas in Swivel.

CHAPTER 2

W ell, that's trouble," said Harley Jackson, and although he was alone in the barn, he spoke the words aloud. In the manner of most long-term bachelors, Harley had grown accustomed to speaking within earshot of no one but himself, and was not at all self-conscious about the practice. In fact, he preferred his conversations thus. How pleasant to speak freely without fear of contradiction. Last thing you want, really: answers.

Despite the barn, and despite a small herd of beef cows, Harley hardly considered himself a farmer. Lifelong bachelor, factory worker, member of the Swivel Volunteer Fire Department, that's pretty much the list. Oh, and college dropout. He forgets that one sometimes. Not out of shame or deception, but because it was a long time ago. One semester short of graduation, he had been forced to withdraw, and he'd never made it back. Fifteen years now he's been employed at the filter factory in Boomler, twenty minutes down the freeway, pulling twelve-hour shifts in a rotation leaving opportunity for other modest pursuits: He hunts some, fishes a little, tinkers on his truck, and like a lot of folks in the area, has taken to raising a few head of beef on the side. The beefers are more of a hobby than a moneymaker, really, although they do earn him a modest break on the property taxes.

Once while they were having porch beers after the evening chores, Harley handed his friend Billy Tripp a bottle of Foamy Viking and asked, "Billy, what's the secret to happiness?"

"Low overhead," said Billy.

Pretty much, thought Harley.

The calf in the straw was wet and wobbly kneed, woozily head-butting its mother's abdomen, intuitively prospecting for the udder it knew to be south of its current location. Problematically, the calf had rotated north. This allowed Harley to inspect the flip side of the animal, upon which he was relieved to see nothing but the standard black-and-white patchwork. Bumping into its mother's fore-shank, the calf paused, tottered backward a half step, then turned to renew its search, and in making this turn it once again revealed the critical side of its hide, upon which could clearly be seen what appeared to be an above-average stencil of the Son of God.

In his time, Harley had been a believer. A born-again believer. There was a time when the sight of this calf would have dropped him to his knees. Now he simply saw a complication in the even keel of things.

Harley sighed, and again spoke aloud.

"I better call Billy."

BILLY TRIPP OPENED Harley's barn door and fully filled the frame. Well over six feet tall and burly with the stature of those men who carry a seventy-pound overage like seven, he arrived clad in grim sweatpants and a capacious parka, and notwithstanding the Christmas Eve snow stood shod in orange rubber clogs. He wore a beard the size of an otter.

Billy was a decorated combat veteran whose wartime injuries had at one point put him flat on his back for the better part of a year. He and Harley were well along in their friendship before Billy shared the whole story. "Anybody who says they're above it all has never been beneath it all," he said by way of conclusion, then never spoke of it again. He lived surrounded by stacks of books and an innumerable census of cats in a single-wide trailer on a sliver of property purchased from Harley's father during the years Harley was away at college in the city of Clearwater—an hour south of Swivel. Upon his return home, Harley resented the presence of the trailer at the far end of the pasture and by default its occupant, but one afternoon as he struggled to repair the frozen apron chain of his father's manure spreader, the sky darkened and it was Billy blocking the sun. "As the worm gear turns, eh?" said Billy. The combination of literate humor and obscure manure-handling technology knowledge appealed to Harley, and a low-key conversation ensued. Now Harley considered Billy his best friend, although Harley never cared for the term, implying as it did that life was a pageant. Like Harley, Billy was also a bachelor. The two of them liked to get together and not talk much.

After a childhood of daily dairy chores, Harley had sworn he would never again milk a cow, but he retained a farm kid's atavistic affection for fresh-skimmed cream over cornflakes. When he broached the possibility with Billy, who subsisted on a military pension and disability drawn on his injuries, Billy saw the milk as a means to defray his prohibitive monthly cat food expenses, and thus offered to split the milking chores. With this agreement in hand, Harley obtained a bred milk cow from one of the few remaining dairy farmers in the county.

Billy was present the day she was led off the back of the cattle trailer.

"Tina Turner," said Billy.

"Huh?" said Harley.

"Tina Turner. We'll call her Tina Turner."

Harley had tried in vain to make any connection, some resemblance of hairstyle or mannerism, a certain strength to the gait.

"But I don't—"

"Not the point," said Billy, seeing Harley there puzzling.

"But why—"

"Respect must be paid," said Billy, his definitive tone making it clear he considered the answer self-evident and the discussion closed. Indeed, it was not uncommon in these parts to choose animal names for honorific purposes. Harley himself had once named a Holstein heifer calf after a high school girlfriend; sadly the relationship ended before the calf was weaned.

Now, as the two men watched, Tina Turner licked her calf from stem to stern, clearing the last of the amniotic fluid. At the moment, Billy was unable to see the image of Jesus, his view being blocked broadside by Tina.

Then the cow laid on an especially aggressive lick, and the calf stumbled into the open. The hair across its rib cage was slicked and whorled, but even thus distorted, there was no mistaking the image made manifest.

"Y'got the Son a God there, bud," said Billy. "With a cowlick."

This was a stylized Jesus, rendered in black-and-white splotches like clip art from the cover of a 1970s family-planning brochure, but immediately recognizable as the standard doe-eyed Lutheran hippie iteration.

Harley looked up at his friend. "Whad'ya think?"

"Get a lawyer," said Billy. "And start printin' T-shirts."

MARKED BY GOD or not, Tina Turner's newborn calf still couldn't locate supper. Harley knelt down and gently steered the calf's snout toward the mother's udder. Sensing sustenance, the calf began to root around with his nose, nursing the air. Harley wrapped an arm around the calf's neck, grasping its jaw in one hand and a teat in the other. Slowly bringing the two closer and closer, he was rewarded when the calf drew the teat into its mouth and began to suck. After several false starts and separations, the calf locked on for a good long pull. Still kneeling beside the calf, Harley noticed that up this close he couldn't make out Jesus, or any face at all for that matter. Just black-and-white blotches. Hide and hair. Odd what tricks the eyes play given a little distance.

Satisfied that the calf was dialed in, Harley rose and backed away to stand beside Billy. Silently the two men watched the animal suckle. Finally Harley said, "That's miracle enough for me," and Billy nodded. Then they lapsed back into silence.

After a significant interlude, Harley spoke.

"Staff meeting?"

"Eee-yep," said Billy.

Harley shook out fresh straw for Tina Turner and her be-Jesused baby. After one more look at the calf, and one more shake of his head, Harley moved toward the door, and with Billy set out for the house. They passed beneath the yard light, a fresh sifting of snow floating a halo through the mercury vapor glow. Across the yard, a small hut was visible at the base of the old water tower. The curtains were drawn, but a slim line of light leaked out, reflecting on a Subaru Outback parked inside the gate of the chain-link fence.

"The wicked witch is up late," snorted Billy.

"Be nice," said Harley.

High above, unseen in the darkness, Carolyn Sawchuck waited until the farmhouse door closed behind the two men, then commenced her descent. Rung by rung she left behind her biggest secret, hidden in full view of an entire town.

CHAPTER 3

In the kitchen Harley uncapped a pair of Foamy Vikings. He handed one to Billy, and the two men seated themselves across from each other at the kitchen table. Harley had blown out a childhood's worth of birthday candles at this table. Even now he could summon the image of his mother leaning in, up to her forearms in matching red-checked oven mitts, to place another cheese-and-tuna macaroni casserole on the vintage asbestos hot pad still stowed at the bottom of the kitchen counter drawer beneath those same oven mitts.

A pile of unopened mail lay in the middle of the table. Billy took a swig of beer then reached out with his non-bottle hand and began riffling through fliers and envelopes. Harley had long ago grown used to Billy's habit of going through his mail and, as he was a loyal friend in all respects, did not object.

While Billy sorted, Harley wondered what his mother would have made of that calf out there. Jesus Christ had been her reason for living. And yet for all her devotion to Him, and to His Father, and their Holy Spirit, and to Sunday-morning meeting, to hymns and vespers, to prayer at every turn, hers was a quiet faith, uncomfortable with show or emotion. Silently she read her Bible every morning, silently she bowed her head over each meal throughout the day, silently she ended the day on her knees in prayer beside the bed, Harley's father kneeling at the opposite side of the mattress, their very marriage bed bookended by worship. His mother's creed—religionwise and otherwise—was pretty much: *Let's not make a scene.*

And yet, for all her spiritual fortitude there were certain things she was unable to resist—caramels, the call of a nonnative bird, an unopened envelope. She'd wolf the caramels, then repent with prayer and tears. At the sound of a braided titmouse, she'd lurch for the binoculars and bird book, leaving the laundry unhung. And the mail? Rarely did she make it all the way up the driveway without tearing open each and every envelope. To her, each sealed packet represented something left undone. Harley, on the other hand, didn't care much for caramels, could identify maybe five birds including crows, and took quiet joy in letting the mail accumulate for weeks. He felt it a way of pushing back time. A passive-aggressive means of refusing interruption.

"Jesus on a T-shirt," said Harley, as a way of resuming the conversation left hanging in the barn. "Ma wouldn't'a gone for that."

Billy looked up from the mail and smiled. "She'd have grabbed your dad's black Sunday-go-to-meetin' shoe polish, headed for the barn, got down on her knees, and rubbed out Jesus." Billy had met Harley's mother only a handful of times, as she died the same year he and his trailer arrived. She was a pleasant woman who wore long skirts and her hair up in a bun, her demure exterior belying a strap-steel spirit that Billy discovered the first time he tried to smoke on her porch and she quietly informed him that he was welcome to smoke beside the mailbox at the end of the driveway, the look in her eyes a cross between schoolmarm and martial arts maven. Billy gave up cigarettes shortly thereafter.

"Yah," said Harley, "then she'd'a told Dad to haul it off to the sale barn and sell it for a runt."

Billy nodded, then raised his Foamy Viking in order to contemplate its character against the light. "You'd'a never had a fridge fulla these back in the day."

Harley grinned. "Never brought a drop into this place until after Dad died. First one I popped, I startled at the hiss. Thought it was Ma giving me the ol' Scandihoovian tsk!" Harley was not one for big drinking, but he enjoyed a beer to settle things now and again. Like now, he thought, and he and Billy sat quietly, deep in their thoughts and shallow in their brew.

Harley had never planned to live in the house he grew up in. He remembered the odd sound of his father tearful on the phone—a rare show of emotion, and an even rarer thing, him calling on the phone—when he rang Harley's dorm room early one morning half-way through the final semester of his senior year, waking him to say Harley's mother had "passed" in the night. His father was always a quiet man, but he turned even quieter after losing his wife, he and Harley eating in silence at this very table after Harley dropped out of college and came home to help on the waning farm. By the time his dad "passed" a year later, they had spoken very little. There was no anger, no "issues," as the professional self-helpers liked to say, just not much talking.

"This looks official," said Billy, using a forefinger to flick a simple white envelope to the center of the table. It bore the return address of the Swivel Village Hall. Harley knew what it was and had left it unopened on purpose.

"Go ahead," he said, flicking the envelope back to Billy. Billy reached into his sock, pulled out a knife the size of a jumbo perch, slit the envelope with a deft *snick* that belied his otherwise ponderous presence, then drew the letter out and smoothed it flat across the table.

Harley watched Billy's eyes work back and forth across the paper. Harley didn't need to read the letter to know what it was about. He recognized the signature of the village attorney, Vance Hansen. Vance was an uncomfortable little man who was forever fortifying himself with day-old doughnuts and burnt coffee, and the letter in question was yet another pretend-polite threat regarding the alleged odor of Harley's beef cows.

The letter was signed by Vance, but Harley knew the real push for this action was coming from Klute Sorensen.

And if Klute Sorensen had his way, Harley would be homeless.

CHAPTER 4

At the moment, Klute Sorensen was strangling in his CPAP straps. He despised the breathing machine, viewing it as a symbol of weakness he would never tolerate in others. He had surrendered to it only after winding up in the Boomler Community Hospital emergency room five years ago, clutching his chest and certain he was dying of a heart attack. Eventually his troubles were (embarrassingly, as far as Klute was concerned) traced to sleep apnea. He was fitted for a mask, and even Klute had to admit he had felt better ever since.

But oh, how he hated the thing, especially when he woke at one a.m. with his head in its twisted grip, the mask wedged off center and squashing his nose. Lurching upright in bed, he tore it from his face and flung it aside. He'd heard the new models were much improved, but that would have meant subjecting himself to another doctor's appointment and fittings, and if there was one thing Klute

Sorensen despised more than weakness it was tweaking his schedule to accommodate weakness, so he continued to use the old model.

Crap, thought Klute as he rose from bed and fumbled into his robe, *up for good now.* He knotted the belt, toed into a pair of bedroom slippers, and stepped to the grand window at the far end of his vaulted bedroom. Below he could see half the city of Boomler. Considering himself an eminence in the town, Klute had sited his commodius manse on the very lip of Boomler Bluff. Klute had built the house (it looked more like a sporting goods outlet store than a house) out of a sense of duty, convinced as he was that the community in general looked to him for inspiration. Even now, he liked to imagine, some grubby urchin was peering up through a grimy window to the dark bulk of Klute's giant skylined castle flanked by a triple-illuminated American flag of a dimension suitable for a Perkins Restaurant, and this sight alone would assuage the child's hunger pangs, replacing them with a healthy appetite for money and success. Klute Sorensen was not a man who considered himself in need of comforting, but he did take comfort in the idea of his helping the children. *Lifting all boats,* he thought, and naturally shifted his gaze toward Boomler's city park lagoon, which really struggled to support the metaphor as it was four feet deep and capped with a foot of ice. At the center of the lagoon Klute could see the lights of the official Boomler Christmas tree, which was mounted on the roof of a junk car. The Lions Club towed the car out there every year. Charged five bucks a pop for a colored light, with the proceeds going to children in Africa. After New Year's they removed the lights and rolled up the extension cords, then ran a two-dollar "pick 'em" on when the car would sink. The lucky winner received a jumbo pack of venison jerky and a $50 savings certificate from the bank, and the rest of the proceeds went to the local playground fund. Each year, Klute found out how much the Lions raised for the playground, then wrote a check thrice as big so everyone would maintain a sense of perspective regarding the trickling goodwill of homespun charity as opposed to the beneficent fire hose of private enterprise.

Christmas by now, I guess, thought Klute, pondering the Lions Club tree as he rubbed his sternum and wondered if he was imagining the slight pain in his chest. Had to be from the CPAP strangle, he thought. He swung his gaze around the lights of Boomler. A steady snow was falling, the flakes reflecting and amplifying the ambient streetlight glow. Just off the heart of downtown, on the banks of Birch Creek, Klute could see the unlit bulk of the grain mill and dairy plant his great-grandfather had built in the early 1900s, his grandfather had expanded in the 1960s, and his father had taken over in the 1970s. Klute remembered playing in the buildings as a boy, the roar and grind of the grain and milk trucks coming and going, the farmers loading supplies, the feed dust so heavy everywhere he could trace out tic-tac-toe games on the scale shield with Eddie, the man who tied off the feed sacks and lugged them to the loading dock. Through the decades the Sorensen patriarchs had parlayed this booming operation into a hardware and appliance store. When the interstate was proposed, Klute's father had the foresight (his seat on the county planning commission informing his point of view) to purchase property at the location of the proposed exit ramp, where he subsequently built a neat little Scandinavian-themed motel and restaurant to greet the initial influx of travelers. Klute remembers the pride he felt as a high schooler back then, watching his father cut the ribbon for that section of the interstate and the customers come pouring through.

For the Sorensens, it was a time of tidy profits. Then, in the 1980s, the small farmers who sustained the mill and dairy began to wane, squeezed out by the crush of high-interest loans and the force of larger operators, and by the 1990s both operations were shuttered. Right about the same time, the first McDonald's went up on the opposite side of the interstate, followed by a KFC. Locals and visitors alike drove past the Sorensens' Swedish restaurant to get their Big Macs and buckets of Colonel Sanders Extra Crispy, and soon the restaurant could no longer sustain itself. Then came a franchise Super 8, which finished off the homegrown motel. And, finally, when the big box stores really got going in Clearwater, the hardware and appliance stores could no longer compete and were rented out to a failing series of used furniture vendors. Being an avowed survival-of-the-fittest capitalist free marketeer, Klute found it difficult to articulate his anger at this turn of events, which had drained the family fortune over the course of a thirty-year drizzle.

KLUTE TURNED FROM the window and walked into the living room, which was so cavernous and bare that even his slipper scuffs echoed. Padding into the kitchen, he drew open the door of a massive refrigerator, which was also bare save for several cartons of chocolate milk. Klute poured himself a glass and returned to the living room to sit on the only piece of furniture in the room, an overstuffed couch.

After years of watching the family fortune seep away, and after the death of his father, Klute had decided bold, decisive action was in order. The real estate boom was at full throttle, and Klute went all-in, tapping his final reserves to set up Sorensen Developments, Inc. The first structure Sorensen Developments built was Klute's own gigantic house overlooking Boomler, because Klute understood that a man led by example. Then, having gotten a line from a banker friend on a distressed farm property conveniently located very near an interstate interchange, Klute drove north, to Swivel, where he went about pitching the Swivel Village Board on a dream development he called Clover Blossom Estates.

Being from Boomler, a village with four—rather than three—digits on its population sign, Klute fancied himself an outside hotshot born to show these rubes in Swivel a thing or two, and indeed he had managed to swagger his way into the obsequious good graces of the Swivel Village Board, which had approved the rezoning plans to accommodate his development, and Solid Savings Bank, which had approved the financing for the development.

Klute's charm offensive had begun the night he pulled up before the Swivel Village Hall in a monstrously jacked-up secondhand Hummer sporting plein air stars and stripes on both doors and personalized plates reading 1MPG. Klute intended this abbreviation as a boastful toast to conspicuous consumption but it went slightly awry when one of the locals peeping out through the nicotine-bleared window of the Buck Rub Bar read it as shorthand for I AM PIG. Even had Klute known this he would not have been deterred, for he was not one to be deterred, as indicated by the fact that before he switched off the Hummer it was reverberating to the sounds of a motivational business audiobook titled *Stomp Your Way to Success: A Clodhopper Walks All Over Wall Street.* In fact, the passenger seat of the SUV was littered with motivational business audiobooks the likes of *12 Steps to the Top Floor, Scream Like You Mean It,* and *Set Sale! Seven Shipmasters Share Their Success Stories.* What Klute lacked in business acumen he made up for in body mass, cologne, and confident aphorisms, and this was enough to convince the Swivel Village Board to approve his plans and the bank to hand over money. There was much talk of jobs and an expanded tax base and repeated invocation of the two most magically twinned words in the star-spangled lexicon, *growth* and *progress*. By the time negotiations concluded, the Swivel Village Board would have been willing to strap on tool belts and raise the houses themselves. In short order Klute Sorensen snapped up Harley's father's farmland (which—not coincidentally—was precipitously close to being foreclosed on by the very same bank financing Klute), divvied it up with poorly built roads, slapped together a dozen split-levels, and began handing out brochures: CLOVER BLOSSOM ESTATES—A SWEET LIFE AT A SWEET PRICE.

And right about then, the real estate market climbed over the railing of a very tall bridge, closed its eyes, and jumped, dragging Clover Blossom Estates with it. Before long there were plastic shopping bags wind-socking in the dying shrubberies and goldenrod growing through the prematurely cracked sidewalks.

While the reasons for Klute's real estate troubles were easily diagnosed through the most cursory review of any given financial news crawl, he chose instead to focus on Harley Jackson's beef cows, which he insisted—despite their downwind location on the other side of the four-lane—set up a stink that was driving away potential customers and rendering his homes unsaleable. Everyone on the village board knew this was utter blowhard hoo-hah, but at the outset they had acquiesced to Klute's demands for significant tax breaks, the sunsetting of which were a decade distant, and as such, they felt compelled to take his side, and were further impelled by the fact that this also shifted the blame from their shoulders to those of Harley, who—although historically local and a member of the fire department—had been viewed with some suspicion ever since returning degreeless from college. Rumors of his attending dance recitals and poetry readings in a converted Clearwater tire factory had exacerbated the general unease. The few remaining homeowners of Clover Blossom Estates, finding themselves deeply underwater with the siding peeling away, were also looking for a scapegoat, and Klute commiserated with them mournfully, rolling down his Hummer window to visit with them beside their fraying ticky-tacky boxes, sniffing the air delicately and shaking his head, never mind that it was the agricultural nature of the setting that had drawn them in the first place.

No wonder my chest hurts, thought Klute, sipping his chocolate milk and allowing himself a little sadness at the way he was being treated. He was an entrepreneur. A job creator, an opportunity builder. And, dare he say, as he sighted the hem of his giant flag luffing in the snowflakes, a *patriot*. Over in one corner of the room was a flapped cardboard box half filled with copies of *Atlas Shrugged*. An anniversary edition. Annotated, with gilt-edged pages and an introduction written by a leading radio talk show host. He loved to hand the books out with a hearty handshake. "All you need to know!" he would boom while crushing the recipient's palm, even though he himself had never made it past chapter five.

Truth was, Klute Sorensen was in a bind. Overextended. Overleveraged. On the verge of being undone.

There was one other thing. A thing Klute Sorensen would never admit, not even if someone said it out loud and it echoed all around his unfurnished barn of a house.

Klute Sorensen was lonely.

CHAPTER 5

Twerp."

Billy had placed the letter from the village flat on the table and was stabbing his forefinger at Vance Hansen's signature.

"What is your intended course of action?" said Billy, leaning in.

Harley shrugged. He despised Clover Blossom Estates, beginning with the faux gold leaf letters on the sign at the entrance that tried to pass off an anemic cluster of red-ink plasti-shacks as "estates," and ignored the fact that no clover had bloomed there since the bulldozers departed. But above all he resented the fact that only by selling out to Klute—a final desperate act—had his father managed to hang on to his buildings and remaining fifteen acres. It was a tough thing to see his dad in his waning years, tilling this sad little patch, hemmed in by asphalt and vinyl siding and crushing debt. On his good days, Harley was grateful for what remained. Fifteen acres of elbow room was better than nothing.

"I dunno . . . ," said Harley. "I don't really have it in me to fight 'em. Don't have the money for it. Don't have the anger for it. Don't want to deal with it."

"I beat 'em on the burn barrel."

"The burn barrel was different. You had leverage, and the stakes were low."

Several years previously, the village board had instituted an annual burn barrel fee of $25. The burn barrel fee had been proposed and flogged into existence by Carolyn Sawchuck, who became environmentally outraged upon discovering the locals' most cherished means of trash disposal was to stuff everything into a fifty-five-gallon drum, spritz it with used motor oil, and drop a match on it. The men of Swivel especially viewed burn barrels as a birthright, and were deeply attached to this version of roughneck recycling as it allowed them regular reason to retreat solo to the backyard. Any inhalation of toxic fumes was viewed as a worthy trade-off for twenty minutes of contemplation and a furtive beer. There was also the satisfaction of reducing responsibilities to ash. "It ain't *re*cycling," Billy once said, as the two men drank their Foamy Vikings and stared into the waning flames of the burn barrel Billy kept strategically located within eyesight of his porch, "it's *de*-cycling." So cherished a tradition was the burn barrel around these parts that when Carolyn Sawchuck took her protest of the "ecologically barbarous" practice before the Swivel Village Board, Harley would have bet his pickup truck that it would never pass, but what he failed to anticipate was that Carolyn Sawchuck had done her homework and arrived waving inkjet printouts of a recent state statute outlining the environmental consequences of open burning and mandating the per-barrel fee. The motion passed on a 4–3 vote and when the next round of tax bills arrived, all burn barrel owners were assessed a $25 surcharge, which Billy refused to pay on principle. Called before the board, Billy stood tall in his orange rubber clogs and insisted he would not pony up.

"Well, it's mandated," said Vern Fosberg, the village president. "State makes us do it."

"And, Vern," said Billy, "if I pull an open records request, I trust I'll find your burn barrel registered? The one out behind your yard barn?"

"That's an *incinerator*," said Vern, sternly. "Elevated and ventilated for a clean burn."

"That's a fifty-five-gallon drum stood on two concrete blocks and shot five times with a deer rifle," said Billy, who in fact had tweaked his and Harley's burn barrels in the identical fashion.

"The burn barrel fee is *mandated*," interjected Carolyn Sawchuck from her folding chair seat in the front row, waving a fresh sheaf of inkjet printouts for emphasis. In general, the Swivel Village Board meetings operated under only the most tenuous tenets of Robert's Rules of Order, and this suited Billy fine, for he simply turned and said, "Yes it is, Carol." He always called her Carol specifically because she insisted on Carolyn. "But your lease on the old water tower is not."

At this, Carolyn yanked her papers from the air. Among her many pet projects, Carolyn was especially dedicated to community betterment—whether the community wanted it or not. When Swivel had erected its new water tower, it slated the old one for demolition. In fact, the local scrap hauler, Margaret Magdalene "Meg" Jankowski, had submitted a salvage bid to the village board and it was on the verge of being accepted when Carolyn

Sawchuck—at that time having been in town for only a matter of months—stormed through the door waving an e-mailed injunction (hers was an active and indignant inkjet) and declaring that in the interest of the "culture of community and the community of culture," she had submitted the old water tower to the state landmarks commission and would henceforth be fighting for its preservation.

Harley, being a closet sentimentalist, cherished the old tower. In contrast to the garish spheroid overlooking Clover Blossom Estates, the old tower better matched his childhood recollections of Swivel as a plain but good and decent place to live. That said, the tower came with liability headaches including drunken teenagers with spray-paint cans engaged in what was lately, even in these hinterlands, referred to as "tagging," so he had come around to the idea of scrapping it. However, he had also come to rely on the monthly lease payment paid by the village for the privilege of keeping the tower on his land. If the old tower was demolished, these payments would cease, and with them his main means of paying off his outstanding student loan. Thus, despite his stoic's trepidation regarding the very outspoken Carolyn Sawchuck, when she proposed—in the name of preservation—to assume the lease, he was secretly pleased.

The village board, seeing an opportunity to wash their hands of the old tower and Carolyn Sawchuck in one fell swoop, tabled Meg Jankowski's scrap bid and voted to have village attorney Vance Hansen draw up paperwork transferring ownership of the tower to Harley Jackson, and within the week, Harley and Carolyn had signed a lease agreement. Carolyn announced she would apply for state funds to restore the tower the very next day, "in the interest of maintaining the legacy of this place, whether you people deserve it or not."

AND SO IT came to be, when Carolyn tried to force the issue of the burning barrel mandate, Billy returned fire by referencing Carolyn's precious water tower lease. Carolyn—well aware of the friendship between Billy and Harley, but unaware that Billy and Harley had never even discussed the lease—took it for a thinly veiled threat and decided to let the burn barrel mandate ride. The issue was tabled indefinitely ("tabling" things was a specialty of the Swivel Village Board).

Back at the trailer, Billy celebrated his victory by stuffing his burn barrel with empty cat litter boxes and inviting Harley over for a Foamy Viking. As the cardboard roared, Billy proudly related how his implied threat to revoke the water tower lease had gotten Carolyn to back down.

"But," said Harley, "it's not *your lease*."

"Had to be done. That woman has the disposition of an eczemic rattlesnake."

"Be nice," said Harley.

"I never could toe the mark," said Billy, straightening defiantly, "and I never could walk the line."

"Okay, that's just a Waylon Jennings song," said Harley.

NOW, AS HE sat at his mother's kitchen table considering Vance Hansen's upside-down signature, Harley imagined himself going before the village board to face these threats. Immediately, his palms moistened. Harley could hold his own on the fire hose, could bull aside a recalcitrant steer, and—ever since his first kiss, which convinced him that some things were more powerful than shyness—he could even crank up the courage to ask a woman on a date. But to actually place himself before the public? In a position of confrontation, no less? This set his heart to fibrillating.

He simply lacked the will to engage. Like many low-key loners, he wasn't cut out for confrontation of even the slightest order.

Billy pointed at the letter again. "You gotta tell 'em something. Or they'll be on you like cat hair on my coveralls."

"Yah," said Harley, still staring at the letter, far from making a decision. He was fighting self-loathing. He tended to be a guy who aimed for the middle and yet somehow still undershot.

"And that calf . . ."

"Normally I'd just steer it. Raise it for a beefer."

"Yah," said Billy. "Under normal circumstances, bein' a bull calf, it ain't worth the gas it'd take to haul it to the sale barn."

"Well, they been up some lately," said Harley. He loved this sort of grammatically relaxed conversation. The easy flow of it.

"But bein' that it's got a big ol' JC tattoo . . ." Billy let that one hang there.

Harley didn't want to think about it.

"I don't think you understand what you've got here, son," continued Billy. "You know how it is—someone sees Jesus on a toasted bagel and the pilgrims come a-marching. What you got there is a golden calf. The *good* kind!"

"Well, I—" Harley used his fingernail to scrape at the label on his beer.

"Hell, I read on the Internet some woman in California spotted the face of Christ in a cheese sandwich and sold it for twenty-eight grand on eBay."

Harley looked up.

"Fossilized grilled cheese. Twenty-eight grand."

Billy let that sink in, then continued. "Whereas you—you have a *calf*. A living, breathing, tangible, touchable *calf*."

Harley sat there. Then shook his head.

"Born on *Christmas Eve*."

Harley shook his head again.

"In a *manger.*"

"Well . . . ," said Harley, "it wasn't a *manger.*"

"It is now," said Billy, raising both eyebrows meaningfully. "I'm *framing the narrative.*"

"You're framing something," said Harley, "but it doesn't smell like narrative."

"Son, sometimes yer thicker than bad slab wood," said Billy, digging around in the mail and pulling out a copy of the *Weekly Dealio,* a local newsprint shopper that had survived the online age, hanging on via anniversary and gag fiftieth birthday announcements, auction notices, pet kennel listings, used car ads, and the overwrought poetry of real estate agents.

"Check this out," said Billy, flapping the paper open and spinning it around so Harley could see the front page. The entirety of it was given over to an advertisement for Clover Blossom Estates. House after house, lot after lot, every single square in the grid was stamped REDUCED.

Harley looked at Billy quizzically.

"If a fella was sittin' on a gold mine . . . ," said Billy, and let it hang there.

Harley looked at the ad again, then back to Billy.

"Undevelopment," said Billy.

"Undevelopment?"

Billy pressed on. "Go whole hog with this holy calf business . . . don't stop with T-shirts . . . charge admission to see him, sell the mother's milk, sell patches of his hair, posters, can coolers—everything you can, right down to his freeze-dried holy turds hung in amber from a necklace. Shoot, you could even rent him out! Reverend Gary down at the Church of the Roaring Lamb would froth at the mouth to trot that thing out Sunday mornings. It'd be a red-hot attendance booster.

"Yah, there's lots you could do. Then, when you've got more money than God and his three leading televangelists, and the worshipful hordes clogging the byways have trampled Klute's property values down even further, you go after that bully with everything you've got and start buying back Clover Blossom Estates, lot by lot, matchbox by matchbox, everything at cut-rate, and finally you bulldoze the whole works right back to the way it was, thus jabbing your middle finger in the eye of history, progress, and—while you're at it—so-called manifest destiny."

"Um . . . ," said Harley.

"UM?!" said Billy. "I lay out God's own plan to lift you out of poverty, to bust free of your usurious manacles by turning a low-dollar bull calf into a multimillion-dollar extravaganza of winning one for the little guys, of bloodying the nose of the muscle-brained bigfoot happily trampling your family history in the name of the almighty dollar and the best you can muster is 'UM'?"

"Well, I just—"

"This is the viral age! You Instagram a single snapshot of that calf, the world will tweet and retweet a path to your door. And we haven't even begun to talk *endorsements*."

"I really don't think—"

Billy snorted, and flipped the *Weekly Dealio* into the trash.

Harley took a deep breath, let it out, then spun the last of the suds around the bottom of his beer bottle.

Low overhead, he thought.

He took the last swallow of beer. It was flat and warm.

Let's not make a scene.

"I gotta think on it, Billy. Right now I'm leaning to black shoe polish."

CHAPTER 6

Christmas morning broke to the rumble of a junk truck. Margaret Magdalene Jankowski came downshifting off the overpass and past the old water tower she had hoped to scrap, her split-shift Ford straight truck squatting to the overloads beneath the weight of a dismantled combine (Meg was ninja grade with a blowtorch), a rusted harrow, and a flattened Ford Festiva, the snug balance of the load testament to the fact that this was a woman who knew her way around ratchet straps and chain boomers. The truck pulled into the Kwik Pump and Meg, a slight and nimble widow in a watch cap and greasy coveralls, jumped out to pump the fuel. After paying cash for the gas (she never used a credit card), Meg turned left out of the lot and drove the truck a block into Swivel, pulled a U-turn, and parked along the curb in front of St. Jude's Catholic Church. Most days, she would disappear into the chapel for ten minutes, where she would light a votive candle, pray a decade of the rosary, then reemerge to return up the road past the water tower, recross the overpass, and hang a left down the southbound ramp for Clearwater and the scrap metal processing center.

But today was Christmas. When Meg dismounted from the truck and walked across the St. Jude's parking lot past the concrete Virgin Mary sheltering beneath the protruding half of a vintage bathtub buried in the vertical, she was carrying her best dress hung and sheathed in dry-cleaner's plastic. Today the truck would sit parked all day long at the curb as Meg assisted Father Carl in the celebration of both Christmas Morning masses. She was weary, having returned from midnight mass only a few hours previously, and prior to that having spent Christmas Eve day dissecting the combine, tamping down the Festiva, and loading the truck, but for Meg, devotion trumped all. If it seemed strange that she had driven to Christmas services in a loaded junk truck, it helped to know that it was her only vehicle. If Meg was invited to remove a beached Buick from someone's yard, she arrived in the junk truck. If she had been invited for cocktails, she would have arrived in the junk truck.

And if she had been allowed to scrap that water tower, the pope would have received 15 percent of the proceeds.

St. Jude's Catholic Church was nothing fancy. No soaring arches like the church in Boomler. No frescoes, no life-size, lifelike, bleeding and be-thorned Christ mannequin nailed to a towering cross of solid plaster. Rather, the crucifix that hung above Father Carl during services was punched from polished brass, the suffering Son represented in abstract fashion, his halo formed of tack-welded wire. St. Jude's had been constructed in the late 1960s from blueprints composed by an architect apparently heavily influenced by early Brutalism and Postwar Basement Rec Room. The exterior was done up in concrete and browns, and the interior ran heavily to blond paneling. The pews were padded with Naugahyde, the carpet was a close-nubbed tan-and-mustard-striped affair the texture of a polyester pot scrubber, and the figurines representing the twelve stations of the cross hung on their plaques like dated bowling trophies, the mustachioed long-haired disciples projecting the mien of gentle folk rockers. In short, you could imagine Michelangelo giving the whole works half a star. There were no bells in the belfry, rather a set of metal horn speakers hidden in a cupola that blared out tape-recorded chimes. But every single time Margaret Magdalene Jankowski stepped through the doors of St. Jude's, dipped her fingertips in the holy water, and crossed herself, she thought—no, *felt*—only one word: *sanctuary*.

Meg had been christened in St. Jude's, her father (hale and hearty and having just purchased his first tow truck) and mother cradling her in a long white gown as a priest in horn-rimmed glasses sprinkled her scalp. The pews were full in those days, most of the congregants' faces windburned from fieldwork. By the time she took her first communion, the priest with horn-rimmed glasses was assisted by the young Father Carl, who in those days had all his hair and a fat set of sideburns. It was Father Carl who married Meg and her high school sweetheart, Dougie Clements, in St. Jude's the summer after they graduated, and it was Father Carl who performed the funeral mass two months later when Dougie was killed by a drunk driver, hit while helping Meg's father tow a stalled vehicle from the shoulder of the new interstate. After Dougie was buried, Meg moved back home with her folks, never remarrying and eventually taking over the tow truck service and salvage yard when her father's health failed. Both parents were gone now.

After hanging her dress in the family room, Meg approached the altar, genuflected, then walked to a small rack of votive candles at one side. Kneeling again, she lit a candle, replaced it in the rack, and bowed her head.

Twenty-some years, and still she came in every morning to light that candle for Dougie. Even as she murmured in prayer, she recalled herself standing at the altar, a young bride with no idea of what life would hold but that God and this blessed church would provide.

HARLEY HAD NO plans for Christmas. In fact, he did not care for Christmas. He did not hate Christmas. He was not at war with Christmas. As with the old water tower, his sentimentalism was in play: he liked the nighttime glow of the lights and decorations other people put up, he liked to buy a bag of angel foam candy in Farm and Fleet and eat it all in one sitting (*There y'go, Mom,* he always thought), and he enjoyed going to the community choir Christmas concert at St. Jude's when his work schedule allowed it. But as for Christmas Day itself, he could do without it—particularly in the way it disrupted the daily normalcy of things. He simply didn't care to turn on the radio and hear music he didn't normally hear, or find his comfortable news and sports talk shows were holiday themed rather than re-chewing the usual well-worn issues of the day. Once Harley found a groove, he liked to ride it, and Christmas Day was a pebble in that groove. There was no mail delivery (although based on his feelings about the mail—or at least the *nature* of the mail— he'd been getting lately, perhaps that was a blessing), the feed mill was closed, the filter factory shut down, and no one seemed to be where they were supposed to be. Everything was thrown off. All in all he preferred any given Tuesday. Thus, even as Margaret Magdalene Jankowski rose from her prayers and prepared to help Father Carl set up for the service to follow, Harley welcomed the chance to shrug into his chore coat and step outside to feed and water the beefers. In the chores he found the comfort of the everyday.

Plus, he had to check on that calf. Harley regularly recalled his father—in a rare moment of low-key speechifying—invoking the word "husbandman" and urging Harley to take the term to heart. It wasn't enough to own animals, his father said. You had to walk among them daily, get keyed into their rhythms so you'd notice if anything was amiss. Harley would never be the husbandman his father was, but he did once pick up on a beef steer with a bad hock while simply watching the animals loaf, and by calling the vet was able to intervene in time to keep the animal on track for the abattoir, ultimately a zero-sum proposition for the steer, he supposed, but still the right thing to do, and he was quietly proud of himself for catching it.

So before he threw hay bales down from the mow, he walked through the beefers. The barn thermometer was tickling single digits, and a stiff breeze from the west had left patches of the barnyard snow scoured and thin, broken here and there by dark brown knobs of deep-frozen cow pies. The beefers were hunched and bunched behind the corrugated steel half shed that served as a windbreak, dispassionately chewing their cud, neither grateful nor ungrateful for his husbandry as far as he could tell. After a quick head count to verify that everyone was in attendance and upright, Harley turned his attention to the stock tank. Finding it full and unfrozen—meaning both the plumbing and deicer were operational—he turned on his heel and stomped through the deeper snow in the lee of the wind and let himself in the barn door.

Even after he switched the lights on it took a moment for his eyes to adjust from the wintry white light to the darkness of the barn. The calf was resting against its mother, both of them fold-legged atop the straw. *Maybe I—*, thought Harley, hoping that somehow overnight the image might have disappeared, but then, *Nope, there it is.*

And indeed the face of Jesus was in clear view, all but the bottom fringe of beard, which was tucked into the straw. *"Jaypers!"* said Harley, unconsciously uttering the severest oath he had ever heard his father utter. He had harbored some hope that here on the morning after, the image might have been less distinct.

Tina Turner got to her feet and lowed at him hungrily. "Yah, okay," said Harley, shaking his head as he turned and climbed the haymow ladder. Unhooking the door that swung out over the barnyard, he pitched down a dozen bales, then dropped a single down the chute above Tina Turner's manger.

Most people these days used round bales, the ones that resembled giant cigar stubs or were wrapped in white plastic and looked like elephantine marshmallows. You spiked them with a tractor and they'd feed the cows for several days. But Harley stuck with the old-school bales, the ones that were a packet of hay contained by two loops of knotted twine. They were more work, but he still liked using his dad's old John Deere baler. Billy would drive the tractor while Harley stacked bales on the wagon, the roar of the engine rising and falling to the rhythm of the plunger. Harley found this mechanical harmony soothing, and evocative of a time when everything made sense. Or was at least *containable*. Plus he figured lugging those bales every day was his equivalent of a gym membership.

When Harley stepped off the bottom rung of the ladder, Tina Turner had her head through the slats of the pen, and was straining toward the hay bale. Harley flicked open his lock blade, snicked the twine, and using one foot, swept several flakes of hay within reach of her looping tongue. Her udder was rotund with colostrum, and Harley noted a fleck of foam at each corner of the calf's mouth—a good sign; he'd been feeding. The calf was standing now too, facing Harley head-on, sturdy as you please, all the wobble gone out of its knees. Harley eased around one side of the pen, once again hoping the image of Christ would be indistinct, or that from another perspective it might appear to be a road-killed muskrat or some such— anything, really, as long as it was more benign than the Holy Savior of Man—but then the calf turned to suckle, and there it was, a hairy Rorschach open to only one interpretation: Jesus Christ.

Back outside in the cold, Harley elbowed his way through the cluster of beefers now tearing at his pile of hay bales. One by one he lugged the bales to the bunk feeder that ran along one side of the barnyard, cut the twine, and kicked the flakes along the length of the feeder. When the last bale was split and distributed, he stood in the feeder and watched the cows eat. There was always a comfort in this moment. He found simple satisfaction in the sound of the cattle snuffling and grinding the hay in their molars, switching their tails in contentment. There was the feeling that he had done something tangible and good. Christmas? Maybe so, he thought, but it was hard to imagine any other gifts so thankfully received.

OVER AT ST. Jude's Meg rose to change into her dress and assist Father Carl.

Christmas, she thought, looking at the abstract brass Jesus. *Happy birthday*.

In his office, Father Carl pressed a button, and the tape-recorded bells rang out the joyous message.

CHAPTER 7

In the little hut—originally the pump house, in fact—at the base of the water tower, Carolyn Sawchuck was pedaling her bicycle and reading *Soulful Declensions*, a book of essays she had written and published at the peak of her academic career, when things were really going her way. Despite her late night atop the tower, she had risen early today, awakened by the rumble of Meg's junk truck. *Bless my friend Meg*, she thought, and found herself taken aback by her unconscious use of the word *bless*, but even more so the word *friend*. She hadn't used either word in a long, long time.

The bicycle was clamped into a wind trainer, one of those roller mechanisms that converts a standard bicycle into an exercise bicycle. The trainer in turn had been modified to spin a small pump. A short hose connected a thirty-five-gallon plastic carboy to the pump's intake valve; the other end of the pump was attached to a longer hose that snaked across the floor and out a small hole in the wall that was stuffed with insulation.

Carolyn pedaled steadily, her book propped on a rack mounted on the handlebars. Outside, a sign on the pump house door said ACCEPTING NO VISITORS. Carolyn had screwed the sign to the door the day she moved in. The first time Billy saw it, he chuckled, elbowed Harley, and said, "Who's offering?"

"*Nice*," said Harley. "Be *nice*."

Billy grimaced. "That woman has halitosis of the soul."

ABOVE ALL AND through it all, Carolyn Sawchuck considered herself A Woman of the People. She had focused on becoming A Woman of the People as a second act after being A Woman of Arts and Letters failed to pan out after four underappreciated (and undersold) books, a pair of Guggenheister awards, a fat curriculum vitae's worth of grants and fellowships, two poetry chapbooks, and an endowed chair at the state university in Clearwater. Until the abrupt end it was a satisfying academic arc, although even at its apex Carolyn was not the sort of person for whom satisfaction was a natural state.

It was the vacation home in a Central American expatriate artists' community that put her on the path to a commoner's ruin, what with it being burned to the ground by the very same Marxist collective revolutionaries to whom she had given safe harbor and free copies of her recent treatise on "Indigenous Empowerment in a State of Transitory Postmodern Meta-Contextualism." Wishing to demonstrate her commitment to the cause (and also unload a few boxes of poorly translated and even more poorly selling chapbooks), Carolyn had set up a fund-raiser based on a sparsely attended poetry reading and free beer, after which (and it was never clear if this was the result of the free poetry or the free beer) the revolutionaries burned her retreat to the ground, and—essentially—the grant money that had served as a down payment. They also unloaded her iPad on eBay.

There followed a crash course in the intricacies of the Central American insurance industry, and when the ash and paperwork settled Carolyn was left with a scorched adobe shell and an underwater mortgage that had been of sketchy provenance in the first place.

It was possible she might have survived this personal setback had she not subsequently suffered a professional setback precipitated by a "think piece" she composed for the literary blog *Haute Ignorati* in which she impugned a female freelance writer for selling out the sisterhood by penning a style magazine article entitled "Six Sexy Steps to Steamroll Cellulite," having failed to take into consideration that said female writer was a self-insured single mother who composed her cellulite article on a card table and pawnshop laptop in a one-bedroom apartment overlooking a Shopko loading dock as opposed to on a fresh MacBook in a writing den constructed from sustainable bamboo and tenure.

It developed that the cellulite scribe was a bit of a bootstraps feminist in her own right, and returned fire. In the ensuing online strafing session, Carolyn was shocked to find herself cast and cornered as a tone-deaf member of the privileged class and in violation of an obscure subsection of the university speech code, which Carolyn herself had helped compose. The professional conflagration that followed made the Central American incident seem a jolly marshmallow roast by comparison, and when the final faculty review session concluded, Carolyn found herself endowed with a modest severance package but otherwise hopelessly outcast on all fronts.

THE PUMP GAVE out a gurgle. Carolyn stopped pedaling, and dismounted. One corner of the small room was taken up by a number of five-gallon buckets. Carolyn selected one, fitted a funnel to the mouth of the carboy, emptied the contents of the bucket within, and returned to pedaling and reading her book.

CAROLYN DIDN'T ALWAYS read her own books. In fact, she did so infrequently. But when she did read her own books, it was to reassure herself. To reassure herself that it was the outside world that failed to understand. That her poor book sales had no relation to the quality of the content. There was also the idea that the printed pages validated the work. So many *talked* of writing; she had done it. The fact that her words had languished in small print runs was secondary to the primary fact that she had put her ass in the chair, as she once heard some would-be rough-boy corduroy-blazered creative-writing workshopper say. Half the men in these workshops tended to project a combination of infantile sensitivity coupled with sublimated machismo. The sort of fellow who would be post-coitally teary but secretly hoping the woman would get out of bed and fix a nice snack. Carolyn often countered this image by conjuring up a mental picture of the guilty individual perched atop a pedal-powered monster truck.

There were those in Swivel who saw Carolyn as a bitter woman, and little she did dispelled this. Publicly she had always maintained that she came to Swivel to live "the simple life," a pronouncement that probably did more long-term damage than the burn barrel ruckus, implying as it did that the citizenry were by default de facto simple.

In truth she was more befuddled than bitter. She had done all the right things, sat on the proper literary panels, carefully doled out career-enhancing book reviews (always reserving the long knives for those outside the winner's circle and off the foundation board), and right there on the dust jackets and back covers were the testaments—the "blurbs" as they were called in the coarser trades—all these eminent pacesetters testifying to her wisdom and perspicacity and artistic essentiality, and yet, and yet . . . she wound up in a defunct water tower pump house riding a bicycle to nowhere.

In the wake of losing her position with the university, Carolyn had retreated to Swivel, where the cost of living—if not the tone of living—was more suited to her means, and rented a modest apartment above Reverend Gary's Church of the Roaring Lamb. It was her intent to simply lay low for a year, do some writing, then begin the reentry process. In the meantime, she took it upon herself to uplift and enhance the citizenry by offering memoir-writing workshops and selling dream catchers on consignment at the gas station.

The citizenry had proved stubborn in their unreconstructed lack of cultural acquisitivity. In that first year she sold but one dream catcher, and that to a drunken fisherman who mistook it for a musky lure. Glen Jacobson, a local handyman (known also for his skills as an unlicensed plumber and electrician), showed up for the memoir workshop, but he ignored Carolyn's instruction, insisting instead that she help him edit a sheaf of handwritten limericks stored in a manila folder that smelled of caulk. Carolyn adjudged the limericks juvenile and told Glen his first assignment was to find a word that rhymed with *misogyny*. Punching it into an online rhyming dictionary, Glen found himself recommended to *androgyny*, which he in turn Googled, and what he saw next made him so nervous he wrote no more, and thus the workshop terminated. On another cultural front, Carolyn got into regular shouting matches with Reverend Gary. Some of the disagreements were theological, but mostly it was over all the speaking in tongues after ten p.m. on Bible Study night.

So it was, when Carolyn heard the old village water tower was slated for destruction, she had seen it as a cultural opportunity. More than that, a *responsibility*: if these people couldn't recognize the treasure of their own history, she'd recognize it for them. And after years of navigating the world of government grants and foundation funds, Carolyn happened to know the governor had recently expanded a state program making funds and tax credits available for the renovation of historic landmarks—exactly the sort of thing about which these shortsighted Swivel knuckleheads were oblivious. She went into high gear, submitting the petition for landmark status, storming the village board meetings, and convincing Harley Jackson to let her assume the lease.

Shortly thereafter, the governor reversed himself, announcing a series of budget cuts and putting the renovation program—and its funds—on hold, and Carolyn found herself stuck with a year-long lease on a rusty water tower full of nothing.

CHAPTER 8

With the chores complete, Harley found himself hungry. What he needed was eggs and bacon and good fresh-ground coffee, but what he craved was the instantaneous fix of a gas station pastry washed down with a Styrofoam cup of industrial drip, both available at the Kwik Pump. For that matter, maybe he'd go for a drive. It was one of his favorite things, driving nowhere particular in his pickup truck with old-school country music on the radio, slowly knee-steering along with the coffee in one hand and a pastry in the other. Nutritional napalm, and no way to navigate, but the sort of unobtrusive decadence that suited him. He closed the barn door, started his pickup truck, and made the short drive across County Road M to the Kwik Pump, where a neon sign in the window promised BEER SALES TO MIDNIGHT, and a banner hung with bungee cords advertised a dollar-off special on twenty-four-packs of Old Milwaukee. Right below that was an official government-issue sign identifying the Kwik Pump as a deer carcass registration point. This was an accurate representation of the ratio of interests in the area, which ran about two to one beer to hunting.

Harley parked before the propane cylinder exchange cage and left the truck idling, the heater blowing. Inside the door of the station, Harley stopped as he always did to read the community bulletin board, filled with homemade posters advertising housecleaning services, babysitting, dock repair, cabin winterization, taxidermy, bowling tournaments, cancer benefits, used snowmobiles for sale, and Pampered Chef parties. Down in one corner a piece of paper stapled to the cork featured a cartoonish rendering of a gooey-looking black teardrop falling toward a sad-faced cartoon Earth. A red circle/slash had been superimposed over the black teardrop. The caption below Earth said:

TOP DOLLAR FOR YOUR USED MOTOR OIL

&

OTHER PETROLEUM-BASED WASTE

I PICK UP, I PAY (CASH)

(NONGOVERNMENT) (NO QUESTIONS ASKED)

Below the caption was a fringe made of the same phone number printed vertically, over and over, each separated by a scissors snip. Harley noticed that several of the strips had been torn away.

Harley knew that number. He dialed it whenever he needed to speak with Carolyn Sawchuck.

MAKING HIS WAY through the ranks of foil-wrapped snacks, gallon jugs of window washer fluid, and artfully stacked rock salt, Harley approached the bakery case and chose a creme-filled, maple-frosted long john, then moved to the coffee stand, where he drew a twenty-ounce Kona Luna from the vacuum thermos. Then he turned around, bumped directly into a woman, and slopped fresh hot Kona Luna across her boots.

"Oh, shoot, I—," said Harley, before the woman cut in with a laugh.

"Nothin'!" she said, pronouncing it *NAH-thin!* and waving her hand dismissively.

Harley stood red faced and mute.

"Look at 'er bead up!" said the woman, pointing proudly to her boot toes, where coffee trembled atop the leather in glossy orblets.

Harley liked few things better in this world than a good pair of boots. But among those things was a *woman* in a good pair of boots. Not spiky pumps or furry winter clompers or thigh-high "bondage waders" (Billy's term), but rather sturdy wafflestompers with some scuff on them. Harley kept his eyes locked on the coffee beads, waiting for the face flush to disperse. It only deepened as the nape sweat sprung.

"Oiled 'em last night," he heard her say. "With the beeswax and whatnot. Set 'em by the woodstove all night long. Melts it in good." Harley stared resolutely at the boots. She stomped first one foot, then the other, and the coffee beads dispersed.

"Christmas breakfast in the Kwik Pump?"

Harley had no choice now but to raise his gaze and the woman was looking him square in the eye. His gut flushed as if he had misstepped on the top rung of the haymow ladder. Trying to focus, he didn't so much see her face as take inventory. Long straight hair. Frank hazel eyes. Blaze orange bomber cap trimmed in rabbit fur, flaps down. A face that seemed wide open. And a grin. Not a smile, a grin. A grin like she knew exactly what he looked like in his skivvies. A buddy-style grin the full opposite of coquettish, crinkling into the very first hints of crow's-feet, the kind of lines a man learned to look for after he wearied of petulance and chirping. And: creeping to the crest of one clavicle and just visible at the flare of her flannel collar, an ivy-vine tattoo.

"Oh. Hey. Yah, I . . ." Harley's ears felt molten as he stood there with a dripping coffee cup in one hand and a creme-filled maple-frosted long john in the other. The pastry was a true embarrassment. "Cow calved last night, and I—" He had this fleeting thought that talk of calving would render him in a sturdier light.

"Don't worry about it, big shot," interrupted the woman, hoisting a plastic bakery bag so he could see her own creme-filled, maple-frosted long john within.

Harley grinned in relief.

"Mindy," said the woman, pulling off one leather chopper mitt and extending the undressed hand. "Mindy Johnson." Harley shuffle-juggled his coffee and pastry to the crook of one arm and met her grip, which was strong and naturally electric, with a coarseness that bore the implications of physical labor. The nape sweat formed a drop and slid down his neck. "Harley," he said.

"Off to see family?" said Mindy.

"Nah," said Harley. "No family."

"Oh."

"No big thing, just no family."

"But on Christmas?"

"Not real big on Christmas. Nothin' against it, but . . ."

"You and me both," said Mindy. "Rather have a quiet night in. Or a *warm* night in."

Harley felt himself seizing up.

"Hey!" Mindy was holding up a wire-tied plastic bag packed with day-old blueberry doughnuts. "Four for a buck!"

She lobbed them at his chest. "Y'know y'want 'em," she said, laughing as he basket-caught the bag with his elbows and another slosh of coffee hit the floor, *splat*.

"Well, merry solo Christmas!" she said, laughing again.

"Yah," said Harley. "You too." He fled for the counter, paid the clerk, and hustled for the warmth of his truck. Backing away from the propane cage he clutched into first and steered a smooth arc around the lot to the exit, but then lingered, hoping to catch a glimpse of Mindy in the rearview. Soon enough she emerged and climbed into a well-worn Ford F-250. Red, with plow mounts. A beefy four-wheel drive but fitted with narrow tires—smart for the snow. A set of tire chains hung from the headache rack.

The cab was warm and the coffee smelled better than it was. He was in the mood to drive. Rather than cross to his driveway, Harley flipped the blinker, turned right on County Road M, and headed for the overpass. And he didn't even mind when he turned on the radio hoping for Loretta Lynn and got Christmas carols instead.

CHAPTER 9

"Yer not a LAWYER, yer a WATER BOY!"

Klute Sorensen's face was a plum shade of purple.

Vance Hansen's face was a Kleenex shade of white.

"But, Mr. Sorensen, these things take time . . . surely a man of your stature underst—"

"A man of my stature shouldn't have to be waiting on a mental midget like YOU!"

The cold coffee in Vance Hansen's Styrofoam cup was a trembling bull's-eye of ripples. Clutching it with both hands in an attempt to keep it from sloshing over, Vance sat hunched in a pilled Christmas sweater on a swivel chair that was set too low for the village hall conference table, an unfortunate circumstance that left him looking like an uncomfortable grade-schooler who'd arrived late for school picture day.

Klute Sorensen's recent sleeplessness wasn't solely attributable to the fact that his CPAP roamed his face like a possessive octopus. In fact, even when the machine hadn't bothered him, he had been up a lot these past few months, trying to figure out how to stave off the failure of Clover Blossom Estates. The banker was getting nervous. Klute was certain that in time, when the economy and real estate markets recovered, Clover Blossom Estates would thrive again. History was on his side. To own property at the exit of an interstate was to own a gold mine. He had seen what had happened in Boomler. But he had also seen how it had come undone. How his father had anticipated how valuable the interchange property would become but had failed to anticipate just *how* valuable. And how by owning only one corner he was vulnerable to other developers. The ones who brought in the chain hotels and the franchise restaurants had understood: this was real-life Monopoly. Whoever controls the most spaces wins.

But how to survive in the moment? How to bank against the future when there was nothing in the bank? Swivel was a dinky little village. Klute knew that. But bigger times were coming. All you had to do was drive on the interstate to Clearwater. Sooner or later, even the most remote interchanges were becoming points of commerce. Rather than bail out of Clover Blossom Estates, Klute believed he had to react boldly. Rather than dump and run, he needed to increase his holdings. Double down. The Kwik Pump was already in place, so that corner was out of the equation. But if he could get the rest of Harley Jackson's farm, he would be up to half. That plan was already under way, although Vance Hansen had been a real slow-moving disappointment. He needed some jacking up.

And the third corner of the exchange—the one owned by

Margaret Magdalene Jankowski—would *really* close the deal. That corner had been costing Klute some sleep lately, too. He had offered to buy Meg out several times, but she had refused.

Klute stood across the table from Vance, leaning in, his jaw jutted to within spittle range, his meaty hands braced on either side of an array of papers splayed across the table. Topmost on the stack was a large plat printout of the interstate interchange. With a flick of his fingertips, Klute spun the plat, intending to rotate it so Vance could read it. Instead, he spun it with such violence the centrifugal effect sent the other papers on the table flying in all directions. Setting aside his coffee, Vance scurried over to a corner of the conference room to retrieve the helicoptering plat, then scurried back to return it to the table, smoothing it before Klute with trembling hands.

"THIS!" hollered Klute, jabbing a finger at a rectangle outlined in purple highlighter, "THIS SHOULD BE MINE!"

The purple border delineated Harley's fifteen-acre farmlet. Vance nodded vigorously. "Oh yes! Yes! I agree!"

"A *farm*! What kind of village has a *farm* in it?"

"Well, it's—"

"It's *backward*!"

"I certainly agr—"

"I'm a *forward* man!"

Now he adopted a more reasonable tone.

"You know I care about Swivel."

"Oh, yes."

"I'm an entrepreneur."

"Yes. Yes you are."

"I'm a go-getter."

Vance nodded. Vigorously.

"But I don't just go-get for *me*."

Vance looked mildly confused.

"I LIFT BOATS!"

Now Vance looked lonely. Klute sighed.

"I don't just make investments, I make *sacrifices*—for the good of the community."

Vance went back to nodding, but the look on his face remained quizzical.

"We're here on Christmas morning, aren't we?"

"Yes," said Vance, looking down and picking at his sweater. "Yes, we are."

VANCE HANSEN JUST wanted to go home. The kids would be impossible and his wife, Katy, would be angry that he had gone in to work on Christmas Day, but he also knew there was a paper plate stacked with green-and-red-frosted sugar cookies on the counter, and all he wanted to do was carry them to his recliner with a fresh cup of coffee and eat them one after the other until they were gone, and then, as the kids screeched around through drifts of gift wrap, he would cross his arms across his crumb-dusted sweater and sleep like a man trying to forget.

He wished he could forget the day Klute Sorensen had first pulled up to the village hall in his star-spangled Hummer. How Klute had flung the door open and strode to the front of the room as if he were six men. How his chest was broad and his suit was tailored. How heavily the gold chain hung around his neck, how solid his wristwatch looked, how his thick black hair gleamed beneath the fluorescents.

The position of Swivel village attorney was a very part-time gig; Vance did wills and probate and small-claims work on the side, but it was slim pickings, and lately Katy had been picking up shifts at the Kwik Pump. In Klute, Vance had seen everything he had ever wanted to be. And if he couldn't be that (he'd need a hair transplant and elevator shoes, for starters), he wanted to be *around* that. *Part* of that.

If I make myself valuable to that man, Vance had mused, *we—I—will go places.*

That seemed a long time ago, he thought, jerked back to the present by Klute, roaring again.

"You promised me this would be done by now! You said you had everything all lined up!"

"Y-yes," said Vance. "Well, we're well on our—"

"YOU DON'T SNEAK UP ON SUCCESS IN FLUFFY SLIPPERS!"

Vance recognized that one. Disc three, track five, *Stomp Your Way to Success.*

Klute slammed his hand down flat on the plat, his palm covering the entirety of Harley Jackson's property. Vance jumped, dumping his coffee across the table. Klute drew his fingers inward, scrunching the purple-highlighted section over and over, working his fingers until the entire map was balled within his fist. Then he flung the wad of paper in Vance Hansen's face.

"GET ON IT!"

As Klute's Hummer roared out of the parking lot, Vance dabbed at the coffee with a wad of paper napkins.

Oh, how he wanted a cookie.

CHAPTER 10

Right about the time Klute crumpled Vance Hansen's map, Carolyn Sawchuck climbed off her bicycle. Enough of that for the day, she thought, as she showered in the mini-stall originally designed for a motor home. After dressing, she brewed a mug of EarthHug tea, and curled up to read in her papasan chair. It was a cozy little setup: A thrumming space heater, a small writing desk stocked with hempen paper and her favorite fountain pens in a fair trade coffee can, a teapot and a hot plate, and over there behind the miniature refrigerator, a stash of Little Debbie Zebra Cakes. She procured the Zebra Cakes via an online vendor known mainly for selling books, and most importantly, that shipped everything in plain brown boxes. Carolyn felt she couldn't be seen buying the Zebra Cakes in public, as their preservative-laced sugar-bomb goodness was inconsistent with her public image as a cultural thought leader. Better that people think she was adding to her library.

When St. Jude's electronic bells rang, Carolyn looked up from her book. She hoped this day would be all her dear friend Meg prayed for, but as for herself, Christmas was rooted in a patriarchal mythology from which she had emancipated herself somewhere around her second year of grad school and she would be having none of it.

It seemed improbable that the two women would have become close, and yet when Meg posted a homemade sign on the Kwik Pump bulletin board asking for volunteers to help her establish a local food pantry, the only person to show up at the planning meeting had been Carolyn Sawchuck. Together they cleaned up the abandoned pool hall kitty-corner from the Buck Rub Bar, together they completed and submitted the paperwork to establish tax-exempt charitable status, together they solicited donations, and together they met every other Tuesday to sort and stack the donated canned and boxed goods. Every other Saturday they sacked up the food and handed it out to anyone who showed up, no questions asked.

They didn't have a lot to talk about at first. Early on, Carolyn had tried to jazz things up a bit, suggesting that they offer poetry workshops and yoga for the "underprivileged." Meg paused, a can of tuna in each hand, looked Carolyn square in the eye, and said, "We are here to feed the hungry."

"But man cannot live on bread alone—"

"—and thus the Lord gave us mac and cheese," said Meg, and turned back to the shelves. Carolyn spent the next twenty minutes stacking cans and trying to figure out if she had been the object of a threat or the butt of a joke.

From that moment forward the two women worked in a mostly

wordless tandem, meeting for the sorting and distribution, and responding to emergency requests when needed, like when a house fire put someone out and the chief called.

In fact, they grew into an effective team: Meg in the service of the Lord, Carolyn in the service of humanism, both in service to their neighbors. But still, they didn't talk much, until the day Carolyn revealed that she had lost her longtime partner to cancer fifteen years previously.

"I'm so sorry," said Meg, and tears leaped to her eyes. Then Meg told Carolyn about Dougie, and after that, they had more to talk about.

RISING FROM THE papasan, Carolyn set her teapot to boil again and crackled open a packet of ramen noodles. When she received her severance package, an acquaintance who ran a small mutual funds shop in Clearwater had helped invest it in a real estate trust. Early returns had been robust, allowing her to accumulate savings even while withdrawing a modest monthly stipend. Then, after taking umbrage at the rank typos peppering the *Weekly Dealio*, she fired off a grammatically airtight and punctilious e-mail to the editor and was to her surprise hired as a freelance copyeditor. Thanks to these twin sources of income and her modest lifestyle, Carolyn was able to afford both her apartment rent and the water tower lease.

But then she had gotten into the oil-recycling business.

The way things were going, it was bound to break her.

The whole idea had sprung from the burn barrel incident, after which Carolyn discovered that the burning of used motor oil was perhaps the least environmentally offensive means of disposal.

It was also being poured down drains, into the grass out behind shops, or down the ravines where many of the locals tipped the rest of their junk. Although used oil collection services already existed, they were targeted mainly toward auto shops and not individuals. And then there was the fact that most of the area around Swivel was rural. Far easier to burn the used oil, or dump it on a roller chain, or use it to keep the dust down on the driveway than it was to lug it to a collection center. Furthermore, because the services operated under the auspices of government-driven environmental protection programs, the populace was generally leery and unwilling to participate. For her part, Carolyn figured if she couldn't hector the locals into environmental consciousness, perhaps she could bribe them.

And so she overcame the skeptics with an old-fashioned tool: cash. Carolyn paid by the gallon, at a rate matching the established services, plus a modest sign-up bonus. She also picked up the oil on site, free of charge. At launch, she financed the program out of her own pocket, dipping into her severance package reserves—at that time still in an appreciated state. And as with her hopes for the water tower, Carolyn was confident that in the long term she would be able to fund the program through outside sources.

Frankly, it took off better than she could have expected. Once word got out that the weird lady in the Subaru was paying good money for bad oil, the phone rang steadily. What she had envisioned as a few pints per month quickly multiplied. Soon her apartment above Reverend Gary's Church of the Roaring Lamb was stacked with containers and plastic jugs of all shapes and sizes.

Meg, who had tried to talk Carolyn out of the project from the get-go, offered to take the oil off her hands. "Just dump it in with mine," said Meg. "Every time I crush a car, I have to drain the fluids, and all the oil goes in a container out back. Eventually I haul it to the collection center in Clearwater."

But Carolyn had refused. In fact, she insisted on collecting Meg's waste oil as well, explaining that it would be easier to get funding support if she could document increased collections. Soon the apartment living room was full, and Carolyn was stacking overflow in the bedroom. The joists were beginning to creak. At one point she considered taking the oil to the Clearwater collection site, but then while researching environmental remediation grants she wound up on a Department of Natural Resources website and discovered that she was in violation of at least sixteen different hazardous waste statutes pertaining to collection, storage, and transportation of toxic chemicals. Prison time was not out of the question, and she became badly spooked at the idea of someone from the collection center making inquiries.

And in a crowning setback, the real estate roller coaster was currently on a downslope, further accelerating the shrinkage of her financial reserves.

It was in this troubled state of mind that she was returning from her rounds with yet another batch of full buckets in the back of her Subaru the day she drove past Harley Jackson's place, looked up at the old water tower, and had an epiphany.

DESPITE THE REVOCATION of state restoration funds, and the waning state of her severance package, Carolyn had maintained her lease with Harley, holding out hope that the governor might reverse his decision, or that she might locate a sympathetic benefactor. This was also a matter of frank stubbornness: after all the public declarations she'd made, there was no way she'd give those goobers the satisfaction of seeing her sacrifice the tower for scrap. Just as she had refused Meg's offer to relieve her of the excess oil, Carolyn couldn't stand the idea of bailing on the lease. Carolyn's biggest obstacle wasn't dwindling funds or lack of storage space. It was pride. She'd be damned if she'd fail the preservation of history, she'd be damned if she'd fail the earth, and above all, she'd be damned if she'd fail in front of these damned locals. From the poetry to the professorship, there had been enough failure. Swivel was her fresh start, dammit.

And now there stood that water tower. Empty. With space for thousands of gallons, she figured. And at its base, the neat little pump house. Having recently viewed a PBS special on the tiny house movement, Carolyn now recognized its potential as a snug, environmentally conscious dwelling that would not only reduce her carbon footprint but would allow her to save the rent money she'd been spending on the apartment above Reverend Gary and his vociferous flock.

Rushing home, Carolyn did some quick online research on water tower construction, fluid dynamics, and the website of a humanitarian organization (run by an acquaintance from her ill-fated stint in Central America) that built bicycle-powered machines for farmers in Guatemala. Then she called Glen Jacobson. If you help me renovate the pump house, she said, I'll help you with your limericks.

Harley Jackson had no inkling of any of this until the day he looked out his kitchen window and saw Glen Jacobson's panel van parked inside the chain-link fence that surrounded the pump house and base of the tower. While he was puzzling on this, there was a knock at the door. He opened it to find Carolyn Sawchuck standing on the mat.

"I put a new padlock on the gate up there," she said, pointing toward the water tower.

"Oh?" said Harley.

"The old one was rusted." She opened her hand to reveal two shiny keys. "Here's your copy," she said, and handed one to Harley.

"My copy?" said Harley.

"I'll be keeping the other one," said Carolyn. "I'm moving in."

"Moving in?"

"Moving in. I represent the tiny house movement. Shrinking our carbon footprint, leading by example."

Harley stared a moment, then nodded. If he lacked the will to fight Klute Sorensen, he certainly didn't want to tangle with Carolyn Sawchuck.

Also: The lease. He could keep chipping away at those student loans.

After Glen completed the renovation, there was much to do. Carolyn spent long hours in the pump house (always behind the locked gate and her "ACCEPTING NO VISITORS" sign) assembling her bicycle-powered pump (so as not to arouse suspicion, she ordered the pump and other parts from the same place she got her Zebra Cakes). (She bought the bike at a pawn shop in Clearwater and snuck it in under cover of darkness.) When it was ready, she made her first Christmas Eve climb, inserting the hose with the PVC "T" (which kept it from slipping down the overflow tube) at one end and plumbing it to the pump at the other.

By New Year's, she was astride her bicycle daily, pumping waste oil into the tank high above Swivel. At first she would stagger to her papasan after only a few minutes, but soon she grew stronger and could pedal for two or three hours straight. She became lean and fit, Zebra Cakes notwithstanding.

She hung on to her apartment for a few months, giving her time to sneak the pent-up oil out a few buckets at a time until it had all been bicycle-pumped into the sky. As for what she would do with all that oil? And her accumulating Department of Natural Resources violations? Carolyn put these things out of her mind. There was a lot of room in that water tower. She had bought herself plenty of time—years, in fact—to figure it all out. Meanwhile, she was living tiny, getting fit, and keeping all of that evil oil out of the soil and air.

The ramen helped Carolyn stretch her budget, but over time she had also come to construe it as a form of character-enhancing asceticism. Harder for her to admit was the fact that she actually craved the salty broth; even now she sniffed the steam rising with its trace aroma of chicken and upended saltshakers. It reminded her of the academy, as so many freshman backpacks smelled of it.

Rubbing the steamed window clear as she waited for the noodles to soften, Carolyn sighted down County Road M to where it intersected with the railroad tracks and became Main Street. She could see Meg's truck parked at St. Jude's and for a moment she wondered what it would be to take comfort from such a place. Carolyn remembered going to church when she was a little girl, but she had spent so much time unlearning church that she didn't think she could sit through a service now without drowning herself in dissenting footnotes. It was tough enough to get these local yokels to stop burning their oil-soaked trash in the backyard and tearing down vintage water towers.

NOODLES IN HAND, Carolyn returned to the papasan, resting her bowl of ramen in her lap and her book on her knees. She sighed (*contentedly*, she realized) with some surprise, and settled in to read.

From St. Jude's the prerecorded bells pealed again.

CHAPTER 11

Harley wished his truck was a beefy F-250, but in fact it was a modest brown Silverado inherited from his father. Four-wheel drive and mounted with a plow, but rust-pocked and on the far side of shot. Rear bumper crimped from that time he backed into the barn while trying to tune in Faron Young singing "Hello Walls." Now and then the truck just flat quit on him, and he had little tricks he'd try: waggle the carburetor flap, jiggle the battery cables, smack the solenoid with a ball-peen hammer he stored beneath the seat. Usually one of these did the trick.

Today the truck was humming along fine, and anyway he wasn't pushing it, just easing up the grade toward the overpass, his house and barn visible off to his left, and closer to the road, Billy's trailer half hidden behind a skein of ratty spruce. He thought about the interior of his house then, the rooms patient and silent, the letter from the village attorney on the kitchen table. There was something to the driving that was resonant of that still life, as if by going mobile he was putting everything else on hold, the only world that mattered contained within the space of the cab. You took your pressure relief where you could find it, he thought.

Harley slowed as he crossed the overpass, bemused as usual by the traffic streaming through what had been the hay fields of his youth. "I wonder sometimes where they're all going," said Harley wistfully one evening as he and Billy drank second beers by the light of the burn barrel and listened to the nonstop rubberized rush. "Walmart, mostly," said Billy.

But Harley liked to think there was more to it than that. Today, with time to spend, he downshifted to consider the matter further and was overcome from behind by a blast of twin air horns. He started, slopping his coffee and smearing maple frosting on the shift knob. *Always SPILLING things!* he thought, even as he looked up to find his rearview mirror filled with the grille of Klute Sorensen's elevated Hummer, the chromium brush buster decorated for the season with a Christmas wreath upon which perched a bald eagle wrapped in the American flag and wearing a gold tinsel halo currently peeled back like a comb-over in a hurricane.

Dabbing at the coffee as Klute charged past him, Harley couldn't bring himself to make eye contact. In fact, the vehicular height differential rendered this impossible and Harley was limited to a glimpse of his own reflection in the Hummer's chrome-plated running board. As he watched the roaring road hog veer left into Clover Blossom Estates, Harley wiped the long john frosting from the shift knob with his sleeve and figured he'd take all the people on that interstate over Klute Sorensen any day.

THERE IS SOME doubt as to whether Clover Blossom Estates ever had a shot at living up to its name, but it was certainly falling short at the moment, paved as it was with a meandering melange of shoulderless dead-end roads and a sparse array of chintzy split-levels, many marked by hangdog FOR SALE signs pitched at a cant in the snow. For the most part, Harley couldn't bear to look at the development. He would see those insta-homes and bereft plastic toys and collapsed soft-sider pools and cheap trampolines and then the image of his father would superimpose itself, the man working from dusk to dawn for all those years just to hang on, and then, in the end, having to give way anyway.

Instead, he cast his eyes to the north side of the road, where Margaret Magdalene's salvage yard sat enclosed within a tall fence constructed of corrugated steel. Meg had been compelled to put up the fence after receiving letters from Vance Hansen citing her operation as an eyesore in violation of heretofore unenforced "smart growth" statutes. Everyone knew the impetus for Vance's newfound esthetic concerns came via Klute, as the salvage yard had been there for all the decades Meg's father ran it, right up through to the present, and not only had no one objected, it was considered a visual fascination what with all the unusual bits and pieces and beached vehicles, and the tremendously entertaining homemade vehicle crusher, which in the context of Swivel's available entertainment options delivered the equivalent punch of a feature at the IMAX. Now nothing was visible above the fence but the boom of Meg's crane. Most days it could be seen dipping and swooping as she sorted steel and dropped cars into the crusher, but today, with Meg off to Christmas services, it stood still.

Meg and Harley had known each other since kindergarten,

having passed thirteen years as classmates, making their way from kindergarten to graduation in Swivel's single school building. Neither was particularly popular among their peers, nor were they unpopular, simply present as such. These days Meg and Harley were on a nodding acquaintance—he had sold her some scrap and an old two-bottom plow after his father died—but he knew little about her beyond what he observed: She worked hard, she worked steadily, and the only person who spent more time at St. Jude's—Father Carl included—was the Blessed Virgin Mary in her bathtub.

Despite himself, Harley glanced back to his left, to where he used to build forts and hunt rabbits along the fence line, and later, when he was old enough to drive a tractor, rake the hay before he and his father baled it. The fence lines were gone now, replaced by nursery shrubberies and stick saplings staked and strung stiff in the freezing wind. The houseless lots were tufted with brown weeds sprung sparsely through the snow crust like back hair on a pale man. A single string of Christmas lights hanging from the eaves of one of the few occupied houses only heightened the spavined grimness of the scene. Accelerating past the gates of Meg's salvage yard, Harley steered into the northward curve with the heel of his hand, determined to put Clover Blossom Estates out of sight and mind.

The roads were spotty with snowpack and ice, but Harley had the back end of his truck loaded down with two tractor tires, several five-gallon plastic buckets of sand, and a decommissioned transmission he intended to drop off with Meg come spring, so traction was no trouble. He rolled along, the heater blowing the aroma of that Kona Luna to all corners of the cab. He purposely held off on the long john and doughnuts. He didn't want to mess with the flavor of that first sip. As good as pastry goes with coffee, Harley always felt the sugars disrupted the palate. *One loses the finer notes,* he thought. Then he grinned at himself: gas station coffee soaking his pants, frosting stuck to his sleeve, the radio blasting "Grandma Got Run Over by a Reindeer."

Yah, he thought. *Like you're the king of finer notes.*

KLUTE SORENSEN SAT parked in his idling Hummer at the far end of Clover Blossom Estates and considered the state of things. It was time to get serious. Jacking up Vance Hansen had been a start, although he wasn't sure even now that the boy was up to the job. If Vance and the village couldn't get it done, Klute might have to bring in a bigshot attorney from Clearwater—or so he liked to tell himself, although whether he could afford the legal fees he did not know. But he figured he had a pretty good shot at dislodging Harley Jackson. That fellow didn't seem to have a lot of fight in him.

And then there was Meg Jankowski. Klute had been applying pressure on her via Vance Hansen's "smart growth" letters, and he had been planning to increase the pressure. But last night, up there all alone in that big house of his, he got to thinking about how the last time he saw her she was paying cash for gas in the Kwik Pump and he noticed her calloused hands and thought, *Surely she is ready for a better life. A life where she doesn't have to lug crushed cars and dress in coveralls.* Klute also noticed her form beneath the coveralls and this too played into the equation. He wasn't sure how to go about acting on this new angle, but the seed was planted. Looking across the road to the salvage yard, he squeezed his eyes shut tight and imagined it replaced with a Burger King and a Motel

6 and then he imagined driving slowly through a booming and blooming Clover Blossom Estates with Meg in the passenger seat of the Hummer, her eyes turned admiringly upon him, her hands manicured and soft, the diamond on her ring finger glittering like a disco ball.

Klute opened his eyes and turned his attention to the actual view. He had hoped for so much more. Rather than this sad batch of houses, he had envisioned a thriving suburb. There should be a profusion of holiday lights, he thought. Festive plywood Santas! Rows of those paper sack thingies filled with sand and burning candles! The curbs should be thick with empty minivans, the occupants inside, ripping into gifts. Instead he got this . . . this . . . this *betrayal*.

"No better time to hoist canvas," intoned the upbeat narrator of *Set Sale!*, which was booming in the speakers, "than when you are becalmed! Be ready for the breeze!"

Klute Sorensen punched the Off button, blew a very wet raspberry at the windshield, and hit the accelerator, drawing great satisfaction from the roar of the engine and the screech of the tires as he hopped the curb, blasted a shortcut through the snow covering one of his many undeveloped lots, and put the disappointment of Clover Blossom Estates in his rearview mirror.

OUT ON THE road Harley had settled into the drive, leaning forward, lacing his fingers and draping his forearms around the steering wheel. As he rolled along, he relived his gas station encounter. This Mindy: he hadn't seen her before. Although he was not dialed into Swivel's social scene much beyond the gossip he eavesdropped on from the back row of folding chairs during the monthly fire department meeting, he figured he would have heard of her before if she had been here long. She seemed the sort to cut a swath. And he wasn't the only single fellow in town whose heart might get the yips over a woman like that in a truck like that.

Harley was no monastic, but neither was he what you'd call a "swinging" bachelor. Lately he had been on a sustained celibate stretch. His last relationship had come to a precipitous and inglorious end in an art gallery in Clearwater. In its wake he felt neither bereft nor bereaved; rather more faded out on the whole idea of trying so hard for so little. At forty-two years of age, he had a long track record of never quite making relationships last, and lately he hadn't even been all that wound up about making them start.

And yet, of course, even the most reticent heart is ressurrectable, and this Mindy had tripped something in him. Her sense of humor, her buddy-movie grin, her roughneck spark, those boots, they all suggested someone who wouldn't necessarily need Harley to supply much maintenance. He was also, he had to admit, tantalized by that tattoo.

Even so, he knew what would happen: What had always happened. Being shy, but determined, he would spend up to three months circling and hoping and working up accidental meetings, and rehearsing her companionship in his head as silly as any lovesick high-schooler, all to build up to the courage of asking her out. It was an established pattern of over twenty years now, no less pathetic for its consistency.

BACK IN SWIVEL, Meg was heading home. The Christmas services had been wonderful. Father Carl had fairly glowed with holiness, and as Meg looked over the congregation she felt as always the combination of joy and wonder at the power of people gathered, of heads bowed, of hymns sung. She admitted to some slight peevishness over the size of the congregation on this day as opposed to any given standard Sunday, and to wondering where everyone disappeared to the rest of the year. It wasn't so much the state of their souls she worried about, but rather the state of her church.

The sideburns Father Carl had worn when he married Meg and Dougie were gone now, as was much of the hair on his head, and over the course of time, the congregation had likewise thinned. Most Sundays entire pews would be empty, the Naugauhyde unwarmed. In fact, St. Jude's was in danger of deconsecration. There were rumblings that the higher-ups wanted to shunt the Swivel congregation to Boomler. While the official line cited attendance, many suspected it had more to do with the fact that the Swivel church had been paid off years ago, whereas the much grander Boomler church still carried a significant mortgage. The matter had yet to be decided, but word in the diocese was that Bishop Burkle was definitely doing the math.

Never mind, thought Meg, shaking her head. She didn't want to surrender her joy just yet. As she crossed above the interstate, she thought of how she had heard the sirens that day, how she had run from the salvage yard to the overpass, and looking over the railing to the south, saw the cluster of flashing red lights and knew, just knew, Dougie was gone.

We never shared a married Christmas, thought Meg. After she pulled through the salvage yard gate, she switched the truck off and sat there for a bit, listening to the engine click and cool. She wondered what it would have been like to share today with Dougie, to hold his hand during the homily, to rise from the pew and sing beside him. She wondered what he might have looked like with some age on him.

She wondered, in fact, where he *was*.

THE MAPLE-FROSTED LONG john and three of the doughnuts were gone and the Kona Luna was down to a lukewarm slosh when Harley pointed his truck for home. He had driven a meandering loop and was now pulling onto the straight stretch of Five Mile Road that led past the Big Swamp and back to Swivel when he noticed Mindy's F-250 parked at the old Nicolet place. Harley hit the brakes again, hanging at the stop sign with his blinker on. The Nicolet place was pretty much a wreck, the barn fallen in and the house not far behind. The sturdiest structure on the place was the granary, and the F-250 was parked right beside it. The granary windows were covered with Visqueen, and Harley could see light within. Outside the granary a table saw was set up beside two sawhorses, and there was fresh sawdust in the snow. Seeing movement behind the Visqueen, Harley blanched at the idea of getting caught looking, casting himself as a stalker before he even got started. He lurched from the stop sign and headed for town. Sneaking one more look in the rearview mirror he perceived the shape of what appeared to be a motorcycle beneath a snowbound tarp, and it occurred to him that he had never even considered the possibility of a boyfriend.

Shaking it off, he looked over to the passenger side of the truck and imagined Mindy riding over there come spring, the window open, her one hand raised to keep the hair from her eyes, her turning to him and smiling, him smiling back. He rehearsed how he might look at her, easy like, toward the space just inside the empty passenger-side window, about where her face would be were she actually present. He worked up a little one-sided grin and bobbed his head back a tad, like they were sharing some old familiar joke.

Oh, the whole thing was silly, he thought, as he rolled past the Big Swamp and up McCracken Hill. Less than an hour since he'd met her, and already he was feeling proprietary—and he hadn't done anything more than pour coffee on her boots and mumble some.

"Besides, son," he said, addressing himself bachelor style, "you have other issues to address."

Specifically: that calf.

Billy's suggestion was preposterous, of course. You couldn't make a million off a birth-marked steer. A few grand maybe. Charge five bucks admission, do the T-shirts, sure, but *millions*? And what if it did take off? *I could use the money*, thought Harley, *but not the trouble*. Even if he took it to the sale barn and tried to sell it for straight-up market rate, there'd be unwanted attention. The thing was, he kept coming back to the image of his mother, quiet and solid in her faith. His father too, working hard and honestly, asking no quarter from anyone even when it meant selling off the land he loved. It had been a long time since Harley believed what his parents believed, but he had watched them live, and he could feel them watching him now. Better he keep that calf under wraps, see if it outgrew the Jesus face, then raise it for a beefer, just like any other.

What he needed to do now, he thought, as he pulled into his driveway, was figure a way to ask Mindy Johnson out on a date.

PART

TWO

CHAPTER 12

On the first Saturday of the new year, Harley attended the monthly fire meeting. Rail shipments of crude oil through Swivel had recently increased, and after a story in the national news about a small town nearly wiped out when several oil cars blew up, Chief Knutson moved the meeting to the weekend in order to accommodate the schedule of an instructor from the regional technical college who was an expert on tank explosions.

Harley served on the fire department because his father told him a man should do something of service to his fellow citizens in which he can take pride. His father was very careful to distinguish this form of pride from false pride and pridefulness, which he viewed as pernicious to the soul. But to take pride in serving others was acceptable.

Harley did as his father instructed. He helped pressure-test hose on weeknights. He always hung around until the last bit of gear was stowed after a big fire. He could be counted on to come down on one of his days off to check the oil in the pumper or do inventory. He figured it was the least he could do what with him not having kids and a family.

He fought fires, too, and helped out on ambulance calls. He was hardly a hero, but he did have the underrated but essential ability to keep calm. That, and he was good at pitching in and taking direction. He had no desire to lead the charge, but he was always a good foot soldier.

BEFORE TRAINING BEGAN, everyone convened for the meeting. Sitting in his usual back-row spot, Harley listened to the discussion of last month's rescue runs, including a case review of the chimney fire out on Kaplinski Road. It was agreed that things might have gone better if the department owned a thermal imager, a device that allows firefighters to detect heat inside walls. Sadly, thermal imagers are very expensive, and despite two raffles and a charcoal chicken dinner the money just wasn't there yet, so the Swivel department had to work old-school, feeling for heat with the back of their hands, and when in doubt, ripping through the plaster and into the walls themselves, a process that sometimes led to difficulties on the public relations front. Chief Knutson also pointed out that the thermal imagers were a critical tool in locating fallen or trapped firefighters, as they could also see through smoke. Boober Johnson piped up and added that because of the warmth of the human body, thermal imagers could also be used to spot lost or fugitive individuals in the wild. Boober was in charge of the Swivel Volunteer Fire Department Search and Rescue Division, which currently consisted of little more than a bag of whistles and a flashlight.

Mostly, however, proceedings were dominated by the Jamboree

Days planning committee. Jamboree Days didn't happen until Fourth of July weekend, but preemptive planning was critical. For instance, Porta-Potties had to be reserved before the Boomler Fire Department snatched them all up for their Buttermilk Bash, and softball tournament entry forms had to be mailed to all taverns within a forty-mile radius. There was also the usual extended debate on beer selection and pricing, as well as the establishment of a subcommittee dedicated to erecting a new bratwurst stand.

And of course, number one on the agenda, fireworks. Nothing dominated discussion like fireworks. Harley never understood the obsession. Pretty, sure, and who doesn't like some boom-boom, but ultimately it seemed like putting a match to money. But there was pride in play. Like the tough trucks contest held between monster truck races at the Clearwater Fairgrounds, where you knew a guy couldn't afford his truck in the first place and yet everyone cheered wildly as he wrecked it.

When Chief Knutson announced that due to budget constraints this year's fireworks display might have to be trimmed back, there were groans of dismay and an immediate hubbub of fund-raising suggestions including donkey basketball, a meat raffle, and a firefighter belly-dancing contest, for which many members of Swivel Volunteer Fire Department were well equipped.

"You already win," said Boober, poking Chief Knutson in the belly, at which point the chief adjourned the meeting and sent everyone off to the main bay, where the tank explosion expert began by showing a PowerPoint presentation that included several GIFs of backyard propane tanks and rail cars exploding in slow motion, to which the Swivel Volunteer Fire Department responded with high fives and approving whoops.

How much of the other information was taken to heart remained in some doubt, although everyone's ears perked up when the instructor hit the section on boiling liquid expanding vapor explosions, strictly defined as an explosion caused by the rupture of a vessel containing a pressurized liquid above its boiling point and known in the firefighting trade by the acronym BLEVE. As many of the slides illustrated, a BLEVE is an astounding thing, hell in a black-capped mushroom cloud, but mostly everyone was giggling at the fact that the acronym was pronounced BLEVVY, which sounded rather silly. "Lookout, she's gonna BLEVVY!" hollered Froggy Simpson, pointing at Chief Knutson's belly, which indeed bore more than passing resemblance to a propane tank.

"That'd be yer HEAVY BLEVVY!" said a guffawing Carlene Hestekin.

After the PowerPoint presentation was complete, the chief ordered everyone to suit up in full gear and put the lesson into practice. It was nearing zero degrees outside, so the troops were loathe to leave the heated hall, but then the instructor announced he had a simulated rail tanker mounted on a trailer that was hooked up to a fog machine and shot fire, and soon everyone was outside battling the mock disaster. Despite the cold, the crews worked up a sweat with all the turnout gear and the hose dragging and knee crawling, and Harley had stepped back to the edge of Elm Street and was taking a pull at a Gatorade when a big red F-250 pulled up beside him. The window rolled down and Mindy stuck her head out.

"Well, lookit *you*, hotshot!"

Harley flushed red as the fire trucks.

"How'd you—"

"Yer name's on the tail of your jacket," said Mindy.

"Ah," said Harley.

"In four-inch-tall all-capital reflective letters," said Mindy, laughing now.

Harley felt silly, but he also felt good. Standing there in his firefighter's gear, his breathing apparatus slung off one shoulder, his helmet tipped back and the visor up, a shine of work sweat—rather than coffee-slop flop sweat—on his brow, steam rising from his temples, he figured if he was ever gonna cut a halfway masculine figure, this would be it. So much better than stumbling drippily around the gas station clutching bad snacks.

"Yah, we're—"

"I didn't know you were a *fire*fighter!" She was grinning mischievously. "The bold and the brave!"

"Wellll . . . ," said Harley, running his eyes around the rest of the crew by way of moderation. Stig Halvorsen was giggling while closing the valve on Buck Johnson's air hose, the Hestckin twins were arguing about how to best gut a buck, and Susie Herrick was giving Boober Johnson a noogie rub. Harley himself knew his main departmental asset lay in the fact that his twelve-hour shift rotation meant he was often home during the day, when the ranks were thin. But Harley loved serving with this bunch: when the real smoke rolled they were a surprisingly serious-minded crew; in between things ran at about a seventh-grade level.

"You got beefers," Mindy stated.

"Yeeahh . . . ?"

"I want beefers," said Mindy. "Wondered if I could come over and look at your setup."

His *setup*! Harley felt a zing that had nothing to do with talking agriculture.

"Well . . . I . . . ah . . . yah! Yah!" In his eager panic to complete a sentence, he went full-on Norwegian.

"A'right dere den," said Mindy, and Harley couldn't quite tell if that was for real or if she was giving him the needle. "I gotta run to Boomler for wire staples and conduit—the wiring in that old granary is shot! Meet you at your place on my way back?"

"Yah! Oh! Wait! No! I think I . . . ," said Harley, skidding into babble. He could feel his ears glowing. The training session had come to a halt and the entire department was staring at the two of them. Mindy smiled at him encouragingly, like one might smile at a puppy too spooked to leave the carpet and cross the linoleum.

"Yah!" yelped Harley, his voice cracking on the upswing.

"See y'then, then," said Mindy, and tromped the F-250, flinging a light spatter of fishtail slush over the mock-disaster scene.

Harley was pretty sure he heard Susie Herrick snort.

"Grab a hose and get in there, son," said Chief Knutson, rescuing him with a command. With great relief Harley lowered his visor and charged the pretend railroad car, grateful to plunge anonymously back into the action.

But even as he belly-crawled through the fake fog, the aquanaut sound of his breath hissing within the air mask, there was a part of him gone giddy at the idea that within the hour, Mindy Johnson would come down his driveway. Again he found himself grateful that she had been able to see him standing all manly in his firefighting gear, an image to countervail the one of him dribbling coffee on her boots.

This could be good, he thought. The giddiness in his liver was joined by eagerness. Anticipation.

Then he remembered that calf.

CHAPTER 13

The moment he finished extinguishing the fake BLEVE, Harley mimed looking at his cell phone, then approached the chief and handed over his accountability tag. "Uhm, I gotta go—my neighbor Billy says one of my beefers is out."

"Ten-four, copy that," said the chief.

The Silverado didn't start right away, but after Harley gave it a whack on the solenoid with a ball-peen hammer it spun to life on the next try. As he drove the few blocks home, Harley found himself leaning forward in the cab, as if his posture could will the truck forward. He was tense with the idea that somehow Mindy would get to his place first, go nosing around, and discover that calf with Jesus on it. And then at the railroad tracks he had to wait for a train. It was a long one, made up mostly of tankers like the one he had just been training on.

What will I do? Harley thought as the rail cars trundled past.

Mindy had asked to see his "setup," which implied she didn't want to only look at the cows, or discuss hay prices, she actually wanted to review the whole operation—which would include the barn.

Where that calf was standing, even now.

What happens when she sees that calf? Harley looked nervously down the row of oncoming rail cars, debating whether it would be quicker to run up to North Star Road and cut around the tail of the train.

What if I don't show it to her? What if I keep her out of the barn?

"Well, you can't count on that," said Harley, out loud now. He couldn't show her "the setup" and yet somehow mysteriously keep her out of the one building central to "the setup." The electric fencer unit was in there, and the feed room, and even the manure spreader, which lately he'd taken to bringing in through the side door so it was snow free and close at hand when it was time to clean Tina Turner's pen. Even if he only showed her the haymow, he'd still have to take her through the front door and right past that cow pen in order to get to the ladder.

Harley thought he could see the tail end of the train approaching. It was harder to tell now that cabooses were a thing of the past. *So many damn things just disappear,* he thought. Rather than go for the North Star Road end-around, he figured he'd wait it out.

Harley knew: there was no keeping Mindy out of the barn. She wasn't the kind of person to let that go without a *why not?*

"So what to do, Sparky?" Harley asked himself. There was one possibility he hadn't considered: hiding the calf. But where? The feed room was already on the tour, and he couldn't risk moving the calf outside the barn, lest someone happen in on him in the process. Besides, Tina Turner would put up a fuss, and moo like mad. It also occurred to him that upon meeting Mindy in the Kwik Pump he had told her he'd been up with a calving cow, and you know she'd put two and two together and ask about the calf.

Harley shook his head. The problems just multiplied.

And then the last rail car rolled past, Main Street opened up with a view clear up to the overpass, and it was as if the answer opened up with it.

"She can see the calf . . . she just doesn't have to see *Jesus*."

He smiled and punched the gas.

THE REVELATION RELIEVED the pressure some, but he was still doing the math on how long it would take Mindy to run her Boomler errand and return. His nervousness spiked when he found his driveway blocked by Dixie the mail carrier. Dixie was a cheerful character who delivered the U.S. mail in a vintage U.S. Postal Service Jeep that allowed her to drive from the right-hand side. A faithful member of Reverend Gary's Church of the Roaring Lamb, she had stenciled an ichthy across the tailgate of the Jeep. Harley learned the word *ichthys* from Billy, who said every time he saw one he got hungry for tartar sauce. Spotting Harley as she pulled away from his mailbox, Dixie stuck her hand out the window and gave him a happy wave.

Harley accelerated right past the mailbox, leaving whatever Dixie had delivered in there. Never seemed to be good news lately anyway, and besides, when he shot a last look up toward the overpass, he saw Mindy's truck approaching the stop sign on the end of the off-ramp.

"Oh man. You gotta hustle."

THE TIN OF Kiwi black shoe polish was in the drawer, still nested in the buffing rag where his father last left it. Harley popped the lid, fearing he'd find it cracked and dry, but saw instead the convex matte disk he remembered. The greasy petrol scent rose to his nose and immediately he became five years old, his shirt tucked into his belted corduroys, his miniature clip-on tie askew, his clunky black Sunday shoes shining beneath the shoe rag in the bathroom light, and his Bible downstairs in its leather carrying case and waiting. His father was a quiet man, and not overly affectionate, but there was a gentleness to the way he buffed out Harley's miniature wingtips before they set off for Sunday morning meeting. Later, while sitting through testimony time with his chin in his hands, Harley studied the reflection of his face in the gleaming tips of his shoes and wondered how Jesus could see everybody all of the time.

Memories such as this always brought on a feeling of displacement, an utter inability to understand how he had gotten from there to here, a common enough emotion that nonetheless reliably delivered a low-voltage jolt. There was also the mystery of his parents, how they could be so true and loving and yet upon reflection remain such strangers. *You are derailing into discount-level self-analysis and that woman is gonna be here any second*, thought Harley. He shook his head, recapped the polish, and ran for the barn.

The red F-250 arrived at the end of the driveway just as he grabbed the barn door handle. He waved and ducked inside the barn and pulled the door closed behind him. For a moment he could see nothing. He flicked on the light switch and fumbled with the cap of the polish, his fingers suddenly twitchy. He could see the calf backed up against its mother now, nervous at Harley's hasty entry. Tina Turner laid back her ears.

Grabbing a handful of feed as a peace offering, Harley held it toward Tina. After her rough tongue sandpapered his palm clean he dug a glob of polish from the tin and reached for the fuzzy face of Christ.

He had failed to anticipate how opposed the young calf—which he suddenly realized he had not named, having instead come to think of it as the Jesus calf—might be to having its hair colored. Tina Turner turned defensive and rousted Harley with her snout, rooting at his tailbone with enough force to send him stumbling forward. Placing the calf in a soft headlock he dipped into the polish again and took a swipe at the Christ-likeness. Then he found himself suddenly freezing at the idea that he was quite literally attempting to wipe out the Son of God. It wasn't the sort of thing you did lightly, no matter how long it'd been since you cracked your Bible. But then he heard the sound of the F-250 outside the barn door and redoubled his swabbing.

In the end it was a pretty poor job. The polish tended to clump, and it was nearly impossible to work in down to the hide. His hands were black and there were smudges all over his pants. Tina Turner was becoming actively aggressive. The calf was unsteady.

Harley backed off for a look. He had hoped for better. It appeared the calf had been rubbed against the underside of an oil pan. Still, Christ's face was no longer recognizable, even at a squint. He capped the shoe polish and dropped it in his back pants pocket.

Hearing the truck door slam, he turned for the door, then stopped. Reaching overhead and using one glove like a hotpad, he unscrewed the lightbulb above the pen until it went dark, stopping before it came out of the socket. There were still two other light-bulbs lit—one down by the silo room and one near the doorway—but by extinguishing the one directly overhead, Harley had created enough dimness and shadow within the pen that when he stepped outside the pen the smudge began to look like an actual black patch. Harley figured he had bought himself some visual wiggle room.

"I'll just have to keep her moving," said Harley.

"And maybe not so much talking out loud to yourself when company's here."

He stepped out of the barn door.

"BEEN WRENCHIN'?" SAID Mindy. Harley was confused, and then she pointed at his pants and hands, both smeared with black.

"Oh—yah!" said Harley, deciding in the instant to lie. "Yah, manure spreader chain was froze up." He hoped this sounded self-reliant. He also quickly pulled his gloves from his jacket pockets and tugged them on.

"So let's see these beefers of yours," said Mindy. Harley was still adjusting to her straightforward nature. But he was also invigo-rated by the idea of a woman who might carry herself at this level of independence in all respects.

"Guess we might as well start out here," said Harley, leading her down the path to the feed bunk.

"You chew?" she said from behind.

Harley rotated his head and looked at her confusedly. He couldn't tell if she was asking or offering. The idea of a woman chewing tobacco wasn't out of the question; when Harley was in high school Swivel hosted a Swedish foreign exchange student who would take a delicate pinch of Skoal in her upper lip. This, combined with the fact that she was a classically blond and blue-eyed Scandinavian wonder who spoke broken English with a lisp rendered her so Nordically exotic the local boys nearly choked on their Copenhagen. Their after-school dreams were feverish with Scandinavian nymphets wafting through wintergreen-scented mists. Harley himself recalled a certain weakness behind the kneecaps over the whole deal.

"Nah," said Harley to Mindy. Unsure of the scale against which he was being measured—or if he was being measured at all—he hoped this wouldn't count against him. "Why you asking?"

"You got a can in your pants," said Mindy, pointing at his back pocket.

The shoe polish! With a start Harley realized it was still in his back pocket and approximated the same outline as a tin of dip. He also realized she had implicitly revealed she was studying his butt.

"Oh, ha," he laughed nervously, "No, no . . . no, that's just shoe polish."

"Oookay," said Mindy, and then nothing more, all her amusement implied.

"Yah, I, I was . . . ," Harley floundered.

"Y'don't seem like a real shoe polisher," said Mindy, the grin right there in her voice, something Harley began to feel was there quite a bit.

"Yah, my dad . . . he . . . I was cleanin' out a drawer . . ."

"So these are the beefers," said Mindy, pointing at the cows and changing the subject in the most obvious way.

"Yahp," said Harley, limp in his relief.

Mindy immediately peppered him with questions. Where did he

get them? What did he feed them? How long did it take to bring them to market? Which breed did he prefer? Why didn't they have horns? Harley answered as best he could.

"I just kinda raise 'em on the side," he said. "It's not really that complicated. Y'know, get 'em their food and water, check 'em now and then."

"Now and then?"

"Well, every day," said Harley. "You really do need to get out among 'em." He hesitated, not wanting to sound too precious, but then he said, "My dad. He called it being a good husbandman. I'd say he was right. You want to know the animals. The way they act day to day. So you can tell early on when something's not right."

"So you're a firefighter *and* a husbandman!" said Mindy.

"Amateur at both," said Harley, kicking the dirt.

"*Husbandman*—that's kind of a male-centric double whammy, wouldn't you say? If I get beefers, can I be a *wifewoman*?"

"Well, it's just a word," said Harley, pulling back within himself nervously and thinking for a moment of a woman he'd dated in college, a motorcycle-boots-wearing feminist with a skunk streak bleached into her hair who jerked the intellectual slack out of him when he used the word *gals*.

Mindy gave him a push on the shoulder. "Oh, don't worry there, big shot."

Harley felt the familiar seep of nape sweat.

HE SHOWED HER the whole deal: the pasture layout, the watering system and the heater that kept the water unfrozen over winter, the portable corrals, and the loading chute he used when he took an animal to the sale barn. She kept firing questions about fencing and grazing and grain supplements and galvanized water tanks versus rubberized, and solar-powered fence chargers, and all in all it was clear she'd done her research.

After he showed her the small shed where he stored his father's old Farmall tractor and John Deere baler, he figured maybe he'd get by without showing her the barn, but then she asked about the fencer unit and where he kept the hay, so it became inevitable.

Keep'er movin', he thought, as he opened the door. In the transition to the interior of the barn they could see only darkness. Harley flicked the wall switch and all but the light over the pen came on.

"Oh!" said Mindy, as her eyes adjusted and she saw the cow and calf.

"Milk cow," said Harley by way of explanation. He was deeply relieved to see the calf lying with his holy side nestled against his mother.

"You mind?" said Mindy, putting her hand on the stall gate.

"I . . . yah, no, fine," said Harley, his heart thudding.

"Look at *yewww*," said Mindy, kneeling down to scratch the calf between his ears. It was the most girlish thing Harley had heard her utter thus far.

"You live here all your life?" Mindy was looking up from where she was cuddling the calf in the shadows.

"Pretty much," said Harley, sidling into the pen and subtly trying to put himself in a blocking position in case the calf got to its feet. "Went to the college in Clearwater for a while. Didn't finish."

"But you're happy?"

Harley realized he didn't really have an answer for that. "I'm . . . I mean . . . I guess, yeah."

Mindy looked at him with a friendly smirk.

"Well, aren't you a balla fire!"

"Nah. Just kinda happy with things the way they are. Could be better, could be worse." The calf was getting to its feet.

"So you set the bar pretty high."

Harley tried to grin, but he was preoccupied with putting himself between the calf and Mindy.

She jumped up and punched him in the shoulder. "Oh, I'm being too hard on ya! Let's see the haymow!" She pointed to the rafters over the pen. "By the way, you've got a lightbulb burnt out."

"Yah, I was gonna . . . ," said Harley, but she was already moving past him toward the haymow ladder.

There was a tricky moment of protocol when Harley didn't know who should go up the ladder first but Mindy resolved that by beating him to it. He tried to follow at a chaste distance without looking up but then did anyway, right in time to catch a chunk of alfalfa chaff across his cornea.

In the haymow he stood with one eye watering and explained how the bales got up there on the elevator and that Billy helped by unloading the wagons, and that he stacked the bales in the same pattern his father had out of habit, and then he noticed Mindy was gazing up at the roof and he trailed off, instead studying her throat in profile, the tip of the northernmost tattooed ivy leaf visible at the base of her neck. The haymow was quiet but for their breathing, all the sound muted within the banks of tightly packed hay.

"Lookit the frostcicles!" she said, in a near whisper.

Harley tipped his head back. High above them the shingle nails protruding through the roof boards were furred with frost, stark and delicate against the rough-cut lumber. This was nothing new to Harley—he'd first seen them as a child when his dad sent him out here on winter days to throw down bales—but he had always loved to look at them, always had a fascination for how the outside cold traveled through the nail and how the nail pulled the moisture of cow's breath from the air and transformed it into white velveteen spikes. It was the kind of beauty that resonated in his heart like a tiny bell, the kind of minute observation he'd jot down for his creative-writing journal in college but not the kind of thing you rhapsodized on down at the fire hall.

Without warning, Mindy flopped onto her back, landing in a pile of loose hay left by a bale that had slipped its twine and broken apart coming off the elevator.

"Doesn't it fascinate you? Little beautiful things like that? Especially in this loud ridiculous world? And isn't it the cheapest sort of heaven to be able to climb into a place like this and lie around like the rest of the world has been put on hold until you're ready for it again?" Her eyes were sparkling like the frost.

Harley agreed, although he didn't know how to say so.

"C'mon, lie down and look up!"

"I . . . ah . . ."

Mindy bounced to her feet. "Aw, I made you nervous. Sometimes I go too fast."

Harley desperately wanted to try something bold and uncalled for but he felt cast in caramel. He thought of flopping to his back but realized he had missed the moment and would look like a clown and might even knock the wind out of himself.

"You!" said Mindy, like a command. "You wanna get together again?"

She had one hand on the ladder, ready to descend.

"Yah?" said Harley, and as weakly as he said it he never meant anything more powerfully.

"Take me to the sale barn? Train me in on how to buy beefers?"

"Yah."

"That qualify as a date?"

"Yah. I guess?"

CHAPTER 14

Klute Sorensen fished around with one arm over the side of his bed until he located his smartphone, raised it against the black of the ceiling, and pressed the Home button to check the time. The screen glowed up overbrightly, causing him to squint, which in turn caused his breathing mask to ride up the bridge of his nose. He cursed.

Three a.m.

He cursed again. Then sighed. The only thing more mentally defeating than tossing and turning until after midnight was falling asleep and waking to discover he'd slept just shy of three hours. His brain felt like damp flannel stitched with dry rawhide. He wanted so badly to sleep. Just sleep. Sleep deeply, and sleep long. But lately, no matter how many exhortative audiobooks he cycled through his system, no matter how aggressively he drove the Hummer, the tenuous nature of his financial existence was worming its way into his mind-set. He found himself breaking out in cold sweats. Beset by tremors in his hands. A feeling of adrenalized worry hummed throughout his chest and the fringes of his liver. He'd catch himself clench jawed, drawing lung-bustingly deep breaths through flared nostrils and holding the air until the ribs of his upper back popped along their attachments like a rack of trick knuckles, then exhaling with such force his cheeks inflated like Satchmo blowing E-flat.

Yanking the breathing mask away and switching off the machine, Klute swiped and tapped at the face of his phone. An app bloomed, and Klute tapped again. After a brief pause as the livestream buffered, a woman's voice could be heard updating the vitals of several international stock exchange indices. Klute adjusted the sound down to a nearly inaudible two bars, placed the phone beneath his pillow, then lay down his head and closed his eyes.

It used to be Klute only listened to the business news app in the mornings as he shaved and showered and made coffee. At that hour the voices emanating from studios somewhere in the heart of New York City were focused on the opening bell here in America, anticipating the day in terms of "break-even spreads," "volatility issues," "basis points," and "convergent data." Even if the market was down, hopes were up, and Klute always caught some of that energy, even here in fly-over Boomler. By listening, he felt like he was part of the grand capitalist team. Sometimes he tried to imagine what it was to be one of the on-air guests, joining the show by cell phone from the back of a long black car crossing the East River, or from the top floor of some glass tower flashing with fresh-risen get-to-work-early sun, capably dispatching questions served up by an obsequious soft-balling host. Even when it played indistinctly in the background—as Klute knotted his tie while looking down on Boomler, or returned to the bathroom to dab at a razor nick—the continuous flow of all that beautiful business-world word jazz served as subliminal reassurance: the great machine of international commerce was rolling along, and Klute Sorensen had a ticket for the train.

Lately though, he had taken to monitoring the streaming business news whenever sleep would not come. Even now, at 3 a.m., the mesmerizing chant of numbers and jargon—*monetary aggregates . . . seven-for-one stock splits . . . the "Footsy" up ten . . . Hang Sen off three . . . analyst's average estimates . . . nominal growth paths*—soothed him like one of those white-noise generators used to calm infants. His mind stopped gnawing on his troubles, slowly succumbing instead to the soothing idea that the business of business was spinning the whole world 'round, and would continue to do so, come weather, war, or worse. Green or red, the numbers rose through his Tempur-Pedic pillow and soothed his mind. And then, with the soft sounds of unceasing commerce whispering in his ear, Klute Sorensen slipped into a state of disassociation, and—finally—sleep.

In the morning he popped the phone into the speaker jack, pipped the volume to its uppermost level, and began his day with the world's good business news echoing all throughout his gigantically empty house.

MEG JANKOWSKI BEGAN her day by putting on her hard hat and crushing three cars. As a child, she stood in awe of the car crusher. She would watch with wide eyes as her father ran the hydraulics and the crushing plate pressed implacably down on the hapless vehicle as it shuddered and screeched and the windows popped until it was nothing but creases and pancake. Nowadays she was more businesslike. Because other salvage yards down around Clearwater operated at much higher volume, and were thus far more competitive, Meg survived by searching the back roads and working the fringes. She went the literal extra mile to drag cars out of the deep weeds, pull old corn pickers from the far borders of overgrown farm fields, and snag the remains of abandoned projects, stripping every resalable part from each before converting it into an iron puck. This operating philosophy was also a hedge against the intersection of international market forces and local bootstrappers: A few years back, when China went on a steel buying spree, prices soared to the point that every knucklehead with a trailer dragged his "backup" car off its cement block perch and hauled it to the larger yards in Clearwater. The roads were filled with ramshackle rigs hauling rust-bucket car carcasses. Mostly, the one-off windfall came right back to town and was invested in the Buck Rub Bar.

To further protect herself from cyclical fluctuations, Meg had also maintained her father's tow truck service. There wasn't much to tow around these parts (much of the towing was performed by people using their own resources, which is to say it was not unusual to see one junker tailgating another at the distance of a logging chain), but the presence of the interstate provided a reliable supply of work in the form of tourists with failed transmissions, folks who couldn't locate their spare tire, or drivers ditched during snowstorms. She also had a standing contract with the fire department to help clear all accident scenes. Meg always crossed herself and murmured a prayer for the injured or deceased.

She was tired this morning, having been called out at three a.m. to tow a Winnebago that had blown a radiator hose at mile marker

72, but even when weary, she enjoyed her work, approaching it with the same dedication she exhibited toward her church, albeit as a different order of devotion.

She supposed it was the work that had kept her head occupied while her heart healed in the wake of Dougie's death. In fact, it didn't heal so much as learn to beat with a hole in it. Nonetheless, it was the work that provided her the momentum to persist. Each day there was something to be done, the work quite literally stacking up one car at a time, the towing calls coming at all hours without respect to day or holiday, but always there was the knowledge that the more she worked, the more she could give to the church and the food pantry. It had long been suspected by many around town that Meg was a secret millionaire, and as a longtime single person, she was a deep tither, but the truth was, once the insurance and taxes and upkeep and accountant and permits were paid, there was less remaining than many of Swivel's gossips believed.

Dougie had been Meg's first and only boyfriend. In the years immediately following his death, the thought of "seeing" someone else was frankly unthinkable, and she had thrown herself into the salvage business beside her father. When he had taken ill and she found herself running the business, her busyness had rendered a social life moot. By the time both of her parents were gone, she had settled into the rhythm of work and church and quiet time alone and found herself quite satisfied. In surprisingly short order, a decade had passed.

Lately though, she had been having doubts. What if she was conveniently deceiving herself? The doubts hadn't come on their own; she had been goaded out of her comfort zone by Carolyn Sawchuck.

AS MEG DROPPED the crusher on a Ford Festiva, Carolyn Sawchuck was returning home from her oil-collection rounds. She was feeling the usual sense of relief that came with not having to drive up yet another driveway to face yet another skeptical farmer or leery shade-tree mechanic. Even though many of her stops were made at the request of someone who had torn off one of her phone number strips in the Kwik Pump, she still felt keenly her outsider status, conferred both by her relatively recent arrival (small towns count by generations: a decade was but a moment) and the fact that she was an overeducated oil-collecting earth mother in a Subaru with a dream catcher hung from the rearview mirror and a CO-EXIST sticker on the bumper.

It had been far worse in the early days, when she made cold calls and was greeted with frank suspicion, scowls, and once, a shotgun. By now she had been at it long enough that while her customers still thought her a tree-hugging oddball, word had spread that her checks never bounced, and in fact, several of her regular customers had taken to scrounging on her behalf. As a result, Carolyn Sawchuck's collection rates were climbing.

Unbeknownst to Carolyn, some of her customers were enhancing the volume of their contributions by mixing in everything from paint thinner to stale gasoline. There were times she arrived home light-headed, unaware she was hauling liquid dynamite.

All she knew was she was wearing out that bicycle.

MEG HAD COMMENCED the terminal crimping of a Chevy Malibu when Klute Sorensen's Hummer nosed through the open gate. The approach was unusual, because usually whenever Klute visited he came barging in, driving with his usual confidence and disregard, bailing out of the four-wheeler while it was still coming to a rest in order to aggressively renew his long-standing offer to purchase her land.

But today he paused behind the wheel for a moment, as if collecting himself. And when he did step out, he smoothed the lapels on his suit coat and instead of the usual bluster his expression and posture were that of a grade-schooler about to recite a poem.

Meg let him stand there while she finished flattening the car. This mild shunning was the furthest Meg would depart from her gentle Christian center. Klute had tried to buffalo her from the beginning, thinking that he could push her off the property by proxy, and if not push her off, bribe her off. He had also spoken ill of Harley, whom Meg knew to be a harmless—if adrift—fellow, and whose father had always been a square dealer with her father.

But now here was a different Klute, obviously nervous. Had he a hat, Meg thought, he would have been holding it at waist level and rotating the brim through his hands. As the sound of ripping tin, snapping plastic, and powdering glass reverberated around them, Meg nodded at Klute. He responded with a ghastly ingratiating grin, which, coming from a man accustomed to neither ingratiation nor grinning, unfurled like a matched set of slow-motion cheek cramps.

When the pop-off valves tripped and the car crusher jaws relaxed, Meg shut down the machine and turned to Klute with a smile.

"Not selling, Klute."

"Oh! I, heh-heh, I, I'm not here to, I, I . . ."

"Perhaps you've come to hand-deliver one of Vance Hansen's 'smart growth' letters?"

Klute flushed and ducked his head. With a shock, Meg realized he truly was nervous.

"Klute, I've never seen you so . . . *schoolboy.*"

Klute stubbed his foot at the frozen ground. "Meg, I've treated you poorly." He was looking right at her now, and it seemed that once he'd started talking he didn't dare stop. "I've tried to push you around like I try to push everyone and everything else around. I listen to these damned—*darned*—CDs all the time, and some-times I think they get me all ginned up to the point where I think I can just twelve-step right over the top of everybody and every-thing."

"Well, you are *forceful.*"

"I know," said Klute. "And I've been thinking that has to change." He paused. "A little."

"You still can't have the place."

"Right now I don't want to talk about that."

"What *do* you want to talk about?"

Klute had begun to ease in the face, but now he looked stricken again, as if he had just inhaled—and was now trying to swallow—a chilled slug.

"Well, I thought you . . . I . . . *we* might work better as a team."

"Klute, I've run this business alone ever since Dad died, and I don't see any reason to do it any differently."

"No . . . well . . . not the *business* . . . well, I mean, maybe the *business*, but I was thinking more maybe we could go somewhere and talk about how . . . what . . . the . . ."

And it was right then, as he trailed off, that Meg realized Klute Sorensen was asking her out on a date.

And then Carolyn Sawchuck arrived.

When Carolyn saw Klute, she frowned. Since she and Meg had become friends, they had often discussed Klute's visits, and his bullheaded attempts to get Meg to sell out. Carolyn had taken her lumps in feminist circles, but that had done nothing to impede her bristling when a man tried to shove a woman around.

"Well, hello there, bulldozer breath," said Carolyn as she stepped out of the car. Meg hid a smile, but Carolyn was surprised when Klute said nothing in return. She had expected him to hurl an insult, or storm off, but instead he just stood there, like he wasn't sure what to say.

"Hello, Carolyn," said Meg, unwilling to embarrass Klute, no matter that he might have deserved it. "Can you please allow Klute and me a moment?"

What's this *all about?* wondered Carolyn as she returned to the Subaru and backed over to the elevated container in which Meg stored her oil. As she drained the oil into a series of five-gallon buckets, she could see—but not hear—Klute and Meg in conversation.

"WELL, THE THING is," said Klute, swallowing and looking as if he wasn't sure what to say next, "the thing is, we have a lot in common."

"Okay?" said Meg in the form of a question. She didn't agree, and she wasn't sure she wanted to hear, but she was curious.

"Well, both our daddies were successful."

Meg looked around at the mangled cars and ancient crane and yard full of dirty slush.

"After a manner of speaking, yes."

"We both know what it is to strive for our own success."

"Out of necessity, yes. Although your definition—"

"We're both on our . . . we don't . . . neither one of us . . . we're—"

"Single?"

Klute blushed brick red.

Now Meg became brisk. "Yes, Klute, I do see overlap in some respects. And there are times when it might be nice to share the company of someone over a meal. But you can't just go from ramming around demanding things in that Hummer to pussyfooting around with dinner invitations."

Klute racked his brain. All those CDs packed with punchy phrases carefully crafted to close the sale, but he drew an echoing blank.

Meg let him gawp a minute, then was surprised to feel a twinge of pity. Harder men had softened, she thought. Who was she to stand in the way of repentance? Did not Christ forgive his persecuters? Perhaps, she thought, Klute was going all Saul of Tarsus.

Carolyn reappeared, the oil loaded. She rolled down the window, and ignoring Klute, said to Meg, "See you Tuesday at the pantry?"

"Yes," said Meg. Both women looked expectantly at Klute. In the past, he had disparaged the food pantry. "Those people don't need free food, they need *jobs*," he had said when they came to the village board meeting to obtain permits. "You keep feeding 'em, they'll never feed themselves. *Teach a man to fish. Et cetera.*"

But today Klute stood mute until Carolyn drove out the gate. Then he turned to Meg. "So you're not saying *no* . . ."

"I'm saying all things considered, over the course of time you've given me a hundred reasons to say no, and none to say yes. But sometimes, well, *comfort the afflicted, the Lord works in mysterious ways . . . et cetera*, well, sometimes we are called to those things we least expect."

"So?" said Klute, hopeful enough that he managed not to take umbrage at the implicit skewering he had just absorbed.

"So I'm going to have to think about this."

Klute's face was red again. But it wasn't an angry red. *I have to get some different audiobooks*, he was thinking.

"Thank you for stopping by, Klute."

"Oh. Yes, yes. I'll . . . I'll stop back by."

"I'm sure you will."

In the Hummer, Klute repressed his desire to stomp the accelerator with both feet. Again it wasn't anger, but rather just a desire to flee. Unfortunately, he had failed to anticipate the logistics of retreat, and between the outsize Hummer and the cramped confines of the yard, he now found himself in the process of executing a laborious five-point turn in the shape of a child's crudely drawn star. While heaving around to look back over his shoulder, he bumped the volume knob on the custom stereo, and the confines of the scrap yard reverberated with the booming narrator of *Set Sale!*

"YOU ARE THE CAPTAIN!!!"

Meg shook her head, smiled, and turned for the crane. She had to get that car loaded up.

Right about the time Klute cleared the on-ramp it occurred to him that perhaps Meg and Carolyn were a couple.

CHAPTER 15

The day after giving Mindy her tour, Harley screwed the loose lightbulb back in and cleaned Tina Turner's pen. As he forked manure into the spreader, the Jesus calf gamboled in and out of Harley's way. It was already bulking up, growing strong and sturdy on Tina Turner's milk. The shoe polish had faded more quickly than he expected. Jesus was looking gray in the face, but was once again clearly Jesus. He'd have to come up with something better than Kiwi black. Especially if Mindy was going to be around more. He held out hope that the calf would outgrow the image on its ribs, but so far it was expanding in proportion. Same visage as the day Harley first saw it, only larger now.

It was good meditation time, cleaning calf pens. Physical labor always helped Harley sort his mind. There was a rhythm to running the pitchfork, a state of physical autopilot that perfused the brain but allowed it to cogitate independently of the task at hand.

He was taking stock, thinking of Mindy, and how he had not felt such anticipation over a woman for a good long while. There was a roughness to her, a coarseness, and a good-humored independence that had him at once hopeful and on edge. Of course this conception was based on little more than initial impressions and his own desires, and was thus unsullied by reality.

Harley might never have dated a woman were it not for a long-legged farmer's daughter named Wendy Willis who asked him to the Sadie Hawkins dance when he was sixteen. Up until that day, he couldn't imagine talking to a girl, but the Sadie Hawkins format flipped the roles. Harley stammered around but finally got to "yes," and later, when Wendy kissed him beside her mailbox on Poleaxe Road, he figured there were joys here worthy of transcending all reticence. When Wendy turned her back to him in the high school library a week later and disappeared into the nonfiction stacks with Scooter Eckstrom, Harley felt he'd never love again, but three days later Kelly Motzer lingered near his locker applying Bubble Gum Lipsmacker and he found his sadness and reservations trumped. In short, he was hooked, and the following year (he and Kelly having fizzled) for homecoming he worked up the courage to ask Jenny Haskins out. That one lasted through basketball season and included several sessions of postgame kissy face in the darkened rear seats of the game bus, but by spring Jenny had lost interest. His senior year was fallow, and he arrived at the university in Clearwater with all of his virginity and most of his naiveté intact. This chaste state was due in part to lack of opportunity, bone-deep Scandinavian reserve, and the old shyness bugaboo, but it was also a product of his old-school Christian upbringing, in which sex was reserved for marriage and those who engaged preemptively were bound to recline long-term upon the coals of doom.

Then, early in the first quarter of his college career, while struggling with his prerequisites, Harley left the library and wandered into the student center, where, in pursuit of beer (the backsliding had begun), he quite accidentally found himself in the middle of a straggily attended poetry reading supported with a cash bar. As he was not allowed to leave the premises with his bottle, he took a table. He had never been to a poetry reading before, and beyond a few childhood nursery rhymes knew nothing of the genre. His first impression of the proceedings was that most of the student poets acted as if they'd never before seen a microphone, and his second impression was that the proceedings would improve considerably were the microphone removed. Just as he was tipping the last of the beer down his throat and preparing to bolt, a woman stepped forward wearing calf-high motorcycle boots with a leather miniskirt and tights, a multitude of jangling wrist bangles, and a skunklike stripe of white through her otherwise jet-black hair. Standing squarely before the mic she read three poems in succession, delivering each in a level, nondemonstrative tone that at first listen seemed apathetic but upon closer attention seemed a fearless determination to let the poems speak for themselves. Contrasted against all the evening's preceding verse (much of it rehashing the disappointments of spring break and the Mysteries of Man as Observed from the Seventh Floor Dorm with a Buzz On), Harley's untrained ear found the skunk-hair woman's poems woven as tough and tight as Kevlar.

But the motorcycle boots clinched it.

Heart high in his throat, he lingered at the exit beside the Pepsi machine and as she walked—alone—to the door he said, "I liked your poems."

"Oh!" she said. "Thank you." She seemed sweetly embarrassed, which Harley was not expecting, what with the bangles and skunk hair and motorcycle boots and all.

"I mean, I don't really *get* poetry . . ."

"Neither do most the people in that place," said the skunk-haired girl, nodding back toward the reading room. "At least you have the good sense to admit it. You want to go for a beer?"

"Well, I just had—," started Harley, and then he thought, *What are you saying, idiot-face?* and then he gulped and said, "Um, yah."

She took him to a creaky-floored joint hung with smoke, where they sat at a corner table beneath a large black-and-white photo of someone Harley assumed was a jazz musician due to the fact that he was smoking a cigarette and holding a saxophone.

Later that night she took him back to her apartment.

In the morning he prayed to be forgiven.

That night he went to her arms again.

HARLEY WAS LEANING on the pitchfork, studying that calf and recalling the skunk-haired girl (*woman,* he corrected himself, recalling her instruction on that point). Over twenty years gone. They had a strong six months, then they ran out of common ground and even poetry and motorcycle boots could not save them. He figured maybe Skunk-haired Girl had broken his heart, but he had to believe she did his head a lot of good. Expanded it, he supposed she would say. To this day he liked a whiff of patchouli now and again, and it was thanks to her encouragement that he had filled one of his humanities electives with a creative writing course on his way to almost getting his business degree. And on occasion he still attended poetry readings at the library in Clearwater.

There had been other women. An emergency room nurse from Boomler—that one ended when the hospital closed and she joined a traveling service. A second go-round with Jenny Haskins after her divorce—that one lasted two weeks longer than the original. He had met the most recent online, thanks to an algorithm that matched them up based on age, a professed interest in the arts, and your basic thirty-mile radius. That one ended in dramatic ignominy at the art gallery, but of all these and the others none had hit him quite like the skunk-haired girl.

But Mindy: this was close. There was a force of impact here he hadn't felt for years. What would it be like, he wondered, to swing by her repurposed granary now and then, for maybe a meal and whatever else followed? To rise in the morning and return to his own quiet house? Or, vice versa, to smile at her from his own pillow as she left his bedroom to begin her own day back at her place? What would it be like, he wondered, to sustain that life right into the future? To never go any more domestic than sleepovers? There were couples who managed it, he knew. And not just for the first two weeks or months, after which things went either solid or sour but rather to live apart happily for years. *Then again,* he thought, *what would it be like to live together in all legal and domicile senses?* To finish dinner and the dishes together, share in the evening chores, take to bed with an eye toward the day and the years ahead?

And what would it be like to share that *secret?* he thought, staring at the Jesus calf. Rather than this shoe polish silliness, rather than a stupid secret, to have her at his side, fully in the know, helping him decide what to do about that calf? A normal person would have called the local TV station. A creative person would have maybe tried to sell the cow to the bank in lieu of all monies owed. *A wise person would have taken that calf out back, and shot it, and buried it deep,* said a voice in his head that sounded suspiciously like Billy.

But Harley Jackson? thought Harley. *Harley Jackson does what he does best: dither. Dither in love, dither in faith, dither in life itself. Dither over Klute's lawsuit, dither over the Jesus calf. You can't keep covering everything over with Kiwi black. Spring'll be here soon, and that'll force your hand. You can't put a wall around the entire pasture like Meg does her junkyard.*

He shook his head. "I'm gonna have to do *something.*"

The barn door opened, and Billy filled it.

"Staff meeting?" said Harley.

"Yahp," said Billy.

Harley jabbed his pitchfork into a straw bale and they walked to the house.

Clear into the new year, and still the letter from the village attorney sat on the kitchen table. Billy flicked it so it spun, stopping with the address right side up before Harley.

"You know this ain't goin' away, right?"

"Yah," said Harley.

"Klute Sorensen is the spiritual equivalent of an orally flatulent bulldog, but a bulldog nonetheless. Masks his effluvial essence with the scent of money—although you'll notice he never actually ponies up—and the locals are willing to overlook a lot of stink for that."

Harley just sat there. There were vast subsections of reality in which he could muster no interest, and this was one of them. And yet he knew he had to do something about it.

"He's got his teeth in. He won't let go. You aren't careful, he'll own this whole works, right down to this table and all it sits on," said Billy.

"I know," said Harley, resignation in his voice.

"I'm telling you, that calf—that calf's yer ticket. You're keeping your million-dollar light under a two-dollar bushel."

Harley stood. "I gotta go clean out my truck."

"Yes?" Billy's question was implied.

"I'm taking a woman to the sale barn tomorrow."

"Is that even legal?"

Harley rolled his eyes.

"Anyone I know?"

"Mindy Johnson."

"Not familiar."

"Red F-250. Headache rack."

"Oh, *her.*" Billy nodded appreciatively. "The newcomer. So you figure this one will pan out? Yer kinda oh-fer in that department. Oh-fer *life.*"

"At least I'm in there swinging."

"First of all, I'd hardly call one date in six months *swinging,*" said Billy. "And didn't your last relationship implode over a wine and cheese party in an art gallery?"

"Well, it certainly crashed."

"You were wearing *khakis,* fer cripes' sake."

Harley couldn't deny that. At the time he had seen it as a form of self-improvement. Although it hadn't been his idea.

"What about you?" said Harley, mounting a counteroffensive. "I've never *once* seen you with a woman."

"I'm saving myself."

Harley snorted. "For what?"

"Not for, from."

"From?"

"Women."

"Why?"

"Because women been my trouble since I found out they weren't men."

"Waylon," said Harley. "Again."

Billy grinned, drained his beer, and departed for his trailer.

CHAPTER 16

I n the food pantry, Carolyn and Meg were mopping out the mop room. Any irony in this was obscured by the stench rising around them. The Swivel town sewer system had been sketchy for years, but lately it was getting worse. Several basements had been flooded with sewage, no treat at any time but especially poignant in winter. So far the pantry had avoided this fate, but now and then the mop room drain belched up foul gas and backwash.

When Klute Sorensen proposed Clover Blossom Estates, and further proposed that the town pick up the tab for new streets and sewers to service the development, there had been objections. But then Klute and the banker from Solid Savings had shown a Power-Point presentation that laid out very clearly how an investment in Clover Blossom Estates (rather than the boring business of spending the money to fix the existing infrastructure) would actually accelerate the generation of tax revenues required to upgrade the old part of town. "You wanna win, you gotta go all in!" said Klute. The soundtrack during his drive over had been *Too Bold to Fold: Poker Champs Up Your Ante.*

Of course the tax revenues never materialized, but the Power-Point presentation had been very nicely put together, including animated graphics of dollar bills spouting out of a toilet. "Usually the government's flushing your money *down* the toilet," interjected Klute knowingly, as the banker, the village board, and several citizens—only moments ago opposed to the whole idea—chuckled and nodded appreciatively. Vance Hansen beamed, thrilled to be in the presence of a man so assured and persuasive as Klute. This was before there had been so much yelling.

Although she was dying to, Carolyn had specifically avoided asking Meg about Klute Sorensen's presence at the salvage yard. Meg was swabbing the last of the residue from the tiles when she said, "So . . . Klute Sorensen asked me out on a *date.*"

Carolyn had a sardonic comment ready, but this revelation stopped her in her tracks.

"He *wha*?"

"Well, he never quite got to specifically asking, but it was pretty clear where we were headed."

"Well."

Meg smiled. It had been a while since she had seen Carolyn reduced to monosyllables. Their friendship had grown slowly, and they still spent very little time in each other's company outside the food pantry, but the hours had accumulated, and they had reached a certain ease.

"I haven't decided what to tell him," said Meg. She meant it, but she was also having some fun with Carolyn.

She was immediately rewarded.

"You're *considering* it?!" Carolyn was looking at her aghast, her mop gripped in both hands like a parade rifle.

"Well . . . he seems very lonely."

"He's a raging buffoon!"

"This does not exclude him from loneliness."

"But, he . . . you . . ."

"I think we both understand loneliness, Carolyn."

Carolyn had been here for ten years now and Meg had never known her to share strictly social time with another person (and reviewing Glen Jacobson's limericks didn't count).

"Well, I can't imagine comporting with that man on purpose," said Carolyn. "That said, you might be exactly what he needs. You might be the one person who can talk some sense into him. Perhaps you could even soften him up and break his heart. That would be nice. Although this presupposes his possessing that organ."

"Oh, I have no desire to hurt him," said Meg, frowning and shaking her head as she dumped the dirty mop water down the sewer drain and then stepped back lest it regurgitate.

"I understand that," said Carolyn. "You are irretrievably decent. But there is also another angle."

"Yes?"

"*You* might need *him*."

Now it was Meg's turn to look shocked.

"Sure," said Carolyn. "You've spent years avoiding relationships."

"No, I—"

"Oh, of course you have, my dear. And for years I've said nothing, because it wasn't my place. But now that it's on the table, there is the matter of you never having any relationship—in the time I've known you—outside of work and the church."

"I'm honoring Dougie," said Meg. "And—I don't mean this to sound dramatic, I simply mean it—and the Lord. And I like my work."

"All worthy. But trade your hard hat for a wimple and you're a *nun*."

"But, Carolyn, I'm content."

"That I believe—to an extent. And contentment is no small thing. So few possess it. But—"

"Are *you* content, Carolyn?"

Carolyn was leaning the mop against the wall and froze for a moment. Then she shrugged. "Not really. It never came naturally. I'm the first to admit I am driven by dissatisfaction far more than satisfaction. I learned the language, but truth is, I've always been far less adept at inner peace than outer abrasiveness."

"Maybe you're hiding behind discomfort as comfort."

"Well, don't you learn quickly," said Carolyn, smiling. "But Klute Sorensen?"

"Oh, I don't know. I was mostly kidding around."

"Maybe you should focus on that 'mostly' and see what comes of it," said Carolyn.

Suddenly a quietness came over Meg. She stared out the food pantry window. "It's odd," she said, "for all I loved Dougie—and I did—we had so little time that in retrospect I'm sure I didn't know who he was." She sighed. "We were so young."

"I say that all the time now," said Carolyn, and Meg was shocked to see tears in her eyes.

MEG FELT SHE should have followed up on Carolyn's unexpected teariness, but she hadn't been sure how to proceed, and then the moment was gone, with Carolyn bustling off to unpack donation boxes. The rest of their conversation was incidental, and after they sorted the last of the cans, Carolyn checked her phone for the time and said she had to get to the post office before the window closed. They bid each other good-bye, and Meg drove away in her truck with a trio of smashed cars lashed to the bed like a stack of rusty latkes. She intended to grab a sandwich at home before delivering the cars to Clearwater, but as she crossed the overpass she spotted Klute's Hummer idling through Clover Blossom Estates. Downshifting, she hit the turn lane and dropped the hammer southbound.

TWO BOXES AWAITED Carolyn in the post office. Back inside the pump house, she opened the lighter of the two boxes first and tucked the Zebra Cakes and ramen packets in their space behind the carboys. Then she opened the second box and brought out a cylindrical object all taped up in bubble wrap. Her oil pump had been making funny noises lately, and she had chased this one down on eBay.

Changing into exercise clothes, she filled the carboy, climbed aboard the bicycle, and began to pedal. The old pump growled, but it was still moving oil. Carolyn propped a book in the rack and took a sip of water. Then she looked at the tubs of oil surrounding her. It was going to be quite a workout.

CHAPTER 17

After Billy departed, Harley changed the oil in his Silverado and excavated the cab, clearing it of coffee cups, doughnut bags, baler twine, and the odd .30-06 cartridge. It's one thing to go on a first date in an old truck, quite another to create the impression one is a well-armed hoarder wired on discount carbs and convenience store caffeine. As a final touch, he vacuumed the seats. He got a little bit of everything, from cookie crumbs to lock nuts.

With the truck ready, Harley spent the rest of the day cleaning his house, because you never knew. Harley didn't live in squalor, but he did tend to let the dishes stack and the dusting lag. It was dark by the time he dragged the vacuum upstairs and started in on his bedroom, the floor of which was carpeted with discarded clothes. The process had the feel of an archaeological dig, and when he finally made it to the farthest corner and unearthed a pair of rumpled dress khakis and a teal polo shirt, he gave out a bemused *hmph!* of recognition.

Taking the khakis by the waistband, he held them up. As Billy had so kindly reminded him, he had worn them on his infamous last date, a trip to the opening reception of an art show at a Clearwater gallery owned by friends of his algorithmically selected date. The frontal pleats of the pants were marked with a dark maroon stain. Harley studied the stain and recalled its source, specifically a cheapish vintage of plonk which he slopped while choking on the inhaled fleck of a cocktail cracker upon which he had unsuccessfully attempted to balance a blot of dilled Brie. As he coughed the crumb and slopped his wine, the Brie bounced off his pastel polo shirt, clinging just long enough to impart a grease print, then fell to the blond hardwood of the art gallery floor. In a spastic attempt to catch the cheese while one-handing the wineglass, Harley fatally head-butted a mixed-media sculpture titled *Transitions: The Meadowlark Weeps* whilst backsplashing the remaining wine into the face of the woman who had dressed him in the polo and khakis and dragged him to the gallery in the first place.

Harley had been compelled to purchase the fractured sculpture by the gallery staff, who comported themselves as if he had farted at a funeral. He was carrying nowhere near sufficient cash to match the price tastefully penciled in the lower-right corner of the display (he noted the absence of a dollar sign, a bit of cosmetic censorship meant to ease the sketchy transition from art to commerce), so although it felt like the least artistic sort of thing to do, he put the whole works on his Swivel County Credit Union debit card. There was a moment of discomfort when his available funds came up twenty bucks short, but after a hushed consultation between the cashier and the gallery owner that included worried glances at both Harley and the maimed art, it was agreed that everyone could be happy with what the Swivel County Credit Union would provide, and Harley was rung up. On the way home, the remains of *Transitions: The Meadowlark Weeps* rode on the pickup truck seat between Harley and his date. Everyone in the cab felt the metaphor spoke for itself, and thus it was a silent passage.

There had been no more dates.

Impulsively, Harley gathered the polo shirt and khakis into his arms, walked downstairs and out the door, then around behind the garage and stuffed the shirt and pants into his burn barrel. Dressing the clothes with a drizzle of used motor oil, he lit and dropped a match, enjoying the soft *whuff* of ignition and the belly-dance waver of the flames taking hold. Sadly, after the motor oil was consumed, the fabric settled to a smolder, so Harley went into the garage, retrieved *Transitions: The Meadowlark Weeps*, and tossed it in. Constructed from renewably resourced balsa wood, indigenously masticated hemp fibers, and locally sourced llama yarn— all united with slatherings of volatile bonding agents purchased on sale at Home Depot—it took with an aggressive crackle, and shortly he had to move back three feet to alleviate the heat on his cheeks.

As the initial flare of flames settled into a steady burn, Harley took up an old hay fork and poked at the contents of the barrel. He felt oddly at peace, as if some invisible wall had been breached. The fork was missing one of its three tines and Harley kept it out here for this very purpose. The truth is that a burn barrel fire needs no tending, but Harley found it a soothing mental exercise even in untroubled times. Tonight as he poked and prodded, nudging bits of khaki and tempera-soaked lath toward the flames, he felt as he always did that relieving sense of finality when trash is reduced to ash. *I got no more business wearing clothes like that,* Harley thought to himself as the pastel collar blackened, *than I do being with a woman like that.*

In fact, if pressed, Harley would admit that *clothes like that* and *women like that* had saved him from the triangular career path of many local men his age: trailer, toil, and tavern. *Yah,* Harley thought, as he forked a strip of scorched Dockers and dandled it through a veil of flames, *you didn't get it right with Wendy Willis, or Kelly Motzer, or Jenny Haskins, or anyone since, but you learned a little something from each one.* Indeed, it was likely Skunk-haired Girl's residual influence—her poetry, her nudging him into a semester of creative writing—that led to his presence at the ill-fated art show, but the trouble there was not the art, it was the clothes and the company. Harley made a mental note to continue to meet art, but to meet it—life, for that matter—on his own terms, which is to say probably in jeans and old boots and certainly not in the company of a woman who would dress him otherwise.

That night Harley was a long time finding sleep. When it came he lay with one arm extended to the empty side of the bed, daring to imagine it occupied.

CHAPTER 18

Come morning, when the chores were complete (thinking ahead, he again unscrewed the lightbulb over the calf's pen), Harley showered, shaved, and dressed: old jeans, a worn T-shirt beneath a flannel shirt, logger boots, and a Carhartt jacket. Returning to the bathroom he paused for a moment, looked at himself in the mirror, then opened a drawer and studied the contents: a comb, a toothbrush, nail clippers, a deodorant stick. Reaching into the back of the drawer he pulled out a bottle of cologne. The cologne had been purchased for him by the art-show girlfriend. *She was really trying to tune me up*, he thought. He sniffed the bottle, then dumped it in the trash.

Mindy had suggested they take her truck since it was newer and more roadworthy, but residual male pride compelled Harley to insist on his Silverado. He also saw this as a chance to beta test his new resolve to meet life on his own terms. If Mindy was the sort of woman to balk at the idea of a first date in a rusty farm truck, well, it would save him—both of them—a lot of trouble on the front end.

He recalled the way the coffee beaded on her boots and figured she'd be fine with it.

SHE STEPPED OUT of the granary as he pulled up, and his breath caught. She was wearing a canvas jacket, the bomber cap, and camo cargo pants.

And those boots.

His heart gave a little *whoopty*.

As he opened the door for her (there was the momentary emancipated male internal debate about whether this was gallant or chauvinistic, then Harley's internal voice said *Tough nuts* and he grabbed the handle; *Meeting life on my own terms*, he thought, although his internal voice quavered a tad) he was struck again by the directness of her gaze, her hazel green eyes jovial and piercing all at once.

"Well, *thank* you," she said, in a tone that somehow simultaneously acknowledged, excused, and encouraged his outdated courtliness.

"How's life in the granary?" asked Harley, not knowing where else to begin.

"Goin' good!" said Mindy. "Wired in the two-twenty today."

"Oh," said Harley. "So now you can get a stove." Mindy had told him she was cooking on a hot plate.

"Um," said Mindy. "The two-twenty is for my welder."

The marvels accumulate, thought Harley.

"You weld?"

"I used to date a welder. The man kind, not the machine kind."

Harley's gut tightened.

"Well, I didn't just *date* him. We lived together for three years. He worked for a bridge-building company, welding up beams. Then he started making sculptures from scrap. 'Sculptwelding,' he called it. Fish with fins made of Volkswagen hoods, cows with oil funnel teats.

"He taught me a few things. Got me my own wire-feed welder. Showed me how to run a plasma cutter. But then we split."

They were pulling back onto the road. Harley busied himself with steering.

"Probably not the way to start a first date, talking about my old boyfriend," said Mindy, after a quarter mile of silence.

"Ach, we're grown-ups," said Harley, with an insouciance he did not feel.

WHEN THEY ARRIVED at the sale barn the parking lot was packed with trucks and cattle trailers. Once again Harley held the door as they stepped inside the vestibule. "Good boy," she said, winking, and he figured that was settled.

A long hallway ran perpendicular to the entry; at the far end of the hallway to the left was a door marked REGISTRATION AND PAYOUT. To the right was a door marked CAFETERIA. Straight ahead was the door leading to the sale ring. In contrast to the chill outside, the inside air was cushiony and smelled of sawdust, fresh manure, and deep fryers. Harley opened the door to the ring and followed Mindy up the stairs. When she stepped into view the auctioneer stuttered a moment, and Harley's ears burned as every cattle jockey in the joint swung around for a look. Mindy was a showstopper on her own merits, but against the greasy-capped backdrop of this crowd (there were no other women present), she was an illuminated angel. The auctioneer resumed, and the assembled heads swiveled back to the business at hand.

The bidding well enclosed the sale ring on three sides. The serious bidders tended to cluster in several rows of vintage theater-style seats nailed to boards in the lower levels; Harley led Mindy to the top row of seats, which were simply varnished boards. Mindy pulled off her cap and shook out her hair. For a moment the warm scent of her conditioner displaced everything else.

"Right now they're selling heifers and cull cows," said Harley.

Mindy smiled at him, then leaned forward, elbows on her knees, chin on her hands, to study the ring below. The auctioneer sat in an elevated booth facing the bidders. His arms were folded on the counter before him and he leaned into a microphone, through which he flowed a steady rattle of numbers, filling any blank spaces with a purr of rolled *r*'s. As each animal entered, hurried along by a man hollering, "Yah-ha! Ha! Ha!" and snapping a noisemaker, its weight flashed on a scoreboard above the auctioneer's booth.

The bidders consulted small scratch pads and participated with nearly imperceptible signs: up-and-down twitch of the head to bid, broken eye contact and a single head shake to withdraw. When bidding lagged, the auctioneer threw out well-worn one-liners to liven things up: "I see Chet Franklin is here—I guess when the fish ain't bitin' there's always the sale barn!"

The regulars chuckled knowingly.

Harley explained how some animals were sold by the batch, others singly. How the thin, ribby cull cows were destined for dog food, what phrases like "as it walks" meant, and that the cattle jockeys made their money on commission after having chased around from farm to farm in the predawn with their aluminum gooseneck trailers.

A cow came halfway into the corral, dipped her haunches, and tried to turn back. While the handlers worked to get her through the gate, the auctioneer made an announcement.

"Any calves still in the dock or in the alley, please bring 'em up!"

"That means the heifers and culls are almost done," said Harley, standing. "We got fifteen minutes. You wanna grab a bite to eat?"

"Yes," said Mindy. "Starved."

The cafeteria setup was straightforward: a few Formica tables, a cubbyhole kitchen run by two women in hairnets, and a Pepsi wall menu that—based on the dated logo and layered flyspecks—had hung there since the seventies. The sign's moveable white plastic letters advertised HBGR, CHZBRGR, FRIES, CURDS, COFFEE, and POP. A dry-erase board propped on an easel beside a tub of plasticware advertised the day's special: ALL YOU CAN EAT TACKO BAR.

"*Tack*os!" said Mindy.

Harley pointed to a card table in one corner of the room, whereupon a stainless steel food warmer held an excavated mound of hamburger; another contained a lump of refried beans, also well mined and drying and cracked around the perimeter. There was a tray of fractured taco shells, a tub of sour cream, two open tin cans of chopped black olives, and several jars of uncapped picante sauce. The rest of the table was sprinkled with bits of lettuce and grated cheese.

"I'll buy!" said Mindy, and handed the cook a ten, which—even after they both ordered sodas—returned to her a dollar and change, which she dumped in the plastic mayonnaise jar labeled TIPS.

As Mindy loaded up her paper plate with taco fixings and tore into the food, Harley marveled. After all his years serving at the Swivel Volunteer Fire Department food tent for Jamboree Days he knew some women who could wolf down half a chicken or a brace of bratwurst, but to see Mindy eating heartily without regard to the state of the facility spoke less to her appetite for food than her acceptance of the roughneck surroundings. *Long ways removed from the damn art gallery,* thought Harley.

With any first-date nervousness diffused by the setting, Mindy and Harley ate in hungry silence. The tables around them were half full. Many of the diners approached the counter with a rocking gait born of bad hips and sprung backs. A group of men were playing cards at a corner table and cursing each other happily.

A dusty speaker hung from a wire above the Pepsi menu crackled, and the auctioneer's voice came over.

"Calf buyers, we're ready to go!"

Returning to the bleachers, Harley and Mindy watched as calves were urged into the ring singly or in groups. "Depends on how the owners want them sold," said Harley. Compared to the older animals, the calves were much more tentative, stopping to sniff the steel tubing of the corral and the sawdust beneath their hooves, their ears cocked in curiosity. If they moved too slowly the wrangler chucked them under the chin or smacked them on the haunches with a flat plastic bat, sometimes while whistling sharply or hissing, *"Cht-cht-cht!"*

"Whoa, folks, take a look right there, we got a set of four bulls," said the auctioneer. "These'll be by the pound, boys—by the pound."

"That means when the auctioneer says, 'Who'll gimme ninety-five,' he means ninety-five cents a pound," said Harley to Mindy.

"Not ninety-five bucks total. You have to watch that. They switch back and forth, depending. You could wind up owning some high-dollar hamburger."

Mindy nodded and smiled. Two men acting as spotters pointed out bidders, hollering "HUP!" every time somebody gave the sign. When the final bidder bailed, the auctioneer slapped his hand on the counter.

"SOLD them calves!"

Harley checked the scoreboard. The four bull calves brought $1.65 a pound. "That's pretty good," he said to Mindy. "I haven't bought calves for a long while—I mostly get my own cows bred and raise those—but there was a stretch when bull calves weren't worth half a *tacko*."

"So that calf in your barn? He's worth a bundle!"

Harley blanched, and his heart thumped with an adrenaline bump. His mind had been a million miles from that calf. It took him a moment to recall that Mindy wasn't in on the secret, and simply meant what she said.

"Ha! Yah!" said Harley, overeagerly, lifting his cap by the bill and running the heel of his hand across his suddenly humid brow.

"What'd ya do, go a tad heavy on the hot sauce?" said Mindy, laughing.

"I guess," said Harley, trying to keep the frantic out of his chuckle.

A lone calf galloped into the corral, then hit the brakes and went into a full-on four-point skid. Blessedly, this drew Mindy's attention back to the sale ring.

"A little crossie!" said the auctioneer. "You betcha!"

"Crossie?" said Mindy.

"Crossbred," said Harley. "Half Holstein, half Angus. Tends toward a smaller calf, easier on the mother. Makes a decent beefer."

The auctioneer was rattling away.

"I can't even tell who's bidding," said Mindy.

"See that guy over there?" said Harley, pointing to a man in a T-shirt. The brim of his cap was tipped down over his face and his hands were laced across his large belly. He was sitting stock-still, with his feet up on the seat back before him. He could have been napping.

"Watch his cap," said Harley. Just then the man twitched, the brim of his cap descending and ascending less than a quarter inch.

"That was a bid," said Harley.

The auctioneer kept rattling. Three seats down from Napper, a man in a cowboy hat touched his ear.

"And that," said Harley, nodding toward Cowboy Hat. "Also, some guys flick their tally sheet."

Napper nodded, and the auctioneer bumped the price again. Cowboy Hat tugged his earlobe. Once again the auctioneer raised. He looked long and hard at Napper, all the while rolling the numbers on his tongue. After a moment's consideration, Napper shook his head tightly, as if trying to dislodge a gnat from the brim of his cap.

"SOLD them calves!" hollered the auctioneer as another batch passed out of the corral. "Put 'em on six fifty-three!"

"Six fifty-three?" asked Mindy.

"Cowboy Hat's bidding number," said Harley. Cowboy Hat was now scribbling in a notebook so tiny it looked like a postage stamp in his paw. "'Put 'em on six fifty-three' means he won the bid, and the secretary—that woman sitting at the computer beside the auctioneer—is generating a sales slip."

"So whaddo I gotta do if I want to buy my own beefers?" asked Mindy.

"Stop down at the buyer's office," said Harley. "Get a bidding number. Then you're good to go."

"I'd like that," said Mindy. "Next spring, maybe. Get some fencing up, try raising a couple."

"Yah," said Harley. "You could do that."

"Maybe find myself some lonely bachelor who owns a hay baler . . ."

Harley blushed.

"Would you come down and help me bid?"

"Well—you bet," said Harley. He hoped his heartbeat wasn't visible through his shirt.

"C'mon!" said Mindy, standing. "Those were some top-notch low-rent tacos, but that coffee tasted like it was poured through a furnace filter. Let's go get some good stuff!"

"Well, there's not much around he—"

"That truck of yours make it to Clearwater and back?"

"Oh, sure. Might have to put your foot over the hole in the floor so the heater can keep up."

"Let's go!"

AT THE COFFEE shop in Clearwater he craved a dry cappuccino but wasn't sure that would give the right impression, plus there was the danger of a foam mustache, so he played it safe with the house blend. Mindy ordered a chai.

"You a straight-coffee guy?" she asked.

Harley decided to play it honest. "Mostly, yah, but a guy does like a triple-shot dry cappuccino now and then." He was embarrassed that he knew what a triple-shot dry cappuccino was, but he figured after the lies about the calf and the lightbulb he should recover the up-and-up.

"Well, whatever," said Mindy, "long's you don't dump it on my boots."

They both chuckled, and Harley realized with a happy shock that they already had shared history. Conversation came easily then.

"So," said Harley. "You're living in a granary."

"Yep," said Mindy. "It's comin' along. I'm gonna convert one of the oats bins into a metalworking studio. Get back to making and selling."

"Selling art? In Swivel?" asked Harley. "Unless it'll double as a beer bottle opener . . ."

"I still have a lot of contacts in the art gallery world," she said. "And I helped the sculptwelder set up his online store, so . . ."

Harley flinched more at the term *art gallery* than he did at another mention of the boyfriend, but he covered with a question. "What do you make?"

"Smaller pieces, mainly. Statuettes. Wind spinners. Decorative wall hangings."

"Maybe I'll have to get something for the bachelor pad," said Harley.

"I accept credit cards or hay bales," said Mindy.

They laughed, and then Harley told her about his history with this coffee shop, how he first came here with the skunk-haired girl, and how she had introduced him to the world of poetry and how he still came down now and then for a reading.

"I'd heard someone joking about you going to art shows," said Mindy. Before he could demur, she said, "I found that attractive."

"Well . . . ," said Harley, thinking in particular of *The Meadowlark Weeps*, "I don't really always get it. The art."

"And you're good enough to say so," said Mindy.

"And I get teased, sure, but no one is *mean* to me. They pretty much leave me be. Helps, I suppose, that I'm on the fire department. That'll buy a guy some slack."

"Well, it sure did with me!" said Mindy, smiling wickedly.

Harley blushed again. "But it's prolly no coincidence that my best friend is Billy, the odd duck from out of town."

"Could be a metaphor for your whole situation," said Mindy.

"And that could be a metaphor for overthinking things," said Harley, relieved when she smiled at his first tentative attempt at a joke.

"So you and the sculptwelder," said Harley. "Three years?"

"Yeah," said Mindy. Harley thought her eyes glistened.

"That's a while."

"It was good," said Mindy, quietly. "First time we ever met, I just knew. Just by the scent of him."

Harley nearly snorkled his coffee. "The *scent* of him?"

"All men have a scent, silly," said Mindy, recovering her humor. "I used to sniff his shirts."

Well, that's kinda weird, thought Harley, although he did recall reading something along those lines in *Cosmopolitan* magazine the last time he was at the dentist's office, the only place you ever saw magazines anymore. The article had been about pheremone dating. You slept in your T-shirt then put it in a Ziploc bag so prospective daters could sniff it.

"I can be a little too frank," said Mindy, chuckling at the look in Harley's eyes.

"Yah, well . . ."

"He was good to me," said Mindy. "I was having some troubles then. He helped me through. I figured we'd be together forever."

"And?"

"And one day I was helping him move some scrap iron, and we bent down to pick up an old car door in the weeds, and I smelled his sweat, and it smelled sour. And that was it. I knew it was over."

"Because his *smell* changed?"

"Or his chemistry. Or mine. Who knows? More research is needed."

That last seemed an attempt at a joke, but her heart wasn't in it.

Harley focused on his coffee.

"It was okay. I like being alone."

THE CHATTER REVIVED as they drove home, the conversation flowing the way it does when a first date goes well. There was also the warmth of the heater and the glow of the dash and the ease of the road. When Harley pulled into the driveway of Mindy's place, he executed a Y-turn to position the passenger door near the granary. As his headlights swept the yard, they illuminated a Kokopelli made of sickle-mower bars and parts of an antique dump rake.

"Whoa," said Harley. "You weld that?"

"The sculptwelder," she said.

"Ah," said Harley, for lack of anything better to say.

"Don't gotta love the artist to love the art," said Mindy, and Harley figured that was fair. Now the headlights shone on the tarped bundle he'd noticed the day he drove past after spilling the coffee on her boots.

"Another sculpture?"

"Nope," said Mindy. "Motorcyle."

"I *thought* so," said Harley.

"Sixty-seven Norton."

Harley whistled. "That his too?"

"All mine, boy."

"Really!"

Now the truck was idling before the granary door, and Harley—even after all these years—wondered what to do, but Mindy took care of it in the instant, opening the door and jumping out of the cab.

Holding the door open, illuminated by the overhead light, she smiled at Harley and said, "That was fun! Let's do it again."

Then she slammed the door and disappeared into the granary.

It didn't even occur to Harley to be disappointed that the evening was over. Instead, as he drove home, Mindy's words spun around and around in his brain: *Let's do it again.*

Yeah, thought Harley. *Yeah.*

CHAPTER 19

Harley rose early for his shift at the filter factory. During his first break he found a voice message waiting on his cell phone. It was Mindy.

"Let's keep it simple. Date number two—we *are* dating, right?—I'll come by your place. I'll bring supper. Lentil soup and bread. Homemade. Tonight okay?"

Harley called back and got Mindy's voice mail. "Yah," he said, deploying the universal Scandihoovian preface, "I'm working a twelve today—a twelve-hour shift. So I won't be back until late. But yah. Supper. That'd be nice."

And then he gave her a time, purposely an hour later than he planned to be home so as to allow himself time to spruce up the house and—just for safety's sake—to dose the Jesus calf with shoe polish.

Man, he thought, *I gotta come up with something better than shoe polish.*

WHILE SCRUBBING THE calf with Kiwi black, Harley wondered about that lentil soup. He may have been considered Swivel's cosmopolitan fellow, and he didn't mind a little dilled Brie when he didn't have to peel it off some art gallery floor, but at base his appetites were still those of a farm boy, and there was the concern that lentil soup might run a bit light, verging as it did toward the hippie vegan side of things.

He needn't have worried. When Mindy climbed out of her truck, she handed him a Crock-Pot, and when he popped the lid he found the lentils keeping company with hearty chunks of pork sausage and diced red tomatoes, and the aroma had him instantly hungry. Mindy was also carrying a fresh-baked linen-wrapped loaf of thick-crusted bread. It was still warm at the center when Harley sliced it, and Mindy didn't skimp when she slathered on the butter. It was nearly ten p.m. when they finished eating, and Harley had yet to feed the beefers, a violation of a rule his father taught him, which was that you didn't sit down to eat until your animals had been fed.

"I can make coffee, if you wanna drink it this late," said Harley, "but first I have to do the chores."

"I'll do these dishes and then give you a hand," said Mindy, already running water into the sink.

"Oh, no need," said Harley breezily as he pulled on his coat and scooted outside. He was secretly relieved that she would be delayed by the dishes. Fresh shoe polish or not, he had no desire to tempt fate, and was hoping to keep her out of the barn. But by the time he threw down the hay and fed Tina Turner, Mindy was already in the corral, bundled up and chucking bales into the bunk feeder. Harley cut the twine and together they kicked hay the length of the feeder. They stood beside each other for a moment then, watching the beefers eat, the breath of both cattle and humans huffing out in white puffs.

The temperature had dropped to single digits, and when Harley checked the waterer he found it frozen over. "Musta thrown the breaker," he said, and turned for the barn, where the electrical box was. Mindy followed him. There was no turning back now, and as he stepped inside the door and hit the light switch, he thanked his lucky stars he had swabbed that calf.

"That lightbulb is still burned out," said Mindy, when only two of three lightbulbs lit.

"Yep," said Harley.

"I oughta fix that for ya," said Mindy.

"Oh, I'll get to it," said Harley, from over by the electrical box. Indeed, the breaker was tripped, and he reset it.

"I can at least make myself useful," said Mindy, opening the gate and depositing a straw bale beneath the bulb.

"Oh, no, I'll—" Harley was trying to sound nonchalant, but Mindy had already stepped up on the bale, and before he could say anything more she reached up to the bulb and gave it a twist.

"Well, it's *loose*," she said. She twisted in the opposite direction and the pen flooded with light. Harley shot a frantic look at the Jesus calf, and was relieved to see the shoe-polished side was turned to the wall. Tina Turner had her face buried in the hay rack. Harley grabbed a pitchfork and began shaking fresh straw around the pen, trying as before to keep himself between Mindy and the calf.

Mindy stepped toward him. "Lightbulbs hardly ever loosen themselves. If I didn't know better, I'd think maybe somebody did that on purpose."

Harley shaded deep red.

"Y'know, to *set the mood.*"

Harley went redder.

"Aw," said Mindy. "Lookit you."

Then she grabbed him, and pulled him downward into the fresh straw.

FOR ALL THE potential scenarios Harley had allowed himself regarding Mindy, making out in a cow pen hadn't been on the list. To the uninitiated it might sound romantic—first cousin to a roll in the hay—but in truth it was a good way to get jabbed in the butt with a ragweed stem, chaff down your underpants, and a stray oat in your sock—to say nothing of triggering latent allergies, or rolling in fresh bovine by-product.

For a while it was your basic high school make-out session (*Nothing very adult about this*, Harley thought at one point, and happily so), no bodice ripping or full-commitment groping, although Harley felt things could rapidly veer in that direction. Mindy was definitely setting the pace. There was an *eagerness* to her, thought Harley. He rolled to his back and she straddled him, and her head was lit from behind by the lightbulb she'd just revived, and he was pondering this nimbus when a fleck of oat husk fell from her hair and into his left eye.

Right then Mindy froze.

"*Jesus Christ!*" she said.

After all those years of being raised never to take the lord's name in vain, Harley still recoiled on behalf of his mother whenever he heard the name invoked out of context, and right now was no different. Then there was a moment, as he stared up at her with his left eye squeezed shut and streaming tears, that he thought her oath was born of passion. And then he realized she was looking straight past him to the corner where Tina Turner and her calf had retreated in the face of this human wrassling. He cranked his head back to follow her line of sight.

Jesus.

A bit dusky and matted, but Jesus nonetheless.

Tina Turner had pulled her face from the hay rack and stood placidly chewing a mouthful of hay. Her nose was covered in dark smudges. As Harley leaned in for a closer look, Tina Turner swallowed, then burped. Her lips parted slightly, and Harley was alarmed to see that her tongue too was dark black. Harley looked back at the Jesus calf and the wet, smudged face of Christ.

Tina had licked away most of the shoe polish. No wonder it had faded so quickly the last time!

One eye still squeezed shut, Harley looked up at Mindy. Slowly she dropped her gaze back to him.

"I . . . is that . . . do you . . ."

Mindy was wide-eyed, and even in his panic Harley realized this was the first time he had ever seen her operating with anything other than aplomb.

"I guess I should explain."

"Yes," said Mindy, dismounting. "Perhaps."

THEY SAT LEANING against the pen, shoulder to shoulder and facing the calf. Harley started at the beginning, at Christmas Eve, through his discussions with Billy, and how he nearly panicked that first day, when Mindy asked about the polish tin in his back pocket.

"Well, you little sneak," said Mindy. "And that loose lightbulb . . ."

"The shoe polish doesn't really work that good," said Harley. "As you can see. I was worried if it was too bright in here . . ."

"But it's amazing," said Mindy, pointing at the calf. "Why'd you hide it from me?"

"I'm hiding it from everybody. Nobody knows but me and Billy."

"Well, it's safe with me, baby," said Mindy, pulling Harley toward her. "It's exciting, to have a secret with you."

Whad'ya gonna do? thought Harley, and rolled back into the straw.

"Tomorrow morning when we wake up, I'll take you to Boomler and we'll buy a decent black hair rinse," said Mindy, smiling down at him. "Something that will last, and can't be licked off."

All Harley heard was *Tomorrow morning when we wake up.*

Shortly afterward they moved to the house.

As they slept it snowed.

They woke to a commotion.

CHAPTER 20

Harley!"

It was Billy, and he was inside the house, hollering up the stairs. Harley looked at the clock: 10:00 a.m. He was late for work.

"Harley!"

Mindy was awake now too, clutching the sheets to her chest and looking at Harley quizzically.

"Yah! Billy!" said Harley. "Just a second!"

"You got a problem, bud! I know you got company, but you got a problem! Look out your window!"

Hopping into his pants, Harley pushed the curtains aside and looked out. The end of his driveway was clustered with cars and people. More people were arriving, some jogging on foot, others in vehicles. Most of the people and vehicles he recognized, but there were a few coming in from the overpass he'd not seen before.

"What is it, Billy?"

"It's that damned Jesus calf!"

"Whaaat?"

"Calf's outta the bag!"

"Ho-lee *crud*!" said Harley, trying to stick his head through the armhole of his T-shirt. Now Billy was at the bedroom door. He nodded at Mindy. "Pleased to meet you."

"And you," said Mindy. "Nice Crocs."

"How?" said Harley to Billy, hopping on one foot and pulling a sock on the other.

"Barn door's wide open. Calf's out by the mailbox."

"Shit!"

Mindy smiled. "That's the most heartfelt thing I've heard you say since we met."

IT WAS DIXIE the mail carrier who had happened upon the calf. She was pulling away from Harley's mailbox when the animal came trotting at her through the fresh snow, tossing its head and skidding on its hooves as it tried to celebrate its freedom. Dixie backed her Jeep across the end of the drive, intending to keep the calf between the snowbanks until she could see if Harley was home or find someone to help her chase it back into the barn. Spooked by the vehicle, the calf tried to turn and run but instead came sliding right toward Dixie's door, finally falling in a heap below her window. Dixie slid her door back and looked straight down into the face of Jesus Christ.

"Lord!" she exclaimed, shooting one hand up into the air, closing her eyes and opening them again to be sure. There was no doubt. Jesus looked a touch smudgy, but it was him all right. Dixie grabbed her phone, hands shaking, and took a photo. And then another.

And then she called Reverend Gary of the Church of the Roaring Lamb. "Bring your Bible," she said, even as she was uploading the first photo to her Twitter account. "And your camera!"

"What is it?" asked the Reverend Gary.

"A sign!" said Dixie. "A sign from God."

"I'm on my way," said Reverend Gary.

Right about that time Dixie's photo posted.

Hashtag, #JESUSCOW.

The next photo went to her Facebook page.

Then she e-mailed the Clearwater television station.

Harley ran downstairs and out the door. *Shit!* he kept thinking. *Shit, shit, ka-shittity, SHIT!* He hated it when he swore like this, even to himself, because he felt it dishonored his parents, but sometimes it slipped out, you were around it so much. And this! He had the feeling this was going to lead to some bad *sh*—some bad trouble indeed.

Running to the end of the sidewalk, he cornered too quickly and his feet shot out from beneath him. He skidded across the unplowed driveway, past Mindy's pickup, and right up to the open barn door. Inside he could see the gate to Tina Turner's pen—also ajar.

So hot to get to the house last night we didn't close up *anything*, he thought as he sprang to his feet. Reaching inside the door he grabbed a loop of baling twine off a nail, slammed the door so Tina couldn't get out, then ran out to the mailbox and side-shouldered his way through the crowd to the calf. Reverend Gary was on one knee, resting a big floppy Bible on the calf's head and praying like sixty. His other hand was raised to the heavens, clutching a bejeweled iron cross be-twined with dangerous-looking silver filigree. The cross appeared to be the length of a hockey stick. Dixie was snapping pictures and posting them as fast as she could tap and swipe.

Harley kneed Reverend Gary aside, looped the baling twine around the calf's neck, and began tugging it toward the barn.

"My son!" said Reverend Gary, tucking his Bible beneath one arm and laying a hand on Harley's shoulder.

Harley whirled on Reverend Gary, surprised at the rage he felt. "Not your damned son, and not your damned calf! Get out of my face, and get offa my property! And, Dixie—I thought you were better than this. You're a *public servant!*"

Several people in the crowd crossed themselves. Harley saw more gawkers incoming.

"Harley, you have been visited with a great blessing!" said Reverend Gary as he and the growing crowd followed Harley up the driveway. "Hide it not beneath a bushel."

Apparently that one's gonna get used a lot, thought Harley. Then Billy appeared, bearing a pitchfork. Like Moses through the Red Sea, he parted the crowd and led Harley and the calf back to the barn. Once inside, Billy shut the door then turned to stand between it and Reverend Gary and all assembled.

HARLEY RELEASED THE Jesus calf and it went directly to its mother. Tina nuzzled it worriedly, and then the calf began nursing. It was quiet then, just the sound of the calf suckling, and in that split second Harley had the thought *Well, this is it,* and with it the chilling realization that he was on the lip of a wave about to curl up and over him and sweep him into circumstances beyond all control.

Someone tapped on a window. As with many of the barns in the area the windows were made of glass bricks rather than panes, so the figure was distorted and diffracted. Now another figure appeared at another window. Someone tried the sliding door he used to bring the manure spreader in and out, and as it rattled, Harley was thankful it was hooked from the inside.

"We want to see the Jesus cow!" It was a voice he didn't recognize.

"Harley!" That was Reverend Gary. "The Lord has chosen to speak through you—let him speak!"

More pixilated figures were peering in through the kaleidoscope windows. He heard the low rumble of Billy's voice. Harley thought surely the sort interested in seeing Jesus on a calf wouldn't turn violent, but they were certainly insistent, and very possibly obsessed, and their numbers were mounting. Plus, who knew who might filter in with them? Harley fished his phone from his pocket and dialed.

"Constable Benson," said the voice on the other end of the line. "What is the nature of your emergency?"

The nature of my emergency is, I've got Jesus on the side of a cow, thought Harley, but he figured that might raise more questions than it answered, so instead he said, "Trespassers."

"Trespassers?"

"I'll explain when you get down here," said Harley. "And, Constable?"

"Yes?"

"Bring your bullhorn." Harley knew that would speed things up. Constable Benson loved his bullhorn.

TRUSTING THAT BILLY was holding back the crowd, Harley opened the door a crack. Immediately it filled with faces.

"The Jesus cow! We want to see the Jesus cow!"

A hand reached through the crack in the doorway. Someone butted the door and Harley stumbled backward. Several figures pushed through. Billy grabbed two of them by the scruff of the neck and tossed them bodily back out, but there were too many people, and now they were crowding in. Harley backed up against the gate of the pen and grabbed a pitchfork for himself. Tina Turner was pressed back into a far corner, the Jesus calf pressed against the wall behind her. Reverend Gary charged forward, the Bible clutched to his chest and his cross raised to the rafters. Tucking the Bible under his arm again, he offered Harley his hand. "We come in peace, Harley. We come in love. We come to witness."

"You come too far," said Harley. It was really getting crowded now. Harley looked for Billy, but he had disappeared. Harley climbed up on the gate and brandished the pitchfork. *This went from shit to Holy Shit pretty fast*, he thought.

Now Reverend Gary raised his Bible high. "Harley, the Lord is speaking here today—"

"So far, Reverend, you're the only one I've heard speaking, and I don't care for your tone. Every one of you is trespassing right now. You're on private property. I don't want trouble. I've never wanted trouble. But I've called the constable. It's time to go."

"Yes," said a voice from the doorway, where suddenly the people were scurrying sideways. *Mindy!* thought Harley, and sure enough it was. *How'd she—* thought Harley, and then she broke through and he understood. She was holding a stainless steel revolver so big it needed wheels.

"Folks, I'm basically a hippie chick in work boots," said Mindy. "Not into violence, not into harshing your vibe, not into running your show. But I am into politeness. And this man"—here she grinned sweetly at Harley—"this man has very politely asked you to leave."

She raised the pistol. "This is a Ruger Redhawk .44 Mag with a seven-and-a-half-inch barrel. Shoots six 240-grain slugs. Slow, yes, but faster than you. As a single lady living alone, I find it a great comfort—although for clearing a room full of you, I'd prefer something more shotgunny."

"Like this?"

Billy had reappeared in the doorway. He was toting a pump shotgun and his chest was crisscrossed with loaded bandoliers. There was a sudden scurry, and the room cleared, Reverend Gary leading the way. Mindy put a hand on his shoulder. "Hold it there, Reverend." Reverend Gary froze.

"Quite a cross you got there."

"It was a gift from my parishioners," said Reverend Gary. "I am told they purchased it online."

"Well I know a thing or two about metalwork, and that's an above-average beauty," said Mindy. Then she pointed to a small hook soldered to the back of the cross. "But you're supposed to hang it on a wall, not wave it around like some nutball archangel."

Reverend Gary just blinked.

"Keep it up and you're gonna put somebody's eye out with that thing."

Reverend Gary bolted for the door. Mindy let him go, then winked at Harley. "That's one of ours."

"Ours?"

"Me and the sculptwelder. Decorative crosses were our steadiest sellers. Based on e-mails, I'd say about ten percent are purchased in irony, the rest in faith. The ex used to say cute frogs and crosses are the metal sculptor's equivalent of a painter's seagulls and lighthouses."

Harley turned toward Billy. "Um . . . *bandoliers?*"

"Bit much, prolly," said Billy, grinning like a kid. "Still, it seemed better to come big than show up short." He dipped his beard toward the bandoliers. "Picked these up in an army surplus store a while back, but have never had occasion. I believe they deliver a certain visual impact."

A red dot wavered across the floor. Harley shook his head and looked at Billy again. "A *laser* sight?"

Billy shrugged.

"On a shotgun?" said Harley. "Really?"

"They all found reverse, didn't they?"

Now Harley turned to Mindy.

"And you?"

Mindy smiled demurely. "It happened to be in my purse."

Harley shook his head. "You don't even carry a purse."

"Okay, a biometric case, beneath my truck seat."

"Good lord. Can you stay with Tina and the calf?"

"Of course," said Mindy.

"Billy, you guard the door."

"An honor and a privilege," said Billy, backing up against the gate and holding the shotgun across his chest.

"Okay there, Rambo," said Harley, rolling his eyes.

Then he left the barn to hunt the constable and face the growing crowd.

Holy cripes, thought Harley, when he saw how the crowd had grown. *I am not cut out for this.* He had figured the calf might be trouble, but no way did he think things would spin out of hand this quickly. Once again, he cursed himself for his dithering, for not disposing of that calf—one way or another—the moment he saw it in the straw.

"Harley." It was Reverend Gary. He seemed to have appointed himself the unofficial leader of the pilgrims now congregated about him, each of them looking at Harley expectantly.

"Harley. Are you a Christian, Harley?"

"Folks," said Harley, "I'm a quiet guy, trying to live quietly. I need you to *leave* quietly."

"But the calf . . . we saw the face. A sign of this import . . ." Reverend Gary was clutching both the Bible and the spangled steel cross against his chest.

That's a big honkin' cross, thought Harley. Out loud, he said, "Pretty sure it's just a calf with a birthmark."

"Would you hide this calf beneath a bushel?"

Okay, that's thrice, thought Harley, but he was spared answering by the sound of Constable Benson's siren, which he left blaring even as he turned down the driveway and nosed his squad car through the pedestrians clogging the drive. When he reached the barn, he swung a U-turn, and mercifully killed the siren. Stepping out of the car he went around to the trunk and removed a giant bullhorn. Raising it to his lips he pressed the trigger and it immediately squealed into a feedback loop with his radio. All around, people fell back and clapped their hands to their ears. The constable squelched his radio, repositioned the bullhorn, and tried again.

"SWIVEL CONSTABULARY, TEST, ONE-TWO-THREE, TEST."

Satisfied, the constable approached Harley, who explained the situation.

"So you want I should disperse them?" asked the constable, finger twitching on the bullhorn trigger.

"Yep," said Harley.

The bullhorn rose. "LADIES AND GENTLEMEN, I MUST ASK YOU TO DISPERSE."

There was scant movement.

"IT'S A SIMPLE MATTER OF TRESPASS, FOLKS."

Still nothing. Then the barn door swung open, and Billy stepped forward with his shotgun, bandoliers, and orange clogs. A murmur went through the near fringes of the crowd. They moved back three steps.

"OFF THE PROPERTY, FOLKS, OR I DEPUTIZE THAT MAN," announced Constable Benson, and now the tide began to turn.

While the others retreated, a pale woman in an ankle-length denim skirt who had been standing off to the side and behind Reverend Gary stepped forward and addressed Harley. "We hope you will do good with this calf," she said. From behind her skirt she produced a young girl with a runny nose and a stocking cap. Now there came a tremble in her tone. "My daughter," she said, pulling away the child's stocking cap to reveal the child's hairless head, softly bald. "Please. Take her to the calf."

"*Whosoever shall receive one of such children in my name, recieveth me!*" called someone from the crowd.

"I . . . folks, I . . . you'll have to . . ."

"Glory to His name! Amen! Amen!" That was Reverend Gary.

The *amens* rippled up the driveway. Harley looked at the little girl again. She was staring at him implacably. "Folks! I don't know what I'm going to do. I have to think it over. But you have to leave us alone now. We'll say more tomorrow."

Constable Benson raised his bullhorn again.

"TIME TO GO, FOLKS."

Billy moved forward. The people moved back.

"AT LEAST TO THE ROAD."

The constable turned to Harley. "You know there's no way I can hold 'em, right?" Even now more people were arriving. A van from the Clearwater TV station had arrived and was raising its antenna. Cars were beginning to back up nearly to the overpass.

"I've radioed the county," said the constable. "They'll send deputies. Likely call in the reserves. They'll be able to secure the barn and property overnight, but the county's not gonna pay to have them sit out here forever. You're going to have to come up with something."

There was the sound of another siren approaching. Harley thought perhaps someone else had called the sheriff. Then Chief Knutson's Expedition careened around a corner, nearly wiping out a row of onlookers. At the end of the driveway the chief flipped his siren from wail to phaser, and the people parted to let him pass. Chief Knutson loved the phaser setting like Constable Benson loved his bullhorn.

The phaser burped to silence and Chief Knutson hit the ground running, his belly leading the way.

"Heard a commotion on the scanner! Whaddawe got?"

Harley explained the situation. The chief, a regular at St. Jude's, crossed himself, and then, looking at all the people and cars and the TV truck, said, "Well, Christ on a calf, this is a mess."

"The county's comin'," said Constable Benson.

"Well, we're gonna need'em," said Chief Knutson.

An idea occurred to Harley.

"We still short on funds for that thermal imager?"

"At this point we can afford the wrist strap and half a battery. What's yer point?"

"Every year the fire department runs the Jamboree Days beer tent and softball tournament," said Harley.

"Yah . . . ," said the chief, puzzled.

"Parking, crowd control, tickets, we do it all."

"You sayin' . . . ?"

Harley sighed, and thought long and hard. He had sworn he wouldn't do this. But then he looked at the gathering crowd. They weren't going away without a look at that calf. And who knew how many more were coming.

"Yeah," he said to the chief reluctantly. "No reason we couldn't use the same setup to run folks through here for a look at that calf."

Now the chief looked at the crowd. "But why—"

"Sell tickets, donate the whole works to the thermal imager fund."

The chief raised his eyebrows, a sign that he was interested.

"Plus, a raffle," said Harley.

That got his attention. The chief loved a raffle. "Can't be any harder than runnin' the beer garden on a Saturday night," he said.

"And lower odds of getting hit in the head with a stray softball," said Harley.

"I'd have to get everybody rounded up," said Chief Knutson.

"That's your specialty," said Harley.

"Yes it is," said the chief, swelling right up. In a trice, he was back in his Expedition, phaser blazing, headed for the fire hall.

CHAPTER 21

Ith county deputies patrolling the property lines, blocking the driveway and posted at both doors of the barn, Constable Benson took to the hood of his squad car with the megaphone and announced that the calf would be made available for viewing the following day, but in the meantime anyone who set foot on Harley's property or blocked the road would be arrested and taken to the county jail immediately. He then repeated this information in a brief interview with the television reporter. These announcements and the coming of darkness cut the crowd to manageable proportions, although by no means eradicated it.

In light of the day to follow, Harley sent Billy home to feed his cats and get a good night's sleep.

Harley let himself into the barn. The lightbulb above Tina Turner's stall was burning brightly. Mindy was seated in a corner of the pen, her revolver at her side. Harley unscrewed the bulb, then sat beside Mindy and studied the Jesus calf in the half-light. It was lying beside its mother, legs folded, neck curled back, chin resting on its hocks.

Harley's cell phone rang. He didn't recognize the area code.

"Harley Jackson?" A man's voice. Businesslike.

"Who's this?" As far as he knew, his phone number wasn't listed anywhere.

"Sloan Knight," he said. "International Talent Management."

"Who—"

"This Jesus cow of yours. We want to represent it—and you."

"But how did you—"

"Calf's viral. All over the Internet. We have people monitoring these things. We like to move fast."

"You want to represent a *calf*?"

"Client, calf, we can work out the details later. Right now we just want to sign you to the agency so we can get started with the licensing and monetization. Sooner the better. I'm about to leave L.A. for Minneapolis now, and should be in Swivel by morning."

Harley sat silent, and the agent continued. "If you can provide me with an e-mail address, I'll send a rough draft of the proposal and contract and we can work out the details in the morning."

"Um, yah, no," said Harley. "I don't want a big thing. We're gonna handle it here. Do a fund-raiser for the fire department over the next couple of weekends until the interest dies down."

There was silence on the other end.

"So," said Harley, as a way of wrapping things up.

"You have no idea what you've got there, do you?" said Sloan finally.

"Well, it's just—"

"We'll talk again," said the man, and the line went dead.

Suddenly Harley was tired. Overwhelmingly tired. He stared at the calf's side long and hard, until Jesus went blurry.

But damn. It was sure enough Jesus.

He took Mindy by the hand then, and after checking that the deputies were in place, the two of them walked into his house and into bed where they slept, and only slept.

CHAPTER 22

In the morning, Meg Jankowski set out for St. Jude's as usual and found her way blocked by a pair of sheriff's deputies directing cars and pedestrians. When she drew even with one of the deputies, Meg rolled down her window and asked what was up.

"Ask that guy," said the deputy, pointing down the road, where Reverend Gary was standing atop a car, waving his Bible and bedazzled cross. When Meg reached him, she stopped the truck.

"Hello, Reverend."

"Meg! Glorious news!" hollered the reverend. "The Lord has given us a sign!"

"Really," said Meg.

"Christ himself, Meg!"

"Really," said Meg again.

"Well . . . His likeness! On the side of Harley Jackson's bull calf!"

"*Really,*" said Meg, putting the truck back in gear.

"Won't you stay? Won't you see Him?"

Meg smiled and drove away. Inside St. Jude's she lit Dougie's candle and prayed quietly.

Then she lit one more.

For Harley Jackson, she thought. *It's likely he'll need it.*

THE SWIVEL VOLUNTEER Fire Department had arrived earlier that morning, fortified with doughnuts and coffee provided by the auxiliary. They set to work immediately, with Chief Knutson barking orders left and right. Several of the members brought their own snowblowers to clear the driveway and paths past the barn where the viewing area would be set up. The village allowed the use of its front-end loader and mounted snowblower, which was used to clear Harley's hay field to make room for parking. All footpaths, driving lanes, and parking areas were marked off using yellow-and-black FIRE SCENE tape strung from posts stuck in pails of sand (there was no driving the posts into the frozen ground). As Harley's driveway couldn't possibly handle all the traffic, the fence along the road was taken down and the ditch was filled in with a few loads of gravel to create two "in" lanes and two "out" lanes. The Jamboree Days ticket booths were pulled out of storage and set up along the "in" lanes. The booths looked garish against the snow, stapled as they were with last year's softball tournament beer posters.

Harley knew he couldn't just stand the calf outside in a pen, so he and Mindy framed up a sheet of Plexiglas that could be placed in the open side door of the barn. Then they built a small pen behind the Plexiglas, and illuminated it with a set of halogen shop lights.

WITH ALL THE action happening elsewhere, Vance Hansen was anticipating a quiet cup of coffee alone in the village hall when Klute Sorensen came roaring through the door. Vance, hunched over the coffeemaker with his back to the entrance, startle-froze like a miniature African antelope at the roar of a lion and half his coffee hit the carpet.

"HOW COULD YOU LET THIS HAPPEN!?" yelled Klute. Vance flinched again, an involuntary spasm causing him to crush the Styrofoam cup in his hand, which caused the rest of the coffee to spill over his fingers, which then led him to dance up and down in pain while sucking his knuckles.

"Let what hap—"

"You don't KNOW?" Klute had just finished fighting his way through the crowds. He had done this with much less equanimity than Meg, blowing the twin air horns of his Hummer and yelling out the window at stragglers. Thus he had arrived at the village hall highly revved and ready to rant.

"It's all over the news! That knucklehead Harley Jackson is running amok! Turning this beautiful village into a tourist trap for Jesus freaks!"

"Well, they're just trying to raise funds for the fire department . . ."

"You *believe* that?"

"Well—"

"You see all those loonballs out there? You see them trampling the snowbanks, clogging the roads, parking every which way?"

"Well—"

"I just came from Clover Blossom Estates—you can't even navigate! It looks like a used car lot after a hurricane! You understand what this will do to property values? They're already in the tank, now they're headed for the *TOILET*!"

"But I don't see any way—"

"You call yourself a *lawyer*?!"

"Well, I prefer village *counsel* . . ."

"Well, lemme *counsel* you, *Counsel*. Anybody come in and get permits for that cluster out there? Are winter parking rules suspended? Community beautification ordinances? Is anyone enforcing *anything*?"

"Well, they just—"

"They just push you around, *Counselor*."

"I—"

"Actually, this is the miracle I've been waiting for," said Klute, his voice suddenly softening. He picked up a fresh Styrofoam cup, filled it with coffee, and handed it to Vance, who accepted it with bewildered caution. Klute took a seat at the conference table and motioned for Vance to take the chair beside him.

"Harley Jackson has been undermining me—this *community*— for some time now," said Klute, shaking his head regretfully. "I grieve to think how Swivel might have thrived had Clover Blossom Estates not been sunk by Harley's stinky beefers and stubbornness."

Vance nodded tentatively, still unnerved by Klute's brief run of gentleness.

"At every turn we have tried to convince him to do the right thing, and at every turn he has ignored us. In short, he has been a bad neighbor.

"Well, now he has given us the opening we require."

And then Klute Sorensen outlined his plan. When he left, Vance

Hansen was on the phone with Klute's attorney in Clearwater. And when Klute found himself reduced to a five-mile-an-hour crawl through Swivel's newfound congestion, he simply smiled and cued up *Sawing Through Setbacks: Lessons from the Lumber Barons of Yore.*

That one always made him feel nostalgic.

BY TEN A.M. things were set to go. Chief Knutson was parked on a small rise beside the ticket booths where he had a clear view of the whole operation. He was wearing a brand-new lime-green reflective vest labeled INCIDENT COMMANDER, and although he had just discovered he couldn't get the Velcro tabs to meet across his belly, he couldn't have been happier about the situation in general. In addition to the vest, he was debuting his new Wheel Commander Incident Command System, a magnetic dry-erase whiteboard that clipped to the steering wheel of his Expedition, allowing him to coordinate operations by radio from the quiet of the cab (at least that's how the chief had pitched it to the fire board; there was also the advantage of having a heater and two cup holders: one for his Kona Luna, and the other for a bouquet of Original Slim Jims).

Surveying his whiteboard one last time, the chief delicately centered the magnetized tab engraved CHIEF in the preprinted rectangle captioned ICS COMMANDER, jotted the time in the column labeled INCIDENT LOG, punched the fully integrated scene-time stopwatch, gave a happy little shiver, and keyed his radio mic.

"Incident Command to Operations."

"Yah," replied Boober Johnson. "Operations."

"Commence operations."

"Okeydoke." The chief was hoping for something more professional, and made a mental note to review radio protocol at the next meeting. Just then Boober's voice came across the radio again.

"Ahm . . . which particular operations?"

The chief sighed and keyed his mic. "Let in the cars and people."

"Copy-copy," replied Boober.

The chief peeled a Slim Jim.

BOOBER OPENED THE barn door and relayed the chief's command, then jogged off to alert the crew at the gates. Harley and Billy (armed and back in his bandoliers) moved the calf into position behind the Plexiglas, and Mindy switched on the halogens. Tina mooed worriedly, and the Jesus calf mooed back, so Harley allowed her inside the pen as well. The Swivel Volunteer Fire Department kicked right into Jamboree Days mode, the only difference being that instead of sleeveless T's and bad shorts they were bundled up in bunker pants and blaze orange deer hunting jackets and their breath was visible in the frozen air.

There was trouble immediately. Rather than file past, the first four people to stand before the calf dropped to their knees in prayer. Harley tapped on the Plexiglas and waved them on. They stayed right where they were. The people behind them began pushing forward, and then there were nearly a dozen people trying to peer through the Plexiglas at once. Spotting the backlog, Constable Benson came over with his bullhorn. "KEEP 'ER MOVIN', FOLKS!" he blared from a distance of three feet.

The line began to move again.

For a while then, things moved smoothly, if slowly. Many of the viewers genuflected, or crossed themselves, or simply bowed their heads. Some spun around with their backs to the calf and snapped selfies. One man was holding a poster advertising a homeless shelter fund-raiser. He hollered through the Plexiglas at Harley, "We want to sell raffle tickets for a chance to sit with the calf!" He pointed to a phone number on the poster. "Call me!"

"MOVE IT ALONG!" blared Constable Benson, and the man shuffled on, but kept casting his eyes back at Harley, who felt a jab of guilt.

By now Tina Turner had settled into placidly chewing her cud, apparently undisturbed by the people passing by outside the Plexiglas. The Jesus calf was resting beside her, positioned in such a way that the Christ image was easily visible. Leaving Billy and Mindy to babysit, Harley went outside to see how things were going.

He was unprepared. Cars were backed clear up and out of sight beyond the overpass, snaking around and waiting for their chance to pass through the ticket gates. Clots of people were standing in the Kwik Pump parking lot and walking down the shoulder of the road. The parking area in the hay field was nearly full and someone was working with the village loader and snowblower to clear even more space. Here and there pilgrims were clambering over snowbanks to circumvent the ticket booths. There were people at his house looking in the windows.

Chief Knutson spotted him and—phaser deployed—came tooling over in the Expedition. "Word's gettin' out," said the chief. Carlene Hestekin was in the passenger seat beside him, flicking at her smartphone, and the chief nodded toward her. "My communications officer here has been monitoring social media, and all them people going through the line are posting photos and messages and it's only bringing more and more people. We're makin' a killing at the ticket booths. Coupla days a'this and we'll be able to buy *two* thermal imagers. Or maybe, *maybe*, an Argo!" The chief had long dreamed of purchasing an Argo—an eight-wheeled amphibious firefighting and rescue vehicle—but so far had failed to sell the fire board on the idea.

"Hey!" hollered the chief, punching his phaser and four-wheeling off to intercept someone trying to sneak through the snow around the ticket booths. Harley could see other people doing the same thing—there was really no way to seal the entire perimeter of the place using only the volunteer fire department. Furthermore, each person left a trail in the snow for the next, so sneaking in was becoming easier and easier.

Harley looked toward the house again. Those people staring into his windows: That had to stop. He walked over and asked them to leave. They looked at him silently and did as they were asked. *There are advantages*, Harley thought, *to dealing with people who are gentle in their obsessions.* He stepped through the front door and found the silence of the kitchen oddly foreign. The house of his entire childhood and most of his adult life suddenly felt like an island afloat in a sea of unfamiliarity. Nothing in here but the sound of the refrigerator, and everything so still, and yet he felt the vibration of all the oddness swirling around him.

A face appeared at the window. A woman, tapping the glass with one knuckle.

Harley recognized the woman who had produced the sickly child from behind her skirt. Her eyes were bagged and dark. Her expression was flat and weary. She stared at Harley.

Harley turned his back and opened the refrigerator, looking for something to eat. He hadn't eaten anything but fire department doughnuts and he was of a mind to scramble some sausage and eggs for Billy and Mindy. He pulled out the eggs, but as he faced the stove he could feel the woman's gaze upon him. He placed the pan on the burner and lit the gas, but still couldn't shake the idea of the woman at the window. He snapped the gas off and looked again. She was still there, unmoving, her gaze steady.

He stepped outside.

"My daughter," said the lady, once again producing the child from within the folds of her skirt. The child looked cold beneath her stocking cap. A clear rivulet of snot ran from one nostril. Harley found this more moving than tears.

"Please," said the woman. "Just let her touch Him."

"I . . ."

"Please."

"I don't think that will . . ."

"I am trusting in *my* faith," said the woman, her voice suddenly firm. "Not yours."

Harley looked at the child. She was nearly translucent in her afflictions, but beautiful. So beautiful.

"Okay," said Harley.

He led the mother and child up the path beneath the yard light and out to the barn. Nodding at the firefighter guarding the door, he led them inside. Mindy looked up from where she was sitting on a camp chair but seeing the mother and child said nothing. *One more reason I like her,* thought Harley. *She simply accepts things. Goes with them.*

Without words, Billy drew open the gate to the viewing pen and ushered the woman and child within. Tina Turner laid her ears back and sidled off a quarter turn.

"Move slowly," said Harley. "We don't want to spook 'em."

But as the child spotted the calf she let out the softest *oh* and dropped to her knees, wrapping her arms around its neck, and rather than startling, the calf, seeming to sense the child's fragility, simply allowed itself to be held. The mother had gone to her knees and was praying, eyes closed and hands clasped.

The child—the child. Harley felt his throat clench, and tears came to his eyes. Mindy and Billy were in the same state. There was no sound save Tina Turner ruminating and the mother's whispered prayers.

Outside the Plexiglas, there was a muffled kerfuffle. The line of people had stopped moving. They were pointing and waving their hands, and despite the constable's nonstop megaphoning, they were beginning to clump up. Harley told Billy to remove his bandoliers and store them in the silo room with his shotgun—"Last thing we need is somebody getting shot"—then sent him out to help the constable.

"We can't see!" one of the people hollered, loudly enough so that Harley could hear it through the Plexiglas. "That girl! Tell her to move!" Harley turned and saw that the sick child had now lain herself against the calf's side and was nestled cheek to cheek with the face of Christ. Her eyes were closed, her mouth was in a half smile, and Harley swore her cheeks had taken on fresh color. The mother had stopped praying and was now gazing at her child through tears that gathered and dropped to the straw.

"We can't see!" The shouting grew louder. Several people were waving their torn tickets. "We paid our money, and now we can't see!" Billy, trying to intervene, was being crowded back toward the Plexiglas. The constable was nowhere to be seen. Someone began pounding on the Plexiglas. Harley hustled up the haymow ladder and opened the door he used for throwing bales down to the beefers. From here, he could see long-term trouble building far beyond the viewing area. The people entering the viewing line from the parking lot were still flowing forward, while at the front of the line below him, things were at a dead stop and swelling, like some aneurysm about to burst. There was pushing and crowding, and it was only growing worse.

"HEY!" hollered Harley. "Hold it! Calm down! We'll have things moving again soon!"

"We *PAID*!" yelled a man holding his cell phone high in the air, trying to snap a shot over the heads before him.

"We can't see the holy image!" cried another.

"RIP-OFF!" screamed a woman jostling for position.

"HEY!" hollered Harley again, surprised at the anger rising in him. "There's a *child* in there! A *dying* child! Give her five minutes and we'll get things moving again!"

The line continued to surge forward, and now halfway back people were stumbling and pressing into each other. Billy was being pushed even farther back. He was nearly against the Plexiglas now. Over by the gates, Harley could see Chief Knutson in his Expedition, a Slim Jim clamped in his jaws, happily scribbling on his Wheel Commander Incident Command System and moving name tags around the board like he was on a magnetic poetry binge. Too late, Harley realized that he should have asked for a radio of his own.

A man fought his way through the line. Reverend Gary, Bible and cross high in the air. Now and then he tapped someone on the shoulder with the cross and they took one look at the razor-sharp filigree and stepped aside.

"HARLEY!" hollered Reverend Gary. "MANY ARE DYING!"

"Well, Reverend, that's stretching it some," said Billy.

Reverend Gary pushed forward again. "NOT IN THE BODY, BUT IN THE SOUL!"

"Back off, bud," said Billy, putting a hand to the reverend's chest.

"O, COME ALL YE SINNERS!" preached Reverend Gary.

The sinners took him at his word. The crowd surged, and Harley saw Billy stumble backward. As Harley spun around to hustle back down the ladder, he heard a *snap!* and a *crack!* It was the Plexiglas, giving way. Harley dropped to the manger just in time to see Billy tumble backward and the pilgrims pour through, led by Reverend Gary. The praying mother looked up in fear and snatched her wide-eyed child from the calf as Reverend Gary, pushed by the tide of people behind him, tripped, and fell head-long toward the calf, throwing his hands out to break his fall, and as he did so the stainless steel filigree raked across the calf's hide, and the last thing Harley saw as the people closed in was blood welling from the furry face of Christ.

Harley fought his way to the calf, elbowing and pulling at the bodies that were in his way, his ears filled with the cacophony of maniacal prayer and praises, of weeping, and, here and there, of cussing.

And then there came a thunderous sound.

BLAM!

Everyone froze.

Mindy was standing upon a straw bale, holding her smoking .44. A bit of chaff floated down from a ragged hole in the ceiling above her.

Everyone turned and ran.

Except for Reverend Gary. He was lying across the bleeding calf, clutching his bloody cross and speaking in tongues.

Harley grabbed Reverend Gary by the shoulders, trying to drag him off the calf. Reverend Gary paused in his babbling and switched to plain English.

"Let us pray! Through Christ shall this calf be healed!" He broke away from Harley and threw himself again on the trembling animal, laying his hands on the split face of Christ and unleashing another torrent of babble.

Harley grabbed the pitchfork.

He pressed the tines to Reverend Gary's neck.

Reverend Gary fell silent.

"Get the HELL off my calf," said Harley.

Reverend Gary blinked, then crawled away over the shards of Plexiglas, taking his Bible and cross with him. Mindy kicked the remnants of the viewing frame out of the way, then slid the door closed and hooked it.

Billy reappeared from the dark end of the barn. He was strapped into his bandoliers again, shotgun at the ready. "They'll be back, and soon," he said. "Mindy, throw a bunch of hay bales down the chute." Mindy scuttled up the ladder. "Stack 'em against the door," he said to Harley. "I'll hold 'em off from above." And before Harley could ask, Billy disappeared into the silo room.

As Mindy and Harley blocked the door, people were already banging on it. Harley heard the sound of smashing glass amidst keening and praying.

The mother and sick child were nowhere to be seen.

The Jesus calf lay trembling in the straw, Tina Turner licking gently at its wound.

"That cross . . .," said Mindy. For the first time, she looked shaken.

CHIEF KNUTSON COULDN'T scribble and move his magnets fast enough; everything had come undone. The radio chatter was unintelligible, everyone yammering over everyone else. The viewing line had deteriorated into a boiling knot of people, some angry, some confused. There arose a babble of voices.

He was out of Slim Jims.

Giving up on the radio, the chief heaved himself out of the Expedition and ran over to the ticket booths. "SHUT 'ER DOWN!" A baying howl of disapproval arose from the pedestrians awaiting admission, and then as word spread, there came a chorus of horn honking. The chief jumped back into the Expedition and phased his way to Harley's barn door, where he clicked over to the PA.

"HARLEY!"

A moment later Harley appeared in the haymow door.

Now the chief rolled down his window and hollered.

"I don't think we can hold 'er anymore, son! You'll have to shut it down!"

"We're done anyway," said Harley. "The calf—"

He was interrupted by the sound of a thin, piercing note, followed by a series of beeps.

Harley's heart sank. The tones were coming from the fire department pager on his hip. Next came the disembodied voice of the 911 dispatcher, echoing from the hip of every firefighter on the property.

Barn fire. At the old Klostermann place. Five miles outside of town.

"That's ours!" said the chief, turning on his heel.

"But you can't—we—all those people . . ." Harley felt sick. In the rush to set up the fund-raiser overnight, no one had considered this contingency. At least for Jamboree Days the Boomler department served on standby.

"Protect and serve!" said the chief as he fired up the phaser yet again and backed madly down the driveway, scattering spectators every which way, steering with one arm, and using the sleeve of his other arm to wipe his Wheel Commander Incident Command System clear in preparation for this new assignment. Every firefighter on the place followed him.

And the crowd closed in.

CHAPTER 23

I t is difficult to know what might have transpired had Billy not climbed to the top of the silo with his laser-sighted shotgun. Once the ticket booths were abandoned, cars poured in willy-nilly and the lot was now a gridlocked snarl. People were milling all over Harley's property.

Billy fired only once, and that in the air and mostly to let Harley know he was up there. In truth, the shotgun wasn't much good at such a distance, but Billy found the laser sight to be indispensable. Just the sight of the ruby dot crossing a person's toes was enough to send him or her scurrying backward. In this manner he was able to establish and maintain a clear perimeter around the barn.

Inside the barn, Harley held the calf, and Mindy held Harley. Tina Turner sniffed at her wounded baby. *I have to call a vet*, thought Harley. But he knew full well: no vet would work on that calf.

At first he didn't notice the man standing in the manure

spreader. He attributed this to the bad light and his preoccupation, but really, it's not the sort of place you'd look for someone.

"I told you it would come to this," said the man. His tone was firm, but not accusatory.

"I don't know who you are, bud," said Harley, bringing his pitchfork to bear, "but I'm in no mood."

Keeping his hands in view, the man dismounted from the manure spreader to stand beneath the lightbulb. He was wearing a long coat, a pale yellow scarf, snug black gloves, and ostrich-skin cowboy boots.

"Sloan Knight," he said. "International Talent Management."

"You're the agent . . . ," said Harley, recalling now the man who had told him things would go wrong.

Sloan nodded.

"Um," said Harley, looking the man over and trying to imagine what it might cost to dress like that, "you know that's a *manure* spreader, right?"

"I'm an *agent*. I don't mind a little shit on my boots."

Harley looked back at the calf, and the bloody, matted gash crossing Christ's face. He shook his head.

"We can fix this," said Sloan.

"But it's . . ." Harley waved his hand over the bloodied hide.

"Oh that?" said Sloan, pointing at the wound. "That's nothing. I mean we can fix this whole thing. The whole operation."

Harley heard a sound. Billy reappeared from the dark end of the barn.

"Billy!" said Harley. "Shouldn't you be up there in the silo? Guarding the perimeter? The doors?"

"Ain't nobody coming through any doors," said Billy. "And as for the perimeter, it's sealed up tighter'n a gnat's ass over a rain barrel. Nobody getting within a hundred yards of this barn."

"But how—"

"I'll get to that," said Sloan before Billy could answer.

"It's the agent," said Harley to Billy, nodding toward Sloan. "The one who called before."

Billy stepped around the manure spreader and leaned against the wall, looking Sloan up and down but saying nothing.

"Pitch time," said Sloan.

"But I don't—," said Harley.

"Five minutes," said Sloan. "Five minutes, and then if you say no I'm on my way back to L.A. and you never hear from me again."

Harley, Billy, and Mindy said nothing. Sloan took this as permission to proceed.

"The key is to strike fast and on all fronts. To operate as if tomorrow that calf gets snatched straight to heaven. A comprehensive plan. Market and monetize. Multilevel, multipronged, multimulti."

"Specifics," said Billy.

"Fine," said Sloan. "There are the obvious things—T-shirts, cups, mugs, can cozies, key fobs, stickers and decals, posters—but you're also going to want to consider the less obvious: official novena candles, holy hair lockets, rosaries, snow globes. Beyond the realm of souvenirs, we'll handle book rights and film development, sponsorship and naming rights, product placement, et cetera.

"Then, as long as you've got them coming in droves, give them something to do. Rides. Food stands. Booth rental for festival peddlers."

"But . . . we'd need pilgrims in the tens of thousands to support that kind of thing," said Harley, shaking his head.

Sloan shook *his* head. "You *truly* have no idea what you've got, do you?" Reaching inside his coat he produced a slim neoprene sleeve, from which he drew an electronic tablet. "Let me show you something." Two taps and a swipe and then he knelt beside Harley so they could both view the screen, upon which glowed a black-and-white photo of a big-boned woman in a cotton print dress and sturdy shoes. Behind her, in plaster atop an elevated plinth, stood the Blessed Virgin Mary.

"Mary Ann Van Hoof," said Sloan. "Rural Necedah, Wisconsin. Claimed she saw visions of the Blessed Virgin Mary in her bedroom. And in a blue mist in the trees. And upon a glowing crucifix."

Harley looked closer at the photo. Mrs. Van Hoof had stevedore arms and a butcher's hands. "There's a woman could throw a hay bale," said Billy, who had moved in to peer over Harley's shoulder.

"After several visions," continued Sloan, "she promised that on August 15, 1950, the Virgin Mother would appear in the sun with a message."

Sloan swiped the screen again. "And this was the result."

The photo was taken from an airplane. Acres of cars parked in endless rows across a pasture. People streaming in from all directions to surround a farmhouse nearly identical to Harley's. "Look at them," said Sloan, pointing at the people who were swarming the house like bees a hive. "Eighty thousand souls. Some claim a hundred thousand. In *one day*. They trampled the fences. Flattened the flowers. Wore the grass down to dirt in an afternoon. Reporters counted six trains, a hundred and two buses, and seventeen thousand automobiles. License plates from nearly every state. The governor called in the state police."

Sloan handed the tablet to Harley so he could study the photo more closely. Even in monochrome the Wisconsin countryside looked parched, with exposed sandy patches and a scrubby stand of oak. And as far as the eye could see, people. Pilgrims. Diffuse and patchy in the outlying areas, but clustering ever tighter and ever more densely the closer they were to the house, which was small and unremarkable, and shaded at one end by the trees. Even in the stasis of the vintage photograph, Harley could feel the invisible power drawing all of the people toward the house of apparition.

"All those people," said Sloan. "And that was a half century before the Internet."

"Anybody ever see anything?" asked Mindy.

"Nah," said Sloan. "A few scorched retinas, and somebody thought they spotted her in a box elder."

"That *is* a crowd," said Harley.

"And all for the promise of a vision," said Sloan. "Whereas you— you have a *calf*. A living, breathing *calf*."

Billy perked up. "That's what *I* told him!"

Harley rolled his eyes and dropped his head into his hands.

"Born on *Christmas Eve*!" said Billy. "In a *manger*! I *told* him!"

"Bingo," said Sloan.

Billy drew himself up proudly. "Framing the narrative," he said.

For the first time all night, Sloan Knight smiled. Then he returned the tablet to its sleeve and nodded toward the calf. "Harley, you've got a multimillion-dollar animal there."

"*Multi?*"

"Easily."

Sloan let Harley absorb that in silence for a moment, then spoke again.

"If."

"If?"

"If we work fast. If we work big. If we start now."

"But those people out there"—Harley waved in the general direction of the road, where a low hubbub could still be heard—"they really believe. They really hope. I don't know . . ."

"We'd do a Jesus Cow app, of course," said Sloan, as if he hadn't heard Harley. "That's a no-brainer. We can have the beta online in under twenty-four hours. We'll set up a secure visitation corral, priced on a sliding scale based on proximity and length of visit—from flyby to petting privileges. For real high rollers you can sell chances to feed the calf. For those who can't make the trip, a webcam setup, just like they have at Lourdes, only ours will be pay-per-view. That way you're monetizing the whole wide world."

"But . . . monetizing? That's twice now you've said that. Aren't we putting a price on belief? Commodifying faith?" Harley had picked up the word commodifying at a poetry reading during college.

"No, we're leveraging faith."

"Well, I'm kinda—"

"Harley, I'm about the free market. Faith will take care of itself."

"Well, that's not very—"

"Thoughtful? Respectful? Introspective?"

"I just want to keep it under control, kinda maybe strike a balance . . ."

"Aaaannd how's that workin' for ya?" said Billy.

"Look," said Sloan, after a pause. "You can do this or not. But the fact is, you're in a bind. You have to let the people see their calf. Because the minute that face appeared in public, it became their calf. You can show it for free if you want, or give it away in the fire department raffle, but the one thing you *can't* do is hide it or get rid of it. They'll storm the barn. They'll run you out of town.

"Bottom line? You don't own that calf, that calf owns you."

From his position at the door, Billy cleared his throat and reached into the pocket of his coat. "This might tweak your thinking," he said, and sailed an envelope toward Harley. Tina Turner flinched when the letter within spilled out in midair and floated to the straw.

"So you've already had a look," said Harley, shaking his head as he retrieved the paper.

"Yahp," said Billy. "Hand-delivered by Vance Hansen. I made him climb up the outside of the silo with it. Between a fear of heights and these snazzy bandoliers, that boy was a whiter shade of pale."

Harley read, and the barn went quiet, save for the sound of Tina Turner sniffing at her calf again, then tentatively licking its wound.

Harley recognized the letterhead of Klute Sorensen's Clearwater attorneys, but the letter was also undersigned by Vance Hansen and the village board president. Harley was being notified that in light of his ongoing refusal to cooperate with the village and the recent developments involving the calf, Klute Sorensen and his development corporation, in concert with the village proper, would be suing Harley for a list of offenses that went on for several pages, from actions negatively impacting property values to willful violations of the village parking and permitting rules and failure to collect state and county sales tax. There was verbiage regarding condemnation, foreclosure, and garnishment of future earnings.

Harley placed the letter on the straw and shook his head. "A quiet life. That's all I wanted."

"Low overhead?" said Billy.

"Low overhead," said Harley.

Tina Turner stopped licking her calf and stared at Harley.

Sloan stood silent in the shadows.

After a moment, Billy shrugged in his parka, shifted his orange rubber clogs, cleared his throat, and spoke.

"Undevelopment."

"Not now, Billy."

Billy snatched the letter from the straw and snapped it in the air. "*Growth and progress, progress and growth!* People like Klute Sorensen hammer it and yammer it nonstop. *Buy, bulldoze, and build!* Undevelopment—buy, bulldoze, don't build—now *that* would be a revolution. You'd be the antideveloper. You'd honor your father. You'd honor the land. And you'd be the hero of underdogs everywhere! A man of the people—the *good* people!"

Harley couldn't recall ever seeing Billy so animated. "But . . . I'd have to take advantage of good people to do it."

Sloan stepped forward. For the first time, he seemed impatient. "Harley, you can't help everybody. You can help yourself, you can help me, and you can help *some* of the good people. Your friend here is more committed to the good than I am—I'd be happy just to cash in. He's giving you a way to cash in *and* do some good *and* kick a bully in the nuts."

"But—" Harley pointed to the lawsuit.

Sloan took the papers from Billy's hand, gave them a quick glance, then smirked. "This is the legal equivalent of a Hallmark card. I put our attorneys on it, they'll pound so much sand up Klute

Sorensen's ass he'll be able to crap out his own private beach. And that village attorney of yours will have his polka-dotted boxers handed to him by a team of lawyers the likes of which his wet dreams are made of. Let's just say they'll be getting a truckload of certified mail from unfamiliar zip codes. Zip codes where Klute Sorensen has no more pull than a two-legged cockroach."

Now Billy spoke. "Your father worked all his life to hold this farm, only to have it shaved away bit by bit. And what didn't get shaved got grabbed."

Billy paused, then spoke again. "*Undevelopment.* You'd be the hero. The weird, rich hero."

Billy went silent then, and leaned against the door. Sloan took a step back into the shadows toward the manure spreader. Mindy had been silent the entire time, her hand light atop Harley's.

Tina Turner nudged her calf. The calf rose, shook off the straw, and turned to suckle.

Harley watched the rhythm of the calf's throat as it swallowed the milk. He thought of his father. Thought of how so much he'd worked for had been bulldozed. Thought of his mother dying, knowing the farm would be lost.

He sighed, and turned to Sloan.

"Yeah. I guess. Okay."

Sloan immediately produced his cell phone. "First thing we do is insure that calf and cow," he said.

"Well, I've always worked with Ken down there at State Farm."

"I'm sure he does good work," said Sloan, using his free hand to pull away hay bales and let himself out the door. "We'll be using a little outfit run by a guy named Lloyd, out of London."

It was quiet in the barn then, just the sound of Tina Turner working her cud, and the muffled sound of Sloan on the phone outside the door.

Billy nodded in Sloan's direction. "If that feller ain't the devil, they're damn sure first cousins."

He was grinning as he said it.

On the straw, the calf dozed, the bloodied face of Christ rising and falling.

AN HOUR LATER, Harley's kitchen was a command center. A bank of rechargeable radios blinked on the countertop, and a group of people were hunched over laptops at the table. A ring of uniformed private security personnel encircled the barn and house.

"This is just the advance contingent," said Sloan. "International Talent Management took the liberty of retaining them in advance—on our own dime—in anticipation of exactly these developments. The real help will arrive tomorrow." The private security members were quiet and efficient and not at all the sort of potbellied mall walkers Harley had—rightly or wrongly—come to associate with the phrase *private security.*

Dusk was falling. Out in the hay field and up and down the road, the mess of cars and people and TV trucks still remained and was still growing, but a large portable LED sign on a trailer had been parked between the house and barn, and the same message crawled past, over and over.

...VIEWINGS TO RESUME ASAP...UPDATES AT JESUSCOW.COM...

"I apologize for swamping your kitchen," said Sloan. "The mobile command center will be here by tomorrow morning, and we'll be out of your hair."

Harley didn't know what to say. Sloan laid it out for him.

"We've done a lot of work with the NFL and the movie industry. We're used to setting up on location and running the show on the fly."

Harley stood there goggle-eyed.

"Best thing for you would be to rest," said Sloan. "Right now we're mostly consumed with logistics. But by morning we'll need you to sign off on some things. Including the surgery."

"The . . . wha?"

"We're bringing in a veterinary plastic surgeon from L.A."

"I was not aware of this profession," said Harley.

"Oh, she's very good," said Sloan, as if recommending a barber. "Her clients include the reupholstered shih tzu of a certain regularly rehabbed starlet, an Oscar-winning stunt monkey, and she is on retainer with several of the stars of *Snow Dogs*. Apart from cosmetics, she specializes in wound remediation."

Harley looked at Mindy.

"My place, baby?" asked Mindy.

"That'd be nice," said Harley, looking around the kitchen and out the window, where the TV truck lights had everything halogen bright.

"I'll get my truck," said Mindy.

"No, no," said Sloan. "Jack here will see to it."

"But—"

"He'll also make sure you aren't bothered," said Sloan. A large man in a dark suit and long coat stepped from a corner of the kitchen and ushered them out the door, where a black Suburban had already been started and was waiting.

Outside it was dark. With Jack at the wheel, the Suburban made its way down the driveway, now clear of pilgrims. As Jack accelerated onto the county road, Harley looked back. His farmlet was a psychedelic mishmash of halogen-thrown shadows. Head-lights beamed through the exhaust of several hundred idling cars in his hay field. Dark figures walked to and fro. The LED sign con-tinued to scroll its message, over and over.

I have no idea what is happening, thought Harley. *No idea.*

In the darkness, Mindy squeezed his hand.

PART

THREE

CHAPTER 24

Klute Sorensen woke to the sound of a hedge fund manager in his right ear, discussing how his portfolio was up 28 percent for the year thanks to prescient bets placed on "key transportation and housing sectors." *I must have forgotten to set the sleep timer*, thought Klute, who was having more trouble sleeping than ever now that he had thrown unrequited love into the mix. Since his tentative visit with Meg she seemed to be avoiding him, and he found himself alternately pouting and longing. *It was easier,* he thought, *when I was only pursuing her property.*

And then there were the rumors he had heard about Harley and that damn calf. After the debacle of the fire department fundraiser, Klute had been buoyant. Surely this was the straw that broke the camel's back. Surely now sentiment in Swivel would swing his way. And yet, Klute had heard rumors that some bigshot group from L.A. had come in to run the show. Certainly the flow of pilgrims hadn't slowed. Vance Hansen said he had hardly been able to make it home from the village hall last night for all the traffic. Of course Vance was timid and drove a minivan, thought Klute.

Klute rose to shave and prepare for the day, which looked to amount to more of the same: berating Vance Hansen in an attempt to get Vance to do what Klute's Clearwater lawyers should have been doing (the truth was, Klute could no longer afford them, but during his final consult he had snagged some letterhead) and figuring out some way to put himself in the path of Meg Jankowski without looking like a complete creeper.

The hedge fund founder had finished his interview now, replaced by news at the top of the hour. It was the usual mishmash of war and worry. Then, right at the end, at the spot reserved for what was called "The Business of Entertainment" but was actually just an excuse to wedge celebrity gossip into the programming, Klute heard something that made him pause with his razor in midair.

"And finally, Jim," said a female newscaster, her delighted smile leaping right out through the speakers, "renowned Hollywood star maker Sloan Knight of International Talent Management has announced that he and the firm have taken on a *four-legged* client, having signed a comprehensive deal to represent a Holstein calf in rural Wisconsin that has been all *over* social media lately, thanks to a series of spots on its hide that many say resembles the face of Jesus Christ. In what's being called a three-sixty arrangement, International Talent Management will handle all rights from film to live appearances, endorsements, and merchandising."

"Holy cow!" said Jim, with a fake-baked chuckle.

"Yes," giggled the female newscaster. "That's what I call a *beefy* deal."

Jim segued seamlessly into precious metals futures.

Klute stared into the mirror until the shaving cream began to burn. Then he slowly raised the razor and finished what he had started. When he was done, he toweled off his face and stared into the mirror again. The business news was still echoing all around him, but he didn't hear it. Instead, he straightened up, looked himself right in the eye, and in a very quiet voice said, "Key housing and transportation sectors . . ."

Then he called Vance Hansen and set up a meeting.

It felt good to yell again.

WHEN HARLEY AND Mindy awoke, Jack the driver was waiting with breakfast and a ride back to Harley's farm for a meeting in the command center with Sloan.

"Good news," said Sloan, as an assistant distributed cappuccinos. "The surgeon found the damage to the Jesus face to be mostly superficial. It was easily repairable on-site. We brought in a hair and makeup person to obscure the stitches. It's all cleaned up now and you can't see the difference."

Sloan went on to report that subsequent to the surgery, three independent veterinarians, a hairdresser, and one notary public were obtained to inspect the calf and then sign a certificate of authenticity. "Any knucklehead could stencil a Jesus face on a calf," explained Sloan. Harley thought of his shoe polish trick as he signed the papers Sloan handed to him. He didn't read them in their entirety, but he did see the sentence that said, "Pricewaterhouse-Cooper cannot verify that this is the face of the Savior, but does verify that the calf and/or the image in question has not been in any way artificially manipulated or modified."

Before the veterinarian departed she implanted a tracking device. "With an animal of this value, kidnapping is always a concern," said Sloan. Then, by way of explanation, he added, "Many of these measures are required by Lloyd's."

The speed with which the operation grew was astounding. Two more busloads of security teams arrived, and cleared the property of people and vehicles. The team hired Meg to do the towing. This resulted in an unexpected financial windfall for her and—she tithed the very next day—St. Jude's and the food pantry, and Harley had the first inkling of how all the things Sloan and Billy had predicted might just pan out. The calf might actually be used for good. By afternoon the wreckage of the fire department ticket booths had been replaced with turnstiles and ticket scanners. Weatherproof tents were erected and torpedo heaters brought in. The remainder of Harley's hay field had been plowed clear and fitted with generator-powered lights, heated Porta-Potties, and parking attendants.

The command center was now operating in a gigantic mobile home. A cleaning crew had been through Harley's house in the wake of the command team's departure, and frankly, Harley couldn't recall it ever looking so good.

"Public relations," said Sloan, nodding toward a cluster of four people working tablets and Bluetooths at the far end of the mobile home. "Apart from handling the news crews, they're coordinating with the state tourism board and arranging visits by dignitaries. I understand the governor has already been in touch, as well as the National Association of Religious Broadcasters. We've also assigned one person to monitor animal rights organizations to anticipate and neutralize any difficulties in that direction."

Another four-pack of people was clustered around flat screens. "Social media," said Sloan. "The calf will have numerous accounts."

"Which reminds me," said Harley. "JesusCow.com?"

Sloan smiled. "We took the liberty of squatting on that one in advance. As well as the Twitter handle @TheJesusCow."

"But it's a *calf*. For a while yet."

"Yes, but when it first blew up—I believe it was your mail carrier—"

"Dixie."

"Yes, well, she hashtagged it #JesusCow, and it stuck. So we went with that. Better in the long term anyway. Our market research did yield affection and loyalty spikes around the term 'calf'—due mainly to cuteness variables—but as a term it puts a hard horizon on long-term marketability thematics. Whereas 'cow' has us covered well into the future."

"Um, also, that's gonna be a *bull*, not a *cow*," said Harley.

"We prefer to think of the term in the generic gender-neutral sense," said Sloan. "Furthermore, and by way of update, during the hide repair surgery we took the liberty of . . . um . . . altering that status."

"You steered that bull?"

"Yes," said Sloan. "While bovine animal husbandry is not my chief area of expertise, it seemed best. Apart from the legendary Ferdinand, bulls in general do not project lovability. Whereas our research indicated the term *steer* charts much higher among children, housewives, and hard-core feminists. There were some outliers—a segment of Christians who prefer the image of a muscular, virile Christ—but there is a downside risk to deploying the term *bull* within a religious context."

Harley looked at him blankly, then it dawned on him. *Bull*. As in *bull*shit.

"You know," said Sloan, "the satirists and haters."

"How do you keep track of all this?" said Harley, looking around himself worriedly. "And what about permits, and sales tax and zoning violations and trip-and-fall lawsuits and who knows what else?"

"Actually, in this case I agree with your archnemesis Klute Sorensen," said Sloan. "In particular the way he proceeded with Clover Blossom Estates; the key is to go like mad, make as much as you can, and seek forgiveness later. You know, 'Make hay while the sun shines.' Sometimes opportunity has the shelf life of a Twinkie in a pigpen."

Harley found himself booked into a lot of very boring business meetings in which he had to sign piles and piles of paperwork, most of it explained briefly and on the fly. Each time the small voice inside told him this was a bad idea, he imagined Clover Blossom Estates blooming in nothing but actual clover and Klute Sorensen driving a used Toyota. *Oh well*, thought Harley, *can't stop now.*

Throughout the paperwork, Harley saw references to JCOW Enterprises, Inc., of which entity he was apparently president. At one point he signed a piece of paper titled "Agency Representation Agreement" and he had hesitated with his pen in the air for a moment when he read the part about International Talent Management claiming 20 percent of all proceeds. It seemed like an awful lot. Then he looked around at the hum and buzz of activity in the command center, and then he considered the scene outside where everything was shaping up for the reopening, and finally he reflected on the train wreck that resulted when he tried to do it himself, and then he figured whatever the deal was, it was a good deal.

Sloan slid another piece of paper into place. "Catchall," he said. "On your behalf we will control film, media, and merchandising rights. In addition to development, we will vigorously pursue any and all unauthorized online videos and sales items."

Harley signed, and the feeling was that of launching a boat he had never seen and could never bring back to dock.

"Last one for today," said Sloan, placing a single sheet of International Talent Management letterhead into place. It was the simplest of forms, in fact one simple line:

> I, the undersigned, grant International Talent Management and their qualified representatives to negotiate on my behalf with the bishop of Rome and all relevant subsidiary institutions and officials regarding the sanctified status of the property heretofore and henceforth referred to as "the Jesus Cow."

"Bishop of Rome?" asked Harley.

"That would be the pope," said Sloan. "Clearly we won't approach him directly—at least not initially. We will initiate the process via our Vatican contact."

"Your Vatican contact?"

"When's the last time you ever heard of tour buses lining up to visit the Mary Ann Van Hoof farm?"

"Well, I . . ."

"You can visit her place. She's long gone, of course, but a shrine remains. And there are plans for a giant cathedral, as directed to her by Mary in the visions.

"But if you go there, y'know what you'll find?"

Harley shrugged.

"A half-finished cathedral, a few laminated Bible bookmarks in the gift shop, and a brochure asking for donations. They're just scraping by. They failed to obtain approval from the Vatican, and in fact, the regional bishop placed them in a state of interdict—one step removed from excommunication. It really killed the business.

"Now then," continued Sloan, "for the sake of comparison, let us consider the Our Lady of Good Help shrine in New Franken, Wisconsin. They were puttering along, maybe seventy-five to a hundred visitors on a good day. Then the bishop issues a decree certifying that the Virgin Mary had truly appeared there as reported, and, *boom!* five hundred to eight hundred visitors per day, even during winter. Bus tours. Faithful pilgrims from all around the world. A mention on *Nightline*."

He handed Harley a scan of a newspaper article containing the story and these details.

"Yeah, but how about this?" asked Harley, pointing to a quote from a local priest: "We don't want to become a kind of circus."

"We at International Talent Management," said Sloan, "are not lumbered with that particular compunction."

HIS MORNING DOUBTS at bay, Klute Sorensen was back in his element, having blared his Hummer through the ranks of pilgrims to Swivel Village Hall, where he was once again fulminating at Vance Hansen.

"But—," said Vance.

"*But* is where you *sit* when you *quit!*" hollered Klute, who had made that one up himself and intended to include it on his own motivational CD one day. Sometimes he liked to close his eyes and imagine himself stalking the stage of a giant conference center, wearing one of those invisibly slim flesh-toned microphones that attach right to your face, looking out at a sea of expectant faces as he boomed out business-savvy piths and gists backed by a Power-Point projection the size of a drive-in movie screen.

"But I don't control the school buses," said Vance. "I can't simply sign them over to you."

"BUREAUCRACY!" hollered Klute. "BANE OF ALL ENTER-PRISE! ENEMY OF PROGRESS! GUM IN THE GEARS OF GREATNESS!"

"Yes, well—"

"Who's the president of the school board?"

"Freda Sigurdson . . ."

"You call Freda *right now,* and you tell her to convene a special session. You tell her Klute Sorensen is going to rent every single school bus on the lot for the foreseeable future."

Vance looked confused. Klute pointed out the window. "You see all those damned cow worshippers? Clogging the streets? Parking all over the place?"

"Yes, it's a problem," said Vance. "Constable Benson is—"

"*You* see a *problem,*" said Klute, "I see an *opportunity!*"

"That's why you're you," said Vance.

"Transportation and housing! Those are your *key sectors* in a situation like this! Right now Swivel has a problem with *both,* and more coming! You tell her Klute Sorensen will cover all the costs and that twenty-five percent of the proceeds . . . ten percent of the proceeds . . . *five percent of the proceeds* will go to the school athletics fund."

"But school is in session . . ."

"We'll be using the buses from nine a.m. to two p.m. for starters, until I can figure out a backup system and procure additional vehicles."

"But I'm not sure the board will approve—"

"Who pledged the entire cost of the new scoreboard down at the football field?"

"You did, Klute," said Vance, reaching for the phone. "This community owes you so much . . ."

There was the tricky bit about the fact that while Klute had *pledged* the scoreboard money, he hadn't actually yet *paid* the money, but Klute was already slamming out the door and Vance could see no reason to detain him on this point.

CHAPTER 25

All the paperwork left Harley unsettled. He called Mindy, and she said to come on out. When he opened the door to the granary, she was wearing a tool belt and was covered in sheet rock dust. She handed him a Foamy Viking and led him by the hand to her bed.

Mindy's bed frightened Harley. Or more specifically, the headboard frightened him. Mindy's sculptwelder boyfriend had made it for her. It was constructed of sheet metal welded inside a channel iron frame. Using a plasma cutter, the sculptwelder had scored designs and figures into the sheet metal, including dancing mountain goats and an army of flute-playing Kokopellis. Harley had spent only one night in the bed, but apart from the idea that it conjured up Mindy's ex, he feared that during some particularly acrobatic escapade he might find himself gored by Kokopelli's steel flute, or intimately strung atop the horn of a dancing goat.

In short, it was the equivalent of making love adjacent to a giant cheese grater.

Harley sat on the edge of the bed and took a swig of his beer. Mindy rubbed his shoulders. Harley sighed.

"That damn calf . . ."

"Damn calf? That damn calf is going to make you a lot of damn money."

"I dunno. It better, I guess. You can't get more all in than I'm all in."

"You rather it had never happened?"

"Kinda moot, I guess. It's just . . . with its . . . its *connotations*. I mean, if the thing had six legs, or two heads, well, y'know, maybe the local TV station would be interested for sixty seconds, and some folks would drop in now and then, but this thing, this thing is about religion, and I just feel like somewhere along the line . . ."

He stopped then, and shook his head.

"I mean, alls I wanted was a damn beefer."

"And a lady friend," said Mindy.

"Well, yah," said Harley, allowing himself a small smile.

"Maybe I could pray on it," said Harley, in a halfhearted attempt at sarcasm he didn't really feel. "Like I learned growing up."

"And how would that go?"

"Our Father, we pray that—"

"We?" interrupted Mindy.

"Well, it was sort of a royal we, I guess," said Harley. "I never really thought about it. It was just the way we did it."

"That's *kinda* faith," said Mindy.

"There was comfort in it, though," said Harley. "Even saying it again now. Even as far as I've strayed." He spun his dwindling beer. "The thing was, we didn't believe in praying for specifics. No asking for help with the rent or your bad leg. Just guidance and humility and . . . well, *concepts*, I guess. I remember in a coffee shop in Clearwater once I eavesdropped on a Bible study group and heard a woman ask the Lord to get her out of a lease, and I just . . ." Harley shook his head.

"Well, I guess you could say our trials ride a sliding scale," said Mindy. "I read a quote once, I think by a yogi: *In certain circumstances the raindrop is a flood.*"

"Yeah, it just seems . . ."

"Like it doesn't really measure up? The bad lease as compared to any given genocide?"

"Yah, I guess that's part of it. Plus the informality. Like you'd use your audience with the Almighty to ask for the spiritual equivalent of Cracker Jacks."

"What drove you away?"

"I drifted more than drove."

"Mm."

"And not my folks, that's for sure," said Harley. "I should be half as good as them."

"But you don't believe."

"I don't think so."

"So? How'd it happen? How'd you go from believer to Doubting Thomas?"

Harley looked at the beer in his hand like he had just discovered it, and took a deep swig. "In college, I had to write a paper. Your basic geography report. I was in the library reading up on Central America. I stumbled over this article that described—and this wasn't ancient history, this happened when I was a kid—entire families being tortured. To death. Including children, with parents forced to watch. After that, the ol' 'sometimes bad things happen to good people' thing never quite cut it for me."

Mindy was silent.

"I was already slipping," said Harley. "But that pushed me over. I couldn't see how you could have it both ways: either God's all-powerful but chose to let those babies suffer, or he *isn't* all-powerful and couldn't stop it."

Harley paused, and shrugged. "It's not a very original path to doubt. First time I discussed it with Billy, he said, 'Welcome to the Epicurean paradox, son, a couple thousand years after the fact. Also, you might want to read up on theodicy.'"

"*The Odyssey?*"

"Ha! No, *theodicy*: t-h-e-o-d-i-c-y. It's a theological deal. Supposed to explain how a good God can allow evil."

"How about your parents? How did they explain it?"

"I don't know," said Harley. "I never asked."

They sat together quietly then, until Mindy spoke.

"How did you wrap up?"

"Wrap what?"

"Your prayers."

"'In Jesus' name, amen.'"

"That's a sweet little poem, that's what that is."

It is a comforting rhythm, thought Harley as he finished the beer and turned to Mindy. She leaned into his T-shirt, put her nose at the level of his clavicle, and drew in deep. "Mmmmm, I love your smell," she said.

He went cold. He remembered her telling him about the sculptwelder's smell. "Mmmm," she said again, nuzzling deeper.

He held her, wanted to be happy, or even just fool around enough to undo the whole theodicy bummer, but she could sense his unease. "What?" She was looking up, both hands flat on his chest. "What is it?"

"You liked the smell of the sculptwelder," he said. "And then one day . . ."

"Oh, baby . . . ," she said, moving her hands around his back. She linked her fingers and squeezed. "Oh, baby . . . ," she said, as if he were a child afraid of the dark. She moved in, and he fell back on the bed, one eye on all the Kokopellis dancing dangerously above.

BACK IN SWIVEL, Klute Sorensen was driving through Clover Blossom Estates, counting empty houses. This was the housing sector portion of his plan. It was his intent to rent the empty houses to Jesus Cow tourists by the day.

Damn, if I had that hotel up, he thought, looking toward Meg's place. He imagined what it would be like to see the parking lot filled with cars, every room full. The cash register singing.

Ahead of Klute, a car slowed, causing him to jam on the brakes. Rather than pay for parking in the village, tourists were parking on the streets of the development, then hiking across the overpass. Klute speed-dialed Vance Hansen.

"Yes, Klute?"

"How we coming on the transportation sector action plan?"

"The which?"

"Have you rented any damn school buses yet!"

"Well, I haven't heard back from—"

"Never mind! I want Constable Benson down here now!"

"Well, I'll just check—"

"I got people parked all over Clover Blossom Estates. I want 'em outta there!"

"Well, those are village streets, so legally they can—"

"Does the village not shut down parking for the Jamboree Days parade?"

"Yes, but—"

"So do it here! *Now!*"

"Well, I'll just get the constable—"

"I'm *fast-tracking* this!"

"I see."

"Not everyone can *do* what I do."

"That is so true," said Vance.

BY THAT EVENING Klute's plan to rent Swivel's school buses still hadn't received approval from the school board, but he did manage to rent three from the private company that leased them to the Boomler school district. He also stopped by Signs-2-Go and had several all-weather banners printed up: some advertising the Clover Blossom homes for short-term rental by the room, others that read SHUTTLE PICKUP. And as long as he was there and had his American Express warmed up, he had the folks at Signs-2-Go crank out two dozen placards that said NO PARKING ON STREET BY ORDER OF VILLAGE CONSTABLE, since the actual constable still hadn't done the job.

One day later, he cleared the snow from two empty lots and began offering off-street parking by the hour. Two days later, his three school bus shuttles were running. Three days later, he rented his first room.

On the fourth day, a trio of state inspectors showed up and shut down the whole works.

AS FOR JCOW Enterprises, Sloan and his crew kept things humming right along. A patch of land between the old water tower and Harley's barn was subdivided into a bazaar where vendors in heated tents sold all manner of religious tchotchkes, from chalices to calf-shaped cheese curds served with bacon halos.

The barn had been transformed into something off a postcard. Sloan had brought in a set designer whose team had applied fresh paint—no easy trick in the cold—and trimmed the eaves in pine boughs, hung wreaths on the windows, and bathed the entire structure in hidden lighting.

A reality television show was in the works, and a documentary film crew had been retained and was shooting several times a week. Harley had refused to sit for interviews of any sort. Sloan said this was fine, that his reclusiveness simply added one more layer of mystery to the entire production. Harley suspected there was a lot of footage of him walking away with his cap pulled down.

After the farm was visited by several national television news-magazine programs, attendance numbers boomed and resulted in some bottlenecks, but within a week or so the whole works settled into a steady, manageable state. Crowds of people were still pouring into town, but some of the congestion had been alleviated by a fleet of officially sanctioned JesusCow tour buses that ran on a regular round-trip schedule from Boomler, where Sloan's people had worked out a package deal with the two chain motels, a development that left Klute Sorensen fuming.

When Harley brought this up with Sloan, Sloan smiled.

"As it turns out, there are some very strict state statutes governing the operation of hotels and shuttles. Through a state senator friend we were able to notify the proper enforcement branches.

They in turn were able to intervene and protect the public. In short, Klute was visited by a batch of bureaucrats with badges."

"But what about our shuttles?" asked Harley.

"Out of gratitude for our notifying him of Klute's illicit operation, the senator was able to expedite our paperwork," said Sloan. "We're good to go."

Harley knew he shouldn't gloat. There was enough residual teaching from his parents and the leftover tenets of his own faith that he knew it didn't do to wish someone ill, no matter how ill that person might treat you. But simply knowing there was a chance that a bully might shortly be relegated to a mighty small corner of the playground left Harley pleased indeed, and rather than the queasy worry he so often felt in the face of opportunity, Harley allowed himself a brief burst of happiness. It was freeing to charge ahead (although, he had to admit, by proxy) without mincing about, and it was thrilling for once to turn the weapons of Klute on Klute himself.

CHAPTER 26

As the days passed, Harley tried to continue on as things always were—doing his barn chores, feeding his beefers, and pulling his shifts at the filter factory—but there was no question that events caused his life to become more circumscribed. He found the routine of his factory shifts a great relief, and he was grateful for the chance to be just another person working the line, but feelings in the break room were divided, with half the crew admiring him for continuing to be one of them despite what everyone assumed to be his new fortune, and the other half, who resented the fact that someone socking away that kind of money would keep a job that would do someone else in tougher straits some good. When Sloan told him JCOW Enterprises could put him on a salary three times what he was drawing at the factory, Harley turned in his notice.

He also kept trying to make calls with the fire department. But even down at the fire hall things were getting tense. Due to the abrupt termination of the calf-viewing fund-raiser, the thermal imager fund was still less than a third of the way to the top of the plywood thermometer. Additionally, with all the transient gawkers coming to town, the department was experiencing a huge increase in calls—be they for fender benders or fainting pilgrims—and the annual operating budget was beyond blown, to say nothing of all the sleep and family time that was being missed. Harley hung in there, but every time he answered a call related to JCOW Enterprises, he felt the grumpiness of the rest of the crew as they missed yet another hour of work in order to tend to some true believer with heart palpitations, or some unlucky visitor who twisted an ankle stepping off an officially sanctioned JesusCow tour bus, or that nun who got the vapors when the Jesus calf appeared to wink at her.

Harley requested a leave of absence. The chief approved it without comment.

THE TUESDAY AFTER taking his leave, Harley attended the Swivel Village Board meeting. In fact, he had been summoned. Although many people in the village were benefiting from the windfall created by Harley's calf, many more were not, and were in fact being inconvenienced by all the traffic and tumult. There had also been concerns raised by Vance Hansen (whom Harley knew was goaded by Klute) that JCOW Enterprises was running afoul of many ordinances and permitting processes, as were many of the citizens running side businesses spawned by the influx of all the far-flung sightseers.

Sloan tried to talk Harley out of attending. "That's what these folks are for," he said, nodding toward a brace of attorneys at the command center conference table. But Harley wanted to do this on his own. These were, after all, his neighbors. He felt a sense of duty, but he also felt embarrassed at the idea of siccing West Coast lawyers on his neighbors.

Five minutes into the meeting, Harley wished he had sicced the lawyers. One by one, his fellow citizens approached the podium and let him have it. Gladys Hough said people were parking in the alley and tromping through her yard. "Someone stole my gazing ball," she said, and then, fixing Harley with a disappointed glare, added, "Furthermore, I used to babysit you." "All this extra traffic is tearin' up the roads," said Vern Trilling. "And we taxpayers are gonna get stuck with the bill for all the extra asphalt patch come spring." Jilly Francis complained about the light pollution from a giant wraparound LED screen that had been mounted on the catwalk railing of the old water tower and was visible from the interstate. (Carolyn had refused to allow the crew access until she was assured in writing by Sloan that the signworks would be bolted to the railing and not the tank itself—she cited several obscure statutes related to historic preservation but was in fact terrified that some poor sap might drill a hole in the tank and her secret would come squirting out). Paul Forster, owner of the Kwik Pump, wondered why the official Jesus Cow tour buses were buying their fuel in Boomler, rather than "availing themselves" of "locally sourced" diesel.

Throughout this litany of grievances, Klute Sorensen sat in the front row, nodding with outsize concern, as if each complaint were an arrow through his own heart. When the last citizen had spoken, Klute rose and faced the room.

"Ladies and gentlemen, it is no secret that I am not from this town." Klute paused a moment, for effect. "But it is also no secret that I have come to *love* this town."

An appreciative murmur ran through the room.

"I *love* this town," repeated Klute, "and so it *wounds* me to see it mistreated. Taken for granted. Everyone in this room knows the great lengths to which I have gone to resurrect Swivel from tough times not of its own making. Clover Blossom Estates is a labor of *love*. Love between a man who may not be *from* this town, but has been *welcomed* by this town and the visionary people in it."

But mostly love between you and yourself, thought Harley.

"The Clover Blossom Estates project has been struggling—that is no secret. Despite careful planning, despite attractive terms, despite the community's goodwill and support, it has struggled, and I think we know why: it is because despite the forward-looking leadership and citizenry of this community, there are some—or at least *one*—who has stubbornly refused to move forward, and instead has clung, clawing, to the past.

"I suppose it could be my fault," continued Klute, after heaving a martyr's sigh. "I suppose there are developers out there who could convince people to buy new homes within sniffing distance of a cattle feedlot"—here Klute looked directly at Harley—"but apparently I am not that man.

"It takes a special kind of man to overcome those odds," said Klute, now regarding Harley openly. "But it takes another kind of special man to stand in the way of progress—after all, what sort of citizen holds his village, adjacent as it is to an undeveloped four-lane interchange, back year after year by insisting that one of its most desirable, potentially tax-generating parcels be kept instead under eight head of beef—a tax dodge!—and a decrepit water tower?"

"No one is a greater champion of private property rights than Klute Sorensen," continued Klute, "and although I have found Harley Jackson's obstinance frustrating and even financially injurious, I could at least understand it in those terms. It was his father's land, after all, and he wished to preserve that legacy—or what was left of it. But now"—here Klute gestured out the village hall window toward Harley's farm—"now we see that when there is big money to be made, he is prepared to grab all he can, never mind what injury might be done to those around him."

"But, Klute," said Harley, surprised he could speak, "success— doesn't it float all boats?" He waved a hand at the assembled crowd. "Isn't that how you sold Clover Blossom Estates to this bunch?"

Harley had to give him this: Klute didn't falter. Rather, he drew himself up with an air of wounded patience and said, "In all things there is nuance, Harley. And in this case, there is the nuance of being a *good neighbor*. Of not just stomping around and raking it in. Of not only taking, but *giving back*. If Clover Blossom Estates was thriving, the tax base would be thriving right along with it, and we'd have the money to rebuild the sewer systems, which—as many of you know only too well—are in a sad state of disrepair. You, on the other hand—you, and your cash-pocketing out-of-state business partners—take profits and pay minimal village and property taxes—I assume you're still taking advantage of the tax break afforded by your beef cows?—while your customers come here by the bus and carload, putting untold wear and tear on our infrastructure, including and especially the sewer system.

You are involved in what we in business circles refer to as an *extractive* industry."

Again, Klute shook his head sorrowfully.

"Why, only last week I spoke with Meg Jankowski. You all know Meg. If there is a more selfless citizen in Swivel, I'd like to meet him—or her. Yes, I spoke with Meg, and although she is a person of great positivity, I sensed an air of worry about her. When I inquired, she said the food pantry was being overrun and was in danger of running out of food.

"It seems that many of the people who come here to see Harley's calf—and pay Harley good money to see that calf—have hardly any money to begin with. They are in need, and they are in hope, so they scrape together what little they have to make the trip, spend the rest on admission and souvenirs, and then wind up at the food pantry seeking sustenance."

I'm about to regurgitate my sustenance, thought Harley.

"And so it turns out that while the Jesus Cow circus is *making* money for some, it is *taking* from most. And so, in conclusion—" Here Klute paused for dramatic effect, and turned toward Vance Hansen.

"Vance, would you be good enough?"

Vance ducked back into his office, and returned with what appeared to be a large piece of cardboard.

"I invited Meg to be here for this, but unfortunately she had to leave at the last minute to tow a tour bus that was blocking access to the food pantry parking lot," said Klute, shaking his head morosely. An angry murmur ran through the crowd, which turned to admiration and applause as Klute Sorensen held above his head a giant cardboard check in the amount of $5,000.00, signed and payable to the Swivel Food Pantry.

AFTER THE SCENE at the village hall, Harley went home and stewed. Sometimes he got so angry at himself. So angry at his politeness, at his circumspectness, at his nibbling around the edges when in fact he harbored a secret admiration for men who cussed and raged and cut right to the heart of the matter. Who called a spade a spade and even better yet called a blowhard a blowhard and a jerk a jerk.

There was this part of him that wanted to be the good boy. Really did. And the good boy *was* good. He tried not to swear, he tried to be polite, and yet perversely found himself wishing to be a person who was profane and scathing precisely because he rarely allowed himself to be either. There was nothing more refreshing than watching a guy like Billy sort someone out right on the spot. Or Sloan, going full speed ahead with never a *hint* of dither. For that matter, there was even something bracing in watching someone as shameless as Klute Sorensen barging along.

He longed to be one of those guys who could just say, *Ahh fuckit.* That's how they always said it, the last two words as one, *Ahh fuckit,* and delivered it with a wave of the hand, but then he recalled that most of the times he'd heard someone say *Ahh fuckit* they had a bottle in one hand and a fistful of trouble in the other, so in the end he wasn't certain of the long-term effectiveness of the strategy.

He wished he could harden his heart. All of it, beyond the scarred edges.

Just once he wanted to go all Bad Johnny Cash. Kick out the footlights. Just let 'er rip. Flip the bird and fly the coop.

Instead he called Mindy. She said she was busy hanging drywall, but could come and see him later.

Then he called Billy.

"Staff meeting," he said, and that was all that needed to be said.

"IT'S LUDICROUS THAT all this disruption should be caused by a birth defect on a cow," said Harley as they uncapped their Foamy Vikings.

"Ludicrous is part of the deal," said Billy, after a swallow of beer.

"Yah, I guess," said Harley, watching yet another busload of tourists debark from a long bus and begin the trek through the barn, which had now been fitted with a climate-controlled flow-through viewing vestibule. "I just wish it was . . . I don't know . . . *quieter. Classier.*"

"Mm-hmm," said Billy.

"I mean, there are a lot of nutty people coming through here."

"Well, sure," said Billy, "but you understand: by and large these are not His top-line representatives."

"I keep thinking of Meg," said Harley. "Going to St. Jude's every day to pray and light those candles. And then back to work. And stocking that pantry. Quietly going about her life. Of all the people in town you'd think would visit that steer, you'd figure it might be her."

"Mm-hmm," said Billy again while scratching his beard, a sure sign that he was giving Harley some rope, letting him work this line of thought on his own. For all his talking, Billy knew when not to talk.

"Even me," Harley said. "You'd think with my background— shoot, I was raised on the Bible, I know it chapter and verse and can still name a fair number of the bit players—you'd think the face on that steer would make me wonder some, but I don't see it as anything more than a furry coincidence."

"And right you are," said Billy, waving his rapidly emptying beer in the direction of the crowds filing through the barn. "What you have there is people assigning meaning to coincidence. Forcing theology into place between nature and chance. There is a mighty space between the known and the unknown, and a lot of folks use theology to spackle the gap."

"Did you just say 'spackle the gap'?"

"Pareidolia, then."

"Para-wha?"

"Pareidolia. A psychological phenomonen. Where your brain fills in the gaps left by your eyes. It's why you can see a man on the moon, or a rabbit in the clouds. It's why people see Jesus in their fish sticks, or their scorched tortilla, or the rear end of a dachshund. We convince ourselves to see what we cannot see. It's scientific fact. And when faith is in play, the inclination kicks into overdrive."

Harley looked at the people again. "Somehow I don't think you'd be able to sell para—pari—well, *that* to them."

"Well, *you're* selling it to them."

Harley fell silent. He had looked into his bank account recently and nearly peed his pants. The number was beyond anything he could imagine.

All that belief, he thought, as another tour bus glided to a stop and disgorged another line of pilgrims.

Belief, thought Harley. *Belief by the busload.*

BY THE TIME Mindy came over, Harley was ready to move, so they went for a walk. It was odd to pass through the crowds anonymously, to hear people talk of the calf and their reasons for coming to see it, even as they were unaware that they were walking beside the man who owned the calf. He heard talk of goiters cured and broken marriages mended and drug-addled adolescents gone straight. He saw people in tears. He heard conversations held in true transcendent joy. And he heard credit card swipers beeping.

"Let's go up in the tower!" said Mindy. "Look at it all from above!"

Harley's first inclination was to demur. The idea of climbing, of being up there as if lording it over everything . . . but then it occurred to him that there would be no more private place. He used his spare key to let himself in through the security gate. Carolyn's car was gone, but he knocked on the pump house door just in case. "She told me she was running a batch of waste oil down to the collection center in Clearwater," said Harley to Mindy when there was no answer. Harley shook his head. "I really can't make the math work on that program of hers."

"I admire her," said Mindy, and reached for the ladder. (In fact Carolyn was not at the collection center, she was at the food co-op buying EarthHug tea. She made these trips once a month after packing her Subaru with empty buckets and telling anyone who would listen that she was off to recycle the oil—a misdirectional ruse intended to provide cover should some Nosy Norbert get curious about where it all went.)

The climb was cold and grew colder rung by rung. Shortly Harley and Mindy reached the trapdoor to the catwalk. Harley raised it and the two crawled through, then turned to lean on the railing and observe the scene below.

The thing that struck Harley first was the orderly nature of the flow. Compared to the photos he had seen in *LIFE* magazine, and compared to how it must have looked the day he and Billy were overrun, everything was well delineated and prescribed. The perimeter of Harley's property had been snow-blown clear, and temporary fencing erected. Security crews in all-terrain vehicles made regular rounds, ensuring that no one was sneaking in.

There were vehicles and pedestrians everywhere, but they moved in orderly rivulets, nobody working against the stream. Off the property things were less organized, odd clusters of people gathered up here and there, signs of freelancers setting up their booths and tables (PARKING, $20/HR.), hawking hand warmers and neon bracelets and bootlegged goods. Sloan always kept a few of his people out undercover, and if any vendor sold them an unauthorized JesusCow item, their goods were confiscated and they were sent packing after a stern talking-to by Constable Benson. The constable had actually come to enjoy this routine as it gave him the opportunity to play the heavy and was much less stressful than breaking up fights at the Buck Rub Bar.

Dusk was fading to dark now. Harley could hear the *squinch* of tires as a steady stream of cars left the lot. Sloan had said it was very important to be businesslike with the hours. Furthermore, the husbandry consultants had warned that the calf mustn't be over-stimulated. The parking lots were illuminated by halogen lights attached to portable trailers, their generators maintaining a steady muffled hum. In the dimmer spots between the pools of white light, parking attendants waved the cars along their way, the cone-tipped flashlights cutting orange arcs above the ground. Two large black SUVs pulled up to the barn and Harley knew these would be the VIPs, allowed in (at a prohibitive rate, and after the rabble had departed) and given a chance to feed and straw the calf, lay their hands upon him, and pose for photographs.

The exterior of the barn was fully lit, bathed in gel lights and upwardly aimed floods and twinkling with strings of white icicle lights. Hidden blowers puffed a gentle dusting of fake snow that dropped past the lighted eaves in a way that couldn't help but impart comfort. And centering it all, an electrified cross atop the silo glowing sacred white. Harley had fought the placement of the cross, but he had to admit Sloan and his Hollywood people had done an astounding job. The barn looked like it was plucked from a Thomas Kinkade refrigerator magnet.

Mindy moved in close.

"I'm so proud of you, baby."

"But I didn't really do anything. That calf fell in my lap. Utter chance. And when I tried to do it on my own, I screwed it up."

"Honey, sometimes you just need to go with happiness and opportunity."

"Yah," said Harley. "Yah, I overthink everything."

"Don't overthink this," said Mindy softly, the glow of the scene lights soft on her cheeks. "Or *this*." She pulled him near and kissed him.

Down below Harley heard a different rumble. It was Meg Jankowski, returning home from the food pantry in her junk truck. She drove slowly, starting and stopping between droves of departing pilgrims, and waiting to be waved through by the security employee doing traffic out by the mailbox. When she finally cleared the last stragglers and accelerated, Harley wondered what in all her faith she made of this garish carnival.

CHAPTER 27

In mid-March, JCOW Enterprises shut down for three days. The entire grounds were cleared, cleaned, and sealed off. The only visible activity was that of the security teams and JCOW Enterprises employees. A special retinue from International Talent Management flew in for the week.

On the morning of the third day, a caravan of white vehicles arrived and drove up Harley's driveway. They were met by the security team, and ushered quickly into the viewing vestibule. For anyone watching from the road, there would have been little to see. But within the vestibule was a team of men—some in vestments, some not—representing the Vatican.

Sloan had asked Harley to take Billy out of town for this one, so they were fueling the Silverado across the street at the Kwik Pump before a trip to the Clearwater warehouse club, where Billy bought kitty litter by the pallet. Just as Harley was topping off his tank,

Meg pulled into the other side of the island and jumped down from her junk truck to fill up.

"Well, hello, Harley," she said. Her smile and gentle familiarity caught him off guard. Like she knew more about him than he suspected.

"Hello, Meg."

"How are you holding up these days?"

"Well, fine, I guess." He nodded toward his farm, which from this distance appeared to be a vacant theme park. An image of the calf (with the Jesus face pixilated) scrolled continuously around the water tower LED screen, followed by a text crawl that read . . . SEE THE JESUS COW . . . JESUSCOW.COM . . . SEE THE JESUS COW . . . Today, a secondary message flashed between the ellipses: . . . RE-OPENING TOMORROW, 9AM!!! . . .

"Quiet today," said Meg, nodding toward the empty grounds.

"Yah," said Harley. "They're doing a bunch of re—" He stopped midword. He had been going to give her some line about revamping, but there was something about Meg's eyes, open and honest in her placid face, that wouldn't allow it.

"Well, it's some of your people," said Harley.

"My people."

"A bishop or some such," said Harley. "They're looking into conferring some sort of official status on the . . . the . . ."

"The situation?"

"Sure," said Harley with relief.

"I'm not so sure about all that."

"But . . . you . . ."

"I go to church every day?"

"Yah."

"I wear the robe and help Father Chuck do all the mystery services?"

"Yah. And yet . . ."

"Harley, the church is a *frame*. It's how I look at things. You know, sometimes we get too caught up in trying to figure out *what* people believe and forget to look at *why* they believe."

Harley didn't have anything to say to that.

"Lighting those candles, going to that church—that's nothing but the outside of what's going on inside," said Meg, racking the diesel nozzle and jogging into the Kwik Pump to pay up. "Good to see you," she said over her shoulder.

Harley climbed back into the truck and looked at Billy.

"You hear all that?"

"Yep."

"How do you *get* that?"

"I suppose you'd just ask her out," said Billy.

"No! Not the *woman*! The goodness! The peace! That pure-heartedness."

"Well, first of all, I reckon she'd tell you it's a tad more compli-cated than that," said Billy. "And I'll tell you that faith and faithful-ness are not the same."

Harley shook his head, as if to clear it.

Billy continued. "It comes back to the people, doesn't it? Em-erson said people are better than their theology. Sometimes he's right. How you treat your neighbors. That's what counts. Meg is good people. End of story."

Harley felt a pang at that, especially in light of what he'd heard about the trouble at the food pantry, and how he was the cause of it. He hadn't moved his truck yet, and Meg was already jogging back to hers. Harley rolled his window down.

"Meg."

"Yes?"

"Um . . . I heard things were tough down at the food pantry."

"Well, things are never *easy* down at the food pantry."

"But all the people . . . a lot more of them, I've heard."

"There has been a steep increase, yes."

"And mostly because of . . ." He trailed off, and yanked his head in the direction of the scene across the road.

"It has played a part."

"Well, I'm going to talk to Sloan. He's the guy in charge. I'll make sure he sends some money."

"That would be nice, Harley." There was something gentle in the way she used his name.

"But, Harley?"

"Yah?"

"What we really need, what we're really short on, is *help*. It's not easy to get enough food and finances, but it's even harder to get enough help. Especially now that we've had to open for an hour daily to help out folks in transit. Mostly it's just Carolyn and me. What we really need is someone else to take a turn. Someone to pitch in, help pick up the food, sort it, hand it out. To run down and swab out the mop room when the sewer blows, which it does about once a week."

For the first time in a long time, Harley brightened. "Well, yeah! I could do that! And, Billy? You wanna pitch in?"

"Gladly," said Billy.

"And Mindy too," said Harley. "She'd love to help out."

"Wonderful," said Meg. "Next Tuesday we're sorting donations. We'll give you the introductory tour, if you can make it."

"You bet," said Harley.

"See you then," said Meg. "And, Harley?

"Thank you."

THAT NIGHT HARLEY called Mindy and told her about the food pantry situation.

"You be willing to do that?"

"Sure!" said Mindy. "I'd like to talk to Meg about buying some scrap metal anyway. Studio's to the point where I can start cranking out some crosses. Maybe set up a tent over there with the others, if that's okay."

"Well, sure," said Harley. "I'll talk to Sloan. See if I can get you a prime spot."

Harley hung up and went out to do the chores. He kept thinking about Meg, and the peace he felt when he was around her. He thought about the little girl with the bald head, and wondered where she was. How she was. *If* she was. He thought about how it was that one summer day when he was running around this very yard with nothing to do but play, those children in Central America were suffering and dying. When the chores were finished he let himself in the pen and sat with the Jesus calf for a long, long time. He found himself wishing for a shortcut. Something to explain all the good and evil in the world, and maybe even more to the point, all the fog and silliness in between.

In the truck after they left the gas station, he and Billy had talked more about Meg, and Klute, and how people figured into the grand equation of life.

"Well, *variably*," said Billy. "But I guess that's obvious."

"And God?" asked Harley.

"Well, if there is one, he's not so much *in* the equation as *above* it."

Harley looked at the calf, staring at the face of Christ until his eyes ached. *What I'd give,* he thought, *for a sign. Just a simple dang sign. Something a wishy-washy knucklehead like me could understand.*

The calf shifted.

Raised its tail.

And into the straw dropped a pat of poop.

CHAPTER 28

JCOW Enterprises continued to thrive. "The numbers"—
as Sloan called them—were down from the initial crush,
but remained strong. Several tour buses still arrived and departed
daily, and the parking lot was never less than half full. Merchandise
sales were strong, with online orders alone generating thousands of
dollars per day.

There had been a tricky stretch during a warm spell when the
ground thawed and the hay field parking lot became impassable,
but Sloan's crew set up an additional shuttle bus arrangement in
which the Clearwater Walmart traded parking lot space for an in-
store appearance by the Jesus Cow (as even Harley himself had
now come to think of it). The in-store went so well that a new International Talent Management team was formed to expand bookings, including one for the Mall of America for which the retainer
amounted to a high six figures.

Harley never stopped marveling at the thoroughness with which Sloan and International Talent Management chased down every possible profit opportunity. One of the most recent additions was an artist with a long blond ponytail who set up an easel at the exit of the viewing vestibule and for fifty bucks a pop painted visitors' faces over those of the shepherds in a luminous creche scene featuring the Jesus Cow. He had a marvelous ability to capture likenesses with a few quick swipes of the brush. In addition to the hard copy, the digitized version could be applied to towels, throw rugs, sweatshirts, wall clocks, or pretty much any other flat surface you wished.

Harley was introduced to the artist by Mindy, who had been given the adjacent booth and was selling crosses as fast as she could cut them out and weld them up.

"Harley, this is Yonni," said Mindy. "Yonni, this is Harley, my boyfriend."

Still not tired of hearing that, thought Harley, then extending his hand to Yonni, he said, "I've always been amazed by caricaturists."

"I prefer *portraitist*," said Yonni.

"Yes," said Mindy. "There's a difference."

Harley felt dumb about that, but even more he felt a tweak of something close to jealousy in the way Mindy had so rapidly jumped to the *portraitist's* defense.

"Hey!" said Mindy. "Let's have him do one of us!"

Harley shook his head and started to pull back, but Mindy grabbed his hand and insisted.

"Come on! It'll be *fun!*"

Harley sighed and moved in beside her against the backdrop. Yonni went to work and in short order handed over the finished work.

Harley looked at himself. He looked glum. Like he'd been parked there short on sleep.

Mindy looked radiant.

Radiant? Flat-out hot.

SWIVEL ITSELF MAINTAINED its ambivalence regarding the ongoing attraction. There was no question that the calf had created a financial windfall. Despite Paul Forster's misgivings about outsourced diesel sales, the Kwik Pump had put on extra staff and added three registers. There were long lines at the Sunrise Café morning and noon, the local churches were experiencing swollen attendance (and their collection plates accordingly), and the Buck Rub Bar was getting in on the action by selling the J-Cow, which was basically a White Russian with a cinnamon cross sprinkled on the top, and served with a beef stick.

Even neighboring communities were feeling the windfall. The motel in Boomler was filled to capacity and the resorts out on Chain Lake the same. There was also a boomlet in the local cash-under-the-table economy, with Swivel residents renting out their bedrooms, setting up food and souvenir stands along the curb, and renting their yards for parking.

There were downsides, of course. Two more constables had been hired and were often put on overtime—although it could be argued that the income they generated by writing parking tickets and clocking outsiders doing twenty-seven in a twenty-five zone helped offset the overhead. There were complaints about the wraparound sign on the water tower, so JCOW Enterprises had agreed to tone down the lumens after midnight. The street maintenance budget was going for broke, and although JCOW

Enterprises continued to maintain its own portable bathroom fa-
cilities, the general increase in visitors to the village had continued to exacerbate the ongoing sewer problems.

"Yep," said Billy when Harley was worrying aloud one day, "but
if you're gonna get swarmed by strangers, religious pilgrims are a
good option. You'll have some issues related to sheer numbers and
fervor, but by and large what you have here is a demographic that
doesn't get drunk, doesn't wreck things, and cleans up after themselves."

On the other hand, they also attracted a certain countervalent
crowd. Animal rights activists picketed the property line daily,
carrying signs and posters decrying the penning of the steer as if
he were in a zoo. Religious groups in modest dress picketed right
beside them, carrying signs and posters decrying the commercial-
ization and profaning of Christ and his image. And now and then
a vanload of atheists showed up. Their signs were generally neatly
printed and witty, if a bit cutting, and they tended to wear Carl
Sagan T-shirts.

And then there were the taunters. People who showed up only
for the fun of making fun. One group of university kids showed
up dressed in sandals, robes, and fake beards, leading two people
in a four-legged cow suit. On the flanks of the fake cow they had
spraypainted RELIGION IS BULL. As the paying pilgrims filed by,
the fake Jesuses taunted them.

Billy got into his bandoliers and ran them off.

"But, Billy, you're not even on the team," said Harley.

"Not on anybody's team. But I don't like cheapness. Tinniness.
I don't care for the sport of needling the squares. The squares
are usually holding the world together for the rest of us. Those

knuckleheads are like kids throwing snowballs at cops. They know that with the exception of a few outliers, they can go all *neener-neener* without fear of reprisal.

"Nothing brave in that."

Later that week when he and Mindy met Carolyn and Meg to help in the food pantry, Harley brought a check from JCOW Enterprises. Meg tried to refuse it, but Harley insisted, joking, "It's not as big as the one Klute wrote, but there will be more."

Carolyn and Meg looked at each other.

"If you won't tell 'im, I will," said Carolyn.

"The one Klute wrote," said Meg, "bounced."

CHAPTER 29

On a warm morning in May, Harley and Mindy were in the killer Kokopelli bed. Birdsong and sunshine were passing through the screen. They had been fooling around some but Harley was in one of his retroactive funks, and couldn't summon the reaction required.

From the moment Mindy had corrected him in front of the caricatur—*portraitist*, Harley had felt an unease in his gut that wouldn't quite go away. Even if he and Mindy had a good and happy day, there would come a moment when some trigger would send him back to that moment, and it precipitated a sense of dread.

Harley recognized the behavior. It tracked clear back to his virginal beginnings, back to the skunk-haired girl, who had not been virginal. After he had slept with her, Harley had found himself obsessing over the men who had been there first. He was haunted by the idea of his handprints overlaying the handprints laid there before him. He would continue with this obsession even as he himself became laid over with handprints. In other words, it was a frank double standard.

He knew this, and it did not help.

In that small instant when Mindy spoke up for the portraitist, Harley felt a shift, as if for that one moment the painter had levered himself between them, and Mindy had in fact acquiesced. He felt the silly twinge in his gut and he knew he was about to disappear into a self-loathing funk, where he not only imagined Mindy with the painter, but with the sculptwelder and with every other man preceding.

He was berating himself about this with Billy one day—Billy, the one person he could trust with this sort of talk, even more than he could trust Mindy (and maybe, he thought, that was part of the problem), and, having had one more beer than usual and trying to be profound, he said, "Billy, what is the statute of limitations on another man's touch?"

Billy grinned and shook his head. "You regard women as visions. As evanescent creatures. Despite all previous experience. Need I remind you of *The Meadowlark Weeps?*"

Harley slumped in his chair, nursing his mope.

Billy continued. "You desire these women, heart, soul, and flesh. Then when they prove to be of the flesh, you become petulant and disheartened."

True enough, thought Harley. He was embarrassed by his inability to avoid the wallow in another's past, embarrassed by the need to worry it like a broken tooth, but even more he was terrified by the grip it put on his heart. The way it squeezed his guts in the worst moments. He would be tracing Mindy's ivy tattoo, and suddenly he would envision the sculptwelder doing the same. Like a drop of dye dropped in water, the sick feeling would spread through his chest, go purling through his liver, and settle acidulously into his guts. And then always the same vision: her acquiescing, lying back, the man lowering himself, and then a dissipation into bitter darkness. He hated himself for his unreasonable weakness, but even more unreasonably he hated the past. He also despised himself for entertaining these feelings in light of his own history. It's not like he had ever been a swinger, but over the course of time and trying there were certain accruals. And then there was the fact that he was grieving over innocence even as he traced the tattoo on a naked woman not his wife. He was, he believed, astonishingly unreasonable and selfish. This understanding failed to ameliorate his self-pity.

"Babe, what's wrong?" said Mindy, bringing Harley back to the present.

He gave her the whole mopey recitation. She listened patiently, then spoke.

"We are who we have become, baby. My history, your history, they lead to now."

"Yah," said Harley, sighing. "But hell. It still hurts."

"C'mon, baby," said Mindy, and pulled him to her. But Harley resisted.

"I worry sometimes you're hanging in there with me because I have all this money now," he said.

He was unprepared for the hurt that sprang to her eyes.

It was followed quickly by anger.

"The day you spilled coffee all over my boots and drove off in a rusty truck—you didn't have all that money *then*."

He felt immediately small.

"I'm sorry, baby," he said. "I never should have said that."

Then, trying to rescue things with a lame joke, he said, "You know I've only ever loved you for your truck. I mean—a *headache rack*?"

She chuckled at that. But even as she came to his arms he sensed the worry stain spreading. He felt the inevitability of yet another failure. A permeant feeling of futility.

The trouble didn't inhibit their appetite for each other, and later as they lay back beneath the scabrous headboard, Harley said, "Hoo. That *and* a truck."

Mindy slapped him right across the face.

Harley's eyes flew open in shock, but Mindy was already laughing. "Mosquito," she said, showing him the crushed bug as evidence.

The wet stretch had triggered a boom in the insects. In fact, Sloan had considered spraying Skeeter-Beater, but then he realized there was more money to be made in *not* spraying it. Instead he set up yet another booth, and at last report insect repellent concessions were booming. The man was a genius.

"I used to walk by the swamp and let mosquitos sting me when I was a kid," said Harley.

"Well, *that's* not too weird," said Mindy.

"Yah, there was something about the sting—it's not really a sting, it's kinda itchy sweet."

"Yer kinda itchy sweet," said Mindy, kissing him on the nose.

His heart full of hope again, Harley started rambling. "Sometimes you hung in there too long and even though a full mosquito lumbers in the air like an overloaded chopper, it got away and you felt kinda cheated, like you'd let intelligence fall into enemy hands, or enemy *proboscises*, because now you—your blood—was going to feed new generations of skeeters."

"Seems like all that blood loss is still affecting your brain," said Mindy, her face close to his, and smiling.

"Sometimes I'd try to see how many I could stand. Just let them land and jab me until I couldn't take it anymore. Sometimes on humid evenings they'd be so thick that when I slapped them they'd leave a gray handprint on my jeans."

"Ew."

"Then I'd run. Sprint down the road. Try to create my own wind, lose them, listen as the whine receded. But the minute I stopped, they'd swarm in again. I'd slap and swat. My forearms would be covered with gray smears of wing dust and thin red stripes of blood."

"If this is pillow talk, put my head *under* the pillow," said Mindy. They both laughed and Harley loved the lightness of it, the relief from the worry, the way her eyes were sparkling just the way he remembered them in the Kwik Pump that first day.

"Tuesday," said Harley. "Can you do the food pantry with me?"

"Sure!" said Mindy. "Maybe afterward I'll take you out on the Norton. There's a hill out by the big swamp—"

"—McCracken Hill," said Harley.

"Yeah, I like to crest that thing going like sixty, then tuck coming off it. I'll put you behind me and we'll do that. Kill some mosquitos with our teeth!"

LATER, AS HE drove away, Mindy waving in his rearview mirror, Harley found himself wanting her more than ever. Her independence, her strength, her laugh, her four-wheel-drive demeanor. Lately they had been discussing his idea of continuing to live in their own places even if they got married. They had also talked about pitching everything and moving to Panama, where Mindy had once hitchhiked. There was something bohemian in all of this that made his heart beat with hope again. And even if they just settled into baling hay and raising beefers, that'd be fine. Suddenly happy in his lightness, he had a hankering for Kona Luna and a maple-frosted long john. He turned on the radio. Patsy Cline was singing, *"Hurt me now, get it over . . ."* Despite his sudden buoyance, the thought occurred to him: is there anything sadder than the way a man walks in the wake of a woman he knows he has already lost?

ONE DAY IN late June, Sloan called Harley into a meeting to tell him the International Talent Management bean counters noted a taper in "the numbers" at JCOW Enterprises. Pilgrims and profits remained abundant, but had settled since the boom days. In response, Sloan outlined a plan to bolster areas of strength (offsite bookings, online sales), pursue new developments (several agricultural biotech firms were interested in harvesting Tina Turner's ova, and there were also discussions with a leading cloning facility) and cut back where possible (reductions in the shuttle schedule and size of the parking lot, thus requiring less equipment and fewer cleanup and security personnel).

Sloan also showed Harley a chart tracking an uptick in lawsuits. People tripped or fell, or got bumped in the parking area, or some other theoretically actionable thing, and a week later the certified mail arrived. Sloan assured Harley the lawyers would handle it, and that he couldn't be touched, but Harley knew his name was on every one of those legal forms, and he was not used to sleeping on that sort of information.

Finally, said Sloan, public sentiment in Swivel continued to deteriorate. Harley already knew that. With the receding crowds came receding profits for local entrepreneurs willing to put up with the disruption as long as they could make a little money on the side. Now that things weren't so flush, they were becoming restless and resentful. There were also moments of heavy-handedness: Gladys Knutson had been selling crocheted Jesus Cow tea cozies and donating the proceeds to the Lutheran Ladies Haiti Fund until International Talent Management's attorneys shut her down. Shortly afterward, her Etsy site was hacked. "Tell me *that* was a coincidence," she said, after cornering Harley down at the Post Office. Finally, the condition of the village sewers worsened weekly (one particularly horrific subterranean burp necessitated the evacuation of the Buck Rub Bar on bingo night), and although the trouble had been bubbling for years, JCOW Enterprises was universally blamed.

Harley had done things here and there to assuage the populace, including setting up a deal in which Swivel's school buses were used to supplement the International Talent Management shuttle fleet, with (and he admitted this was a dig at Klute) 100 percent of the proceeds going to the school. He had also written a check to the Swivel Volunteer Fire Department to cover the remainder of the thermal imager fund, and, while he was at it, he threw in enough to cover a brand-new Argo with all the trimmings. The chief—who hadn't spoken to Harley since he submitted his letter of leave—insisted on a ceremony featuring a giant check so that he could get a photo in the *Weekly Dealio*.

Harley cringed at the memory.

AFTER THE MEETING with Sloan, Harley drove the Silverado over to gas up at the Kwik Pump and Chief Knutson flagged him down in the parking lot.

"There's been a little grumblin' about the fireworks."

"Oh?" said Harley, confused.

"Well, some of the fellers were sayin' that if you could front the cash for that infrared camera *and* an Argo, fireworks would just be pocket change."

Harley felt a mix of sadness and anger. How much would be enough?

"Due to unexpected expenses brought on by high call volume related to elevated levels of transient populations," said the chief, nodding his head meaningfully as another shuttle bus unloaded across the road, "The village cut our fireworks budget by fifty percent. We were gonna make up the difference with a raffle, but what with all the extra calls, we just don't know when we'd do it. Plus I believe the boys—and by boys I mean the ladies too—are kinda raffled out."

"Well, I suppose I could . . ." Harley trailed off. He felt like something had been pulled from beneath him. He thought how even though he had always operated on the fringes of the department it had been the one place where he felt part of the crew, the club, the bunch. But now this damned calf had managed to cut him out of even that herd.

Harley looked at the chief. "Even if you did raise the money, wouldn't the village be better off spending it on a new sewer system?" But even as he asked the question, Harley knew better. He knew that like dirt track stock car races and demolition derbies and heated deer stands and camouflage brassieres and for that matter faith itself, there were some things that were simply part of a place and a people and didn't bear scrutiny.

Harley also knew pride and history were in play. Boomler's fireworks display had grown larger and larger over the years, until it had even begun to draw viewers from Swivel. Given the right budget, Swivel had a chance to put Boomler in its place.

"I'll see what I can do," said Harley, knowing already he'd do it but not wanting to seem an immediate pushover.

In the end he simply walked into Scooter Eckstrom's fireworks tent and bought everything in sight. Scooter set up the tent every year right beside the interstate off-ramp and hung FIREWORKS, EXIT NOW banners in the trees so they could be seen from both north and southbound lanes. Scooter was not so much an entrepreneur as a serial divorcé trying to bolster his alimony reserves.

"Call Chief Knutson, and let him know this all belongs to the fire department now," said Harley after writing the check. Scooter was looking at him like he couldn't believe his luck.

"And now," said Harley, "let's talk about the real stuff." Harley knew for a fact Scooter made a trip out of state each year and returned with armaments not legally available over the counter or beneath the tent. After some quiet discussion in the cab of Harley's truck, Scooter placed a lengthy phone call, and by the following Monday a cube van rolled into Swivel. On the sides of the van it said OFFICE SUPPLIES but in the back were sufficient munitions to rattle the boots of those losers clear down in Boomler.

And so it came to be, after a long day of bad news and bad vibes, Harley found himself afoot at two a.m., walking to the overpass. Long before the arrival of the Jesus Cow, he had liked to walk out here and watch the occasional car come and go, liked to track the running lights of some lonely trucker deadheading for home. Sometimes he stood at the rail and looked up at the stars and drew the cold air in, and wished with all his heart he could stay there staring up at infinity forever, and then in the moment he'd say the only thing he could think to say, which was a quiet and a reverent *"Goddamn."*

RECENTLY HARLEY HAD been noodling around online when he discovered an Internet video of film footage shot at the Van Hoof farm during the height of the Virgin Mary sightings. The film was soundless but shot in color. The hues were saturated and the sights were a marvel: There were the buses Sloan had described, and when the camera panned right, a train—an actual passenger train—could be seen in the background, stopped in the middle of the field through which the track cut, stopped so people could debark and walk directly to the farmhouse. Several people were seated and watching from the rail bed berm itself. Harley spotted a military jeep and some sort of van with rigging and a tower of speaker trumpets, and there were rows and rows of cars shining like beetles in the sun.

But mostly Harley focused on the people. There were ladies in hats and demure scarves, and the men too had a general formality to them, many in fedoras and ties. In one cut, a high-school-aged boy in a satin jacket could be seen standing behind a temporary fence handing out what appeared to be tickets or maybe Bible bookmarks to passersby. There were no signs of hysterics. The crowd appeared orderly. Even without sound, Harley could tell when Mary Ann Van Hoof must have stepped out to await the latest sign from heaven because the crowd tightened, perceptibly knotting themselves around the farmhouse. Harley found his heart beating harder as he felt—even through all the removes of time and technology, and the silence of the moving pictures—the *yearning* of all those people. Their heartfelt desire to hear their God speak.

What he saw in the video, of course, was what he saw every day in his own driveway. Just with different cars and clothes.

The people who really unsettled him were the ones who looked furtively faithful. You could see in their eyes they truly came in hope. Or in quiet desperation from some life that had turned against them at every opportunity. Mary Ann Van Hoof's visions, his Jesus Cow—if these were not their last hope they were surely rattling around in the bottom of the bucket. These people were *starved* for hope. *And what am I feeding them?* thought Harley.

He was astounded at how quickly he had let himself follow the lead of money and revenge. How quickly he had dismissed faith or how little faith had played into this. He was beaten down at the time, but still . . .

He thought of calling Billy and trading the overpass for the kitchen table and beer, but it was late, and besides, they'd talked around the edge of these things already.

"What would it be like to really be God?" he'd said to Billy during their most recent staff meeting. "To wave my hand and make all of this go away?"

Billy was silent.

"Why must things *passeth all understanding*, Billy? Why not lay it all out there? Why all the mysteries and puzzlement? The outright *deception*?"

"Agreed: some Cliff's Notes woulda been nice," said Billy.

Harley was on a roll. "You know—give a guy a shot at working it out without the intercession of popes and bishops and churches big as football stadiums and pamphlets and people with name tags knocking on your door, men on the AM radio crackling and fading in and out in their own sort of sonic metaphor for the confusion and uncertainty and tenuousness of the whole dang deal." He was drawing real heavily on that one creative writing course.

"Just as with your women, you attempt to render existence in terms of perfection," said Billy. "Life is a rough approximation of things hoped for. You need to revel in the misfires. In the scars and dings. You need to develop a taste for regret. It's the malt vinegar of emotions—drink it straight from the bottle and it'll eat yer guts. Add a sprinkle here and there and it puts a living edge on things."

TONIGHT, AS HE placed his forearms on the bridge rail and leaned out over the four-lane, the moon was coming up full. As another set of taillights slid away beneath him in the dark, Harley knew part of the attraction of this spot was the implication that he could always catch that southbound lane, push the foot feed to the floor, drive off into the night, and just keep driving. He glanced back over toward his farm and saw the security light glow, and above it all the scrolling pixilated steer, chasing its own message: . . . SEE THE JESUS COW . . .

Suddenly the southbound lane seemed more attractive than ever.

But of course he couldn't go. "You can't just quit, son," said Billy, when Harley had broached the idea once before. "Look at all the people you're employing. Look at all the mouths you're feeding. And recharging the government coffers, for which we the taxpayers and we on some form of the dole thank you."

"But I—"

"You're also helping a lot of those people *believe*. It might not be for us, but for many of those people you have brought great peace. Great *hope*."

"Yah, but I—"

"I, I, I," said Billy, shaking his head. "Lemme put it another way: You ain't the only one bleedin' here."

"Waylon again."

"Nah. Ray Wylie Hubbard. My sorta prophet."

And then there was Mindy. They'd had a good stretch lately, but he'd still get in those funks, and no woman should have to put up with a self-pitying infant of that order. And that damned crack he made about her wanting him for his money; he worried what kind of rotten little seed that might have planted. He moved closer to the railing, leaned over just enough to catch the vertiginous zing in his gut. Then it faded, and he stared off toward the rising moon, tannin brown and looking as if it had been dunked in tea. He was recalling a line from a poem now, or it might have been some gospel blues song, he couldn't recall the source—something from back in his college days—but in his head it was the voice of a strapping, strong woman, and the line, or the fragment of the line, went *You ain't prayed in so long.*

You ain't prayed in so long. He said it aloud. Softly, and to himself. There was another line that came on the heels of that one, but he couldn't recall it.

He looked over the railing again. There was the desire to fling himself over, that barely repressible urge. He quailed at the idea of his body going smack, but the image he received of his easy double gainer through the silent air was beautiful and calming. He wondered how amazed folks might be, having watched his stolid movement through life thus far, to know how close to the edge he sometimes ran.

You ain't prayed in so long. Once. Twice. Three times he said it. Then he went silent, and let it echo in his head: *You ain't prayed in so long.* Now it was the strapping, strong woman again. Her tone was gentle, but bore reproach. She spoke gravely, and with disappointment. *You ain't prayed in so long.* Soft, like she was shaking her head. *You ain't prayed in so long.*

And then the next line came to him.

Why bother with fancy now?

She sounded stronger on that one.

CHAPTER 30

Carolyn Sawchuck was laying on the horn of her Subaru, stiff-arming it with grim determination. Once again her egress had been blocked by pilgrims. Ever since the calf had gone public, Carolyn's pump house hideaway had become more like a panic room. She had been forced to paper over the windows to spare herself from prying eyes. She had put out a rack of dream catchers with an honor box for payment but twice it had been ripped down by fundamentalists who viewed it as a pagan danger on the order of incense or books about wizards. She counted herself among those citizens of Swivel ready to see that calf go.

The morning had begun badly. She had failed to order Zebra Cakes and, after a rigorous oil-pumping session, had found herself sneak-buying a midnight box at the Kwik Pump, where she had run into Billy, who was buying an emergency tin of cat food. "Those will go straight to your thighs, Carol," said Billy.

"I am proud of my thighs!" said Carolyn.

"That was never in question," said Billy. In truth he had to admit she had never looked fitter. This was a mystery further confounded by those Zebra Cakes.

Carolyn finally navigated the gauntlet of tourist believers and drove down to the food pantry. The village sewer had backed up yet again, flooding clear into the back room where all the canned goods were stored. Now that the weather was warmer, these episodes were even more odorific. Meg had said she'd meet Carolyn for the cleanup, and as Carolyn drove past St. Jude's she saw Meg's truck at the curb.

INSIDE THE CHURCH, Meg knelt with her head bowed and hands clasped. She loved the peace of the church on a fresh sunny day such as this, when the grass was deep green and smelled of mowing, the trees were thick with leaves, and the weekday traffic of Swivel—usually only a pickup truck or minivan now and then but these days more active with tour buses and pilgrims driving in to see that steer—could be heard through the screens. There was something even more holy about worshipping, about kneeling before the altar, when the rest of the world was otherwise occupied. There was the sheltering sense of the cathedral, the stillness so lacking in the world these days, a sense that the momentum of time had been allayed. There was also something about the church with no priest presiding. No intermediation. Just her and her Lord.

She chose a candle and struck a match. Her rough, cracked hands cupped the flame as she touched it to the wick.

BACK IN HIS house, Harley heard Carolyn's horn. Meg had called him about the sewer. He said he'd come down to help, and now he was in the shower. He had called Mindy to see if she could help out but she said she was busy with a project. He asked her if she needed any help, and she said no. That maybe if she got done early she'd come in and see him.

"Bring me some of that lentil soup?" said Harley, hopefully.

"Yeah," said Mindy, "maybe so."

There was something in her voice—or *not* in her voice. Harley felt the old unease.

MEG WALKED BRISKLY to the food pantry, where Carolyn was unstacking and swabbing off cans.

"Hello, Carolyn," said Meg, opening the broom closet and pulling out a mop.

"Hello, Meg," said Carolyn. "How was church?"

"Peaceful."

"Mm."

"Klute Sorensen has been around again," said Meg.

"And?"

Meg giggled. "Oh—I don't know. He's such . . . he's so . . ."

"Overmasculinized?" asked Carolyn.

Meg giggled again. "That'd be *one* way to put it."

"Has he officially asked you out?"

"No, he's been pestering me to sell. Wants to put in a hotel."

"Big money?"

"Big enough," said Meg. "I wouldn't ever have to crush another car. But after the giant cardboard check, he'd have to bring me a much smaller one from an actual bank."

"What do you think? Will you do it?"

"Mm," said Meg. "I've been praying on it."

"But no decision yet?"

"No."

"So how do you tell?"

"How do I tell what?"

"When you get the answer to your prayer? You hear a voice? You get a feeling? Holy text message?"

Meg smiled. "Oh, I don't know. I'm not sure you do get an answer. The Lord has more important things to do than advise me on land deals."

"And yet you pray."

"It helps to settle my mind. To *sort* my mind."

"Those candles you light every day—what do they mean to you?"

"They mean that in the midst of whatever cares or troubles or other distractions might surrounded me, I have to pause at least long enough to cup that flame until it takes," said Meg, holding the mop in both hands but staring at the floor as if she were not speaking but rather thinking aloud.

"I like that," said Carolyn.

It was quiet for a bit, then Carolyn spoke. "You know . . . about Klute . . . I shouldn't be so hard on him. All that loudmouth grandiosity, you know a lot of it's rooted in disappointment. Especially the way things have been going lately. The real estate going bust. And the way he's been foxed by that Sloan fellow at every turn.

"So much of my life has been spent in *pursuit*. In pursuit of a career. In pursuit of a life in arts and letters. In pursuit of tenure and an office and publication. But above all, I loved words. Books. Language. That is what drove me, even when I got sidetracked with grant applications and faculty jockeying and padding my CV.

"The anger we see in Klute, the bullheadedness and lack of social grace, it may—as mine does—all trace back to disappointment, and the disappointment traces back to belief. Belief that all the hard work will result in some pinnacle moment. Some achievement of long standing. When in fact . . ."

She paused, realizing Meg was just staring at her.

"The thing is, the guy might be worth a shot."

"Sometimes," said Meg, smiling, *"you're* the Christian one."

Carolyn laughed.

They worked in silence then, and Carolyn found herself filled with gratitude. She still missed the place in Central America now and then. She still longed for the thrill of seeing her name in print. She wouldn't mind some companionship, heartwise and otherwise. But as she looked at her new friend—a rough-handed woman in coveralls who believed in what Carolyn could most charitably classify as fairy tales—for the first time since she could remember, Carolyn felt as if she was letting life come to her.

"It's a good life we have, eh, Meg?"

"Yes," said Meg, smiling as she swabbed the floor.

"I could do with a few less pilgrims."

"Yes," said Meg, and they were both giggling when Harley came in to help finish up the mopping and start sorting the food.

"Mindy coming?" asked Carolyn.

"No," said Harley, trying to sound blasé. The two women looked at each other.

"Something wrong?" asked Meg.

"No, I—"

"Oh please," said Carolyn, waving a hand between herself and Meg, "look who yer talkin' to here."

Harley admitted then to his unease. To his sense that all was not well. That Mindy might be losing interest. That maybe—once again and to his shame—he was frittering a good thing away.

"I can tell you one thing," said Meg. "Something I learned from my dad. Do something *nice* once in a while. Not big, not flashy, just *nice*."

"Without being *asked*," said Carolyn, and both women nodded.

"Sometimes Pop came into town and bought Mom a gas station rose," said Meg. "Took him all of five minutes, across the overpass and back, two bucks and it wasn't much of a rose, but oh, how my mother smiled."

AFTER THEY HAD stacked the last can, Harley went straight to the Kwik Pump and bought a rose. *Perfect*, he thought, as he drove out Five Mile Road past the Big Swamp. *Bring her a rose from the place where we first met.*

He smiled. Thought of his latest financial statement, the one Sloan gave him each month. How the last time he looked it had two commas. And now here he was proving his love with a gas station rose.

Mindy and the caricaturist—*portraitist*—were just coming out of the house.

"You remember Yonni," said Mindy, sunnily.

Harley did remember. He shook Yonni's hand. It was soft, and Harley did his best to crush it.

"We're collaborating on a sculpture," said Mindy.

"Yah, cool, well, catch y'later," said Yonni, easing off toward his car as Harley followed Mindy inside.

In the morning when he came out and got in the pickup, the rose was still on the seat, the petals limp against the plastic wrap.

TWO WEEKS PRIOR to Jamboree Days, Mindy ended it.

"Is it the cartoonist?"

"Baby, sometimes there is no reason," she said, ignoring the insult and holding both of Harley's hands. "That's the fear and beauty of love." She had ridden over on her Norton, and it was parked at the end of the sidewalk. He was standing on his porch, she was standing on the top step.

"If you need time . . .," said Harley.

"Maybe ten years ago I'd have told you that," she said. "And maybe ten years ago you'd have believed that. But now we both know—something has gone out of this. Time apart won't fix it."

"But all the things you said? About baling hay? About living together apart? About taking our beefers to the sale barn together to save on shipping? About Panama? About—fer Chrissakes—how I *smelled* right?"

"I meant them when I said them," she said.

Harley flashed with an anger he knew he'd regret. "Isn't that just a fancy way of saying you lied?"

Mindy didn't match his anger. In fact, she spoke softly. "Technically, our relationship began with a lie. Or *lies*. Remember saying that stuff smeared on your hands was manure spreader grease? Remember the shoe polish can in your pocket? Remember you told me you were just cleaning out old drawers? Remember fooling around in the pen right beside that calf with the truth blacked out? Remember the damned loose lightbulb?"

"Was it what I said about the money?"

"What you said about the money hurt," said Mindy. "And then it pissed me off. But no. We all say things we want to take back. I'm afraid this is much more mundane. This is just your garden-variety petering out."

It didn't feel like petering out, thought Harley. It felt like he was stepping off a cliff and there was nothing but icy fog below.

"I never got that motorcycle ride," he said.

"Good-bye, Harley."

He heard the Norton fire up and she drove away.

THAT EVENING THE security guard let him into his own barn to stand with the Jesus Cow. It really was getting to be more of a cow than a calf now, a youthful, fuzzy steer, nearly three-quarters the height of Tina Turner but still nursing now and then. The steer was big enough he sometimes got down on his knees to reach the udder. When the pilgrims saw this there was much joyful laughter, as of course everyone thought he looked as if he were kneeling to pray.

Jesus' face was as recognizable as ever. You would never know this was the same calf that had been gashed with Reverend Gary's crucifix. Sloan kept a hairdresser on retainer to maintain the steer's hide and hair in top condition—what the cattle jockeys would call a "good bloom"—but Sloan was very strict on the matter of not manipulating the image in any way beyond combing and conditioning. What the paying customers saw was truly what they paid for. It was perhaps the most principled part of the entire operation.

Harley moved out into the viewing vestibule and parted the curtains. He wondered how many thousands of people had filed past here. He thought of all those driving this way even now, or sleeping in the hotel in Boomler, or parked out back behind someone's house on Elm Street, paying twenty bucks for the privilege of sleeping in their car. He wondered what the pope was doing right now. If he had reached any decision regarding the main attraction of JCOW Enterprises.

So many people, he thought again. *So many souls*. From every state, and many countries. And every time he saw a child holding the hand of its mother, he thought of the little girl who disappeared that day back when he was still trying to do everything himself and it all went terribly wrong.

He wondered how she was doing.

He wondered if she was still alive.

He wondered if she still had faith.

He looked at the empty parking lot. The generators were extinguished for the night, but there was enough moon and ambient light from the scrolling LED on the water tower that he could make out the plastic ropes and lath posts, the grass trampled flat, the dirt showing through, here and there a candy wrapper, or a Bible bookmark, or a souvenir catalog, rolled up into a tube and discarded, blown open maybe to a page listing the prices for a Genuine Authorized Jesus Cow laminated prayer card set (*Get the Whole Series! All Saints, Every Apostle, Plus Archangels!*) . . .

His beefers were huddled by their shelter. *I'll have to buy my hay this year*, thought Harley. *First year the baler hasn't been used since Dad bought it new the year I was born.*

He thought of his father now, recalled the quietness of him, how when Harley was a boy every day ended with his father sitting on the edge of Harley's bed, the Bible open across his knees. He could see his father's work-thickened finger pointing to the book of John, chapter eleven, thirty-fifth verse.

"Shortest verse in the Bible, Harley," said his father.

Two words. Harley thought of them now.

Jesus wept.

I bet he did, thought Harley.

I bet he did.

CHAPTER 31

 It was the Fourth of July, and Jamboree Days was in full swing. As part of an agreement with the village, the entire Jesus Cow operation was shut down for the duration of the celebration, and the LED wraparound on the water tower and the barn illumination were all switched off for the first time in months. Harley stood alone in the dark, head rolled back on his shoulders, contemplating the ponderous black bulk of the tower. Far above, almost straight up, at the very dome of the tower, Harley could see the flag of the United States of America. Lit by one bright white light, the flag shifted like an uncomfortable grade-schooler caught in the spotlight during a recital, not so much unfurling or waving as fidgeting in the glare.

The flag had been Sloan's idea. When the new water tower went up, the VFW had moved the village flag with it. Apart from celebrating the Fourth, Sloan felt that raising a flag atop the old water tower again would bolster the image of JCOW Enterprises and help diminish some of the criticism it had been weathering lately.

Initially, Sloan contacted the local VFW to arrange the flag-raising, but when they showed up and asked Carolyn to unlock the gate so they could figure out how to access the pole, which was mounted at the very peak of the tower beside the vent cap, she refused, at which point Snook Hustis accused her of being un-American.

"I am no such thing," retorted Carolyn. "In fact, I'll run up that flag myself. I don't object to the flag, I object to the invasion of my privacy on *behalf* of the flag." As when faced with the mounting of the LED sign, she also made vague reference to landmark preservation statutes. In conclusion, she recited three verses of a Wendell Berry poem. No one at the VFW was interested in continuing the debate, and Carolyn—who didn't want anyone within forty feet of that vent cap—was true to her word, scaling the tower with a fresh flag and lanyard. While she was up there, she surreptitiously pried open the vent cap and snuck a look. Everything was in order, the PVC "T" straddling the overflow tube and showing no sign of cracking or breakdown. She returned to the ground very pleased with herself. In fact, halfway down the ladder it struck her that should the need arise, she could now climb the water tower at any time on the pretense of tending the flag.

Harley was aware that Sloan's motivations were less than patriotic, but he was still happy to see the red, white, and blue flying above his buildings again. Harley figured he was a low-key patriot. Residual of his father's admonishments regarding pridefulness he never cared for the PROUD TO BE AN AMERICAN bumper stickers, but he was certainly *grateful* to be an American.

He had the place to himself tonight, with the exception of a small detachment of security guards on duty to redirect those pilgrims who arrived unaware of the shutdown. More than one set of those saw the bright lights of the softball field and rather than genuflecting before a holy calf, wound up in the beer tent. Harley's father and mother had donated the land for the park, and used to enjoy watching the softball games from their porch. The view was still available, but was latticed by the new security fence running the perimeter of Harley's property.

It had been a helluva year, he thought as he stood watching his neighbors at play and the sounds of celebration floated his way: the drum-thump of the cover band, the drunken *woo-hoos*, the calls of encouragement from the stands, the "hey-battah-battah" the "ducks on the pond," the aluminum plink of the bat connecting with the ball, and the beery cheers for the occasional close play. Someone jacked a home run and Chief Knutson, manning the PA system, bellowed "TOUCH 'EM ALL, WARTHOG!" Clouds of moths whirled through the light banks, and the whole scene was lit so beautifully, so greenly, it was simply lovely.

Harley looked back at the old tower now and thought of all the Jamboree Days it had presided over since it was raised in the 1950s, and his ever-burbling sentimentality kicked in. He felt himself longing for a time he never knew, that futile sweetness of the deep yearn. He wondered for a moment if this was why all his relationships wrecked; perhaps he was better at longing than *be*longing.

This train of thought led him to consider the state of his life only seven months ago, how it compared with the present. Everything a guy might dream of in the bank account, but his heart and— by all standard measures—his soul overdrawn. He suddenly found himself resenting the villagers on the other side of the fence. It struck him that while people from all over the world had come to see that calf, most of the interest from his fellow hometown citizens was limited to how they might peel off a few bucks for themselves and, failing that, how to shut the whole works down. He looked over at the park again, and instead of a small-town celebration, he saw a drunken family reunion of vaguely irritating in-laws.

Those people, thought Harley, even as he recoiled at the phrase. *Those people care more about fireworks, softball, and beer than a vision of the Christ they claim to follow. Take a poll and they'll rate themselves 97 percent Christian. But how many of them actually show up for church on Sunday? And of those who do, how many of them really mean it? How many trouble themselves with any thought of why they're even in the pews? Jesus Cow? For most a' them, it ain't nothin' but Harley Jackson's weird damn steer.*

He heard the first of the fireworks go then, the first pop and bang. The band stopped playing, and the crowd went quiet as they turned to watch. Someone killed all but a single softball light, and Harley could see everyone standing in shadow, beers in hand, the ballplayers with their fingers hooked in the backstop fence, batting gloves hanging off their butts as they spit and gazed at the sky. At first there was just a boom or two, a flower and a flare. Some nice rooster tails, some silver bursts, a green spatter. Then came the first fine, orange slips of light as the larger charges rose, followed by the concussive *whomp* and blistering sizzle as the coppery sparks strewed themselves against the black. Scooter Eckstrom had never before operated with a budget that allowed him such pyrotechnic power and was in his glory, running from spot to spot in a crouch, punk stick in hand, touching off fuses in no apparent order and reveling in the *ooohs* and *aaahs* that followed. It was in this spirit of undertrained enthusiasm that he prematurely lit the 100-SHOT FAST-FINALE-IN-A-BOX INCLUDING 20 TITANIUM-SALUTE ENDING, which in his haste he had placed at a bit of an angle atop a molehill, thus releasing a stroboscopic thunderstorm on a trajectory just clearing Harley Jackson's farmhouse. *Those are coming in kinda low,* thought Harley as sparks and ash dropped around him, and he caught the scent of burned powder.

IT'S TOUGH TO maintain an existential grump beneath a skyful of fireworks, and Harley was back to enjoying them like everyone else when he noticed a flicker atop the water tower. A small, wavering orange flame was showing at the cap.

At first Harley was dumbfounded. Flames? Shooting out of a water tower? Then he saw a rectangle of light as Carolyn Sawchuck threw open the door of the pump house. Framed in the light, she tipped her head back. The flame was stiffening and straightening, like a horsetail blown by the wind.

Oh my God! thought Carolyn, irrespective of her disbelief. *The vent cap! The day I put the flag up. I never shut the vent cap!*

She dashed back inside. Fueled by volatile fumes, the flame was now about ten feet tall and issuing a jetting sound audible between the screech and thud of the fireworks. From over on the softball field Harley heard a murmur as people began to notice the flame. Harley was reaching for his phone to dial 911 when he heard pagers going off all over the Jamboree Days grounds. Carolyn must have beat him to it.

Harley knew the volunteers would be running for the trucks parked around the edges of the softball field, as they always were during Jamboree Days. Sprinting to the nearest security fence gate, Harley punched in the combination and threw it open. Chief Knutson roared through on the Argo, lights flashing, siren screaming, all the trucks following him.

The fireworks had ceased. Through the open gate Harley could see that everyone was standing agape, staring at the water tower. The hiss of the flame was now a roar, and the cap of the water tower was beginning to glow. The American flag was aflame.

"BLEVVY!!!!" hollered the chief. "She's gonna BLEVVY!!!!"

Carolyn, thought Harley.

KLUTE SORENSEN WAS parked in the darkest corner of Clover Blossom Estates.

It was over. He had seen the paperwork, and within the week, Clover Blossom Estates would belong to Solid Savings Bank. He thought of his father and his grandfather before him, and his great-grandfather before him, and the big hulking mill that still stood where they built it, and then he looked at the sad distribution of houses dotting the mostly empty lots, and he felt generations of disapproval pressing down on him. Every effort to provide parking, lodging, or transportation for the Jesus Cow tourists had failed. Each time Vance filed the paperwork, it was rejected on some obscure technicality. And how ashamed his immediate paternal ancestors would have been about the giant food pantry check: When that one bounced, Klute knew there was no pulling this thing from the fire. You can't hide when you bounce a four-by-six-foot check.

The giant house too would soon be gone. Bankruptcy laws would allow him to keep it, but he couldn't imagine living there anymore.

The very size of it was a monument—a hollow, unfurnished, *empty* monument—to the scope of his failure.

And Mary Magdalene Jankowski? He'd never know. In the face of all his failure, he simply couldn't face her now. Of all Klute's grand goals, his attempt to court Meg was the first to grow directly from his heart. He had no idea what to do with the remaining ache.

He started the Hummer. That too was bound for the bank. He figured he'd be driving some miniature tin can on wheels soon, so he might as well enjoy it. He turned the key. His old favorite, *Set Sale!*, came through the speakers, but he couldn't face the upbeat hoo-hah and switched it off.

He pulled out of Clover Blossom Estates and headed for the overpass. Across the interstate fireworks splashed across the sky. Klute thought of all the people laughing and drinking and enjoying the show and realized . . . he wouldn't even know how to act with those people if he didn't have his Hummer and his big ideas to hide behind.

He was about to enter the on-ramp when he saw another light, bigger than any fireworks, and pulsing against the near horizon above Harley Jackson's place. And then, a ball of fire, rolling to the sky.

He accelerated past the on-ramp and across the overpass toward Main Street.

"SHE'S GONNA BLEVVY!!!!" hollered the chief again.

And it did.

From Harley's perspective, the explosion was apocalyptic. A ball of flame rolled upward, spinning into the night sky, illuminating everything all around. The water tower peeled open like a soda can blown up by teenage boys with a cherry bomb. For a split second the scrolling LED sign relit at SEE THE JESUS then melted into darkness. As the first flame ball expired, a second belched skyward, and now gouts of liquid fire were pouring from the tower, splashing to the ground, raining down on Carolyn's Subaru, and flowing downhill toward Harley's buildings. Harley saw Carolyn appear at the door of the pump house again, then yank it shut, unable to get past her burning car, let alone unlock the gate. Harley screamed at the firefighters running all around him, trying to get their attention, but no one seemed to hear him. *I'll have to get her myself,* he thought, and ran to the nearest fire truck, where he grabbed a helmet and spare jacket.

CAROLYN WAS PREPARED to die. Not *ready* to die, not *wanting* to die, but in the moment it took to see that her only exit was blocked by her flaming Subaru, she was surprised at the calmness with which she accepted the fact that this was it. *Brought it on myself,* she thought. *Always trying to save the world, but really trying to save my pride.* She looked across the room at her short stack of books, soon to be nothing but ash. *How little we—*

She never got to complete the thought, because outside there was a mighty sound of squealing wire and rending steel followed by a horrific crash, the sound of twin air horns, and a man's voice, hollering.

"CAROLYN! RUN! NOW! RUN!"

Carolyn cracked the pump house door. Klute Sorensen was in his Hummer, gesturing wildly through the passenger door, which he had flung open. The chain-link fence was draped over his windshield and her crumpled Subaru was wedged and flaming in the bars of his chromium-plated brush buster.

"JUMP IN!" hollered Klute, and Carolyn did. Klute roared through the wall of flame and went skidding up to the nearest pumper, where Swivel's finest buried the Subaru, the Hummer, and, for that matter, the heretofore unfriendly couple in a mountain of fire-retardant foam.

THE SWIVEL VOLUNTEER Fire Department had not retreated. Under Chief Knutson's direction, one team had hosed down Harley's house and the JCOW command center with foam. Another team lay down swathes of the foam on the ground between the buildings to serve as a buffer. But there was no arresting the fire itself as it skidded downhill from the water tower in a hellish rolling tide, igniting souvenir booths as it went, leaped the driveway, and splashed against the side of the barn.

Immediately, flames fingered their way up the siding, and in moments the barn was ablaze. Nearly unnoticed, one thin rivulet split off from the main to follow one of the channels worn in the gravel driveway over the years. In a flickering trickle, it meandered its way out to the road, where it came to a storm drain and flowed out of sight. Shortly thereafter Main Street exploded, splitting right down the middle, unzipping the asphalt all the way to the Buck Rub Bar. Barney Parsons would later say the force of the explosion lifted him right off the men's room toilet, causing him to spill his beer.

THE FOOD PANTRY was blown to smithereens.

HARLEY'S BARN BURNED to the ground, and Tina Turner and the Jesus Cow with it.

CHAPTER 32

I t was such a mess. There was so much to sort. Klute served
up a fresh lawsuit, as did the village and any number of terrified citizens. There were endless meetings with Sloan and the
International Talent Management team. Lloyd's of London took
depositions for days, and it was not entirely clear that everything—
or anything—would be covered. There was hope that the natural
disaster clause might be circumnavigated, as this was clearly a disaster of the most unnatural sort, but there was also some concern that payment would still be withheld because the village had
transferred ownership of the water tower to Harley and thus the
illegal storage of toxic (to say nothing of profoundly flammable)
materials was technically his responsibility and violated numerous
clauses.

After Sloan released him from the final meeting, Harley went
straight to the Kwik Pump, bought one of those dollar-off Old

Milwaukee twenty-four-packs, returned to his kitchen, and started drinking. He couldn't even find it in himself to summon Billy. He was lonely. He was devastated. He couldn't see his way forward. He had gone against his better judgment, sought revenge, and the thing had swallowed him whole.

And failed at love.

Again.

He was becoming bleary, and the beer wasn't numbing the pain but rather deepening it. He was feeling sorry for himself, maudlin over his own state, and for the first time in his life he didn't care to go on. His phone kept ringing. He dropped it on the floor and stomped it with his heel. He wanted only to escape.

Taking the box of beer from the refrigerator he went to the Silverado, spared from the flames along with his house and garage. At first it wouldn't start, but he wiggled the battery terminals and then it took. Leaving the truck to idle, he went back into the house, up to his bedroom, and deep into the back of his closet, where from beneath a pile of socks he withdrew his Bible case, hand-tooled by his mother and given him—with the crackling new Bible in it—for his fifth birthday as a reward for learning how to read. Dropping the Bible case on the seat he wove his way out through the blackened yard and around the remains of merchandise booths. When he got out to County Road M, he drove up past the twisted wreckage of the water tower, out across the overpass, beneath which the traffic flew back and forth with all disregard. There was no sign of activity in Clover Blossom Estates. Klute's Hummer was nowhere to be seen, and the empty houses looked even more forlorn now, decorated as they were with all those sagging banners advertising services Klute had never been allowed to provide.

The gate to Meg's junkyard was closed, and the boom of the crane was motionless. Even in his fogginess, Harley knew where Meg was—down at St. Jude's with Carolyn and Mindy, setting up a temporary food pantry in a shipping container on the parking lot. He felt another wave of despair and took another suck on his Old Milwaukee.

He drove on, silent and forlorn, until he came to the old abandoned farmhouse where he had gone to Sunday-morning meetings as a boy. Harley pulled the truck over to the shoulder, pulled his Bible from its case, walked through the rank grass to the building, and stared in through the window. The plaster ceilings were sagging. He could see mildew on the walls and porcupine poop on the curled linoleum. He could also see himself in a straight-backed chair, singing the meaningful hymns, bowing his head in prayer, rereading his chosen Bible verses for the week, readying himself to give testimony, his shoes polished and shining.

How clean-limbed it all seemed, that simple faith. He thought of his mother and his father and their quiet dedication to charity and humility, and the extrapolations required to go from there to a birthmarked calf worth millions and the conflagration of all he had known.

It made his heart hurt, and he wanted another beer. He returned to the truck, twisted another bottle open, ground into third gear, and lurched forward.

He drove until he came to Five Mile Road. He sat at the stop sign a moment before looking up and realizing he was at the old Nicolet Place. *Mindy's* place. The F-250 was parked by the granary, but the Norton was gone, its tarp in a heap on the ground.

Food pantry, he remembered. *Food pantry. Helping out.*

He felt the tears rising.

Then his emotions swung the other way. He leaned out the window. Flung the beer bottle to the asphalt, watched the shards skitter through the foam. Straightened up. Grabbed the wheel with both hands. He was done dithering. Done letting events direct him rather than the other way around. He'd drive to St. Jude's. Lay it on the line. Give Mindy some Bad Johnny Cash. Let her know he was ready to hit life running. Split for Panama.

Get that damn motorcycle ride.

He turned right, and headed south, back toward Swivel. On either side the Big Swamp stretched out, a morass of cut-grass, cattails, swamp water, ooze, and bubbling methane. Harley bore down in his focus, determined to keep his truck centered on the road so as not to wind up in the swamp, which festered right up to the edge of the road on both sides. It was dusk now, the sun laying a final red line across the horizon as he approached McCracken Hill, which would take him up and away from the swamp and into the last hilly stretch toward Swivel.

Right at the base of the hill, barely into the climb, the truck coughed and bucked, roared ahead again, then died. Harley stuffed the clutch and twisted the key. The starter wound but the engine wouldn't fire. He turned the key off, then on again. Still nothing. Because of the grade, the truck was losing momentum rapidly, so Harley popped it out of gear, steered it quietly to the shoulder, and set the emergency brake.

Lifting the hood, he waggled the carburetor flap, jiggled the battery cables, and tried the starter again. Nothing. Fetching the ball-peen hammer he crawled under the truck to smack the solenoid. After a few whacks, he shimmied out and tried the starter again.

Still nothing. He'd have to call Billy, then. Tow the thing home. Foggily he fished through his pockets for his cell phone, but found nothing. He slapped his pants fore and aft, slow in his tipsy concentration. He searched the truck cab, the dash, under the seats, ran his hand in the crack behind the seat and the backrest. He shook his head as if to clear it but couldn't recall where he might have left the phone. Then he remembered dropping it to the floor. Smashing it.

There would be no calling for help, then. *Probably for the best,* he thought. *Last thing I need is the constable coming to find me out here in this kinda shape and my truck engine still warm.*

Okay, he thought. *Walking.*

Leaning into the grade he imagined Mindy seeing him in this condition of drunkenness and dedication, interpreting it as a sign of the depth of his love, and relenting on the spot. He had this heroic vision then, her throwing her arms around him, drawing deeply of his scent, kissing him with tears in her eyes, and then she would kick-start that Norton, and they would ride, ride, ride.

With sunset, strands of fog had begun to drift across the swamp, and a few threads hung over McCracken Hill and the road ahead. He was about halfway up the hill when the glow appeared, a white hint of shine, growing and growing.

The glow waxed steadily, expanding and brightening with ethereal constance. It was a good night for the dispersion of light, the fog strands thickening in the humid evening air, the heaviness of everything serving to muffle all but Harley's footfalls. There was no sound associating itself with the swelling light, and this heightened Harley's susceptibility to the idea that it was more than headlights hoving. In the silence, everything seemed premonitory. Despite himself, Harley felt a surge in his chest. A little *what-if* ticklishness.

Maybe it was the beer, but for now he was willing to turn himself over to hope and belief. In his parlous spiritual state he managed to convince himself of at least the possibility that the glow was not that of a vehicle but rather of a nimbus backlighting the genuine Son of God, that the rapture had come, that it was northbound on Five Mile Road, and that if Harley kept walking, he and Jesus would meet right at the crest of McCracken Hill. Or perhaps it was the Virgin Mary inbound. Perhaps Mary Ann Van Hoof hadn't been the crazy one.

He knew one thing: he was ready for something other than what this dirty world had to offer.

Maybe it was time to believe again.

"I believe," slurred Harley aloud, "I am fifty yards shy of meeting Jesus."

He did not hurry. He walked stolidly, with study and purpose, as a man does when forced to think of balance and foot placement. But as the light grew, his gut grew more and more weightless, and as he stumped toward the luminous horizon he imagined what it would be to top that hill and see the light bust wide open to reveal the real-dang Jesus—not some pariedolic fake Jesus in a nimbus, a broad, encompassing halo of light, a portable aurora borealis with maybe a smattering of sparks, Jesus there beneath it with his arms spread wide as a lake, returned to lift all the good-hearted and weary from their struggle, to levitate Harley out of a world of dead cows and twisted metal and ash and scorched dreams and charred hearts, and Harley had this image full and thrumming in his head, and then the light exploded into view and rather than the Second Coming the mystery broke as a single headlight popped over the horizon, followed by the sound of a motor, and it was Mindy on her Norton.

And Harley thought, *Well, that will do.*

He staggered leftward toward the centerline to wave her down, but she had gone deep into her tuck, the way she always said she loved to come off McCracken Hill, and so focused was she that she did not see him, but in the fading light Harley saw another body behind her, a man spooned tight to the curve of her back and gripping her with all his might, and as the two of them zoomed past, Harley recognized Yonni's ponytail blown straight back in the wind. They locked eyes in the gloaming and in that split second he took a sliver of comfort from the fact that the cartoonist looked terrified.

And then he felt his heart evaporate like cotton candy in a blast furnace, and he spun on his heel, and went stumbling back down the hill.

HE STOPPED AT the truck for another dose of beer. To the north, Mindy's taillight was a patch of red fuzz in the fog, dwindling and dwindling until the glow was gone and with it the last echoes of the engine and then all Harley could hear was the sound of mosquitos and his own heart thumping and the gurgle of the beers as he drained them one after the other.

HE STEPPED INTO the ditch and fell immediately face-first into the swamp water. It was lukewarm and amniotic slick. There was the sensation of larvae. Had it been colder, perhaps it would have shocked him back to sense, but it was medium soup, viscous with frog eggs. He staggered to his feet and spit. The water drained from his head down, sluicing and spattering around his shins. The air smelled of salt and rot. He loosed a reverberant belch.

It was tough going but he operated with the plodding

determination common to drunks and, for that matter, pilgrims. When his feet stuck in the muck, he pulled himself forward by gripping the saw grass hummocks, and soon his hands were a razored, bloody mess and his thighs burned. It was dark now, his only guidance the bulk of dark shapes and darker shapes and the reflection of starlight here and there in the water. Mosquitos came at him from all angles. At one point he stumbled into a channel where the footing was solid beneath the mud and he made good progress but soon the watercourse became choked with cattails and he plunged into them, the velvet-brown tops batting him lightly about the head, the spear-point leaves jabbing him painfully even as their whisking gave him a temporary reprieve from the mosquitos.

He broke through into a placid pond where the stars were so accurately reflected between strips of dissipating fog he became disoriented regarding the position of the heavens for a moment before he stumbled forward waist deep into the water and set the stars to rippling, as if the cosmos were cast in gelatin. As he crossed the open water, the mosquitos returned in a fuzzy swarm, whirring and jabbing, and he inhaled a few. Kneeling, he scooped muck from the pond bottom and smeared it through his hair and on his face and neck and arms. It helped. The mosquitos still buzzed but did not land. The far side of the pond was bordered by a floating bog. When he reached it he threw himself forward and into a half-twist Fosbury flop, landing on his back and using his elbows to crab himself out of the water and onto the bog, which undulated gently beneath him in ever-receding echoes of his movement. He began settling almost immediately, the water rising around his body as it pressed into the bog. Above him the fog had cleared and he saw all the constellations.

He remembered his Bible, then, in the pickup with the empty bottles.

Crap, he thought. *I was gonna read that.*

HE FIGURED THEY'D never find him, which was fine. For the first time since he didn't know how long, he was at peace. Now and then one of the mosquito horde would find its way past the mud pack and he would feel the itchy pinch of the proboscis penetrating his skin, but he was beyond swatting now. He felt peace was within reach. As another mosquito bored in somewhere above his ankle, he wondered idly how much blood a single mosquito might extract, and by virtue of extrapolation, how many mosquitos it would require to bleed him dry. *The things we don't know*, he thought. For a passing moment, he felt fuzzy amusement at the idea of the mosquitos catching a buzz off the beer in his veins. Then he caught sight of the moon, which drew him to focus simply on the apparently infinite universe framed in a saw grass fringe, a perspective that led him to think of Billy and what he'd said about being beneath it all or above it all, and then he recalled the image—it played like a brief video clip—of Mindy flopping on her back in the barn to admire the frosty nails the first time she visited, and how keen his hope and hunger had been in that moment, and how it could all have come to this. From crystalline hope to mucky failure. *So* many *failures*, he thought. So many opportunities to be bold, and it was possible tonight's excursion would be the bravest thing he'd ever done—and even that driven by the twin catalysts of beer and heartbreak.

The mosquitos kept working at his above-water bits and he found himself caring less and less. Soon, enough water had seeped into the depression formed by his head that it ran in and blocked his ears. A gurgle, and the sound of the mosquitos muffled into nothingness, although they spun above him now in a cloud sufficient to dim the stars. *So odd,* he thought, as the last three beers he chugged began to take real hold, *what things come to. How a guy might live like I did and then wind up like this.*

The water was tickling his nostrils now.

He'd miss the burn barrel sessions. The stirring of the flames, the dance of the orange sparks rising. He'd miss Billy and Billy's declaratives. The Waylon Jennings wisdom.

He wondered what lay ahead. What he would find. There was peace in that too. After a life split between utter belief and just wondering—and even more time spent just living and not thinking about it at all—he'd find out soon what the deal was. Or find out nothing. This too, he decided, was acceptable.

He had lost track of time. He couldn't figure out how long he'd been there. The mosquitos coated him like writhing gray velvet and he noticed he could no longer feel their sting, not even when they bit his lips, and he blinked them from his eyes and tried to determine if the stars had changed position since he took to this mushy mattress, just how far the earth had rotated since then, and gazing up as he felt the water rising and closing in around more of his body, it slowly dawned on him that it wasn't about the earth spinning but the universe spinning, and if you let yourself go, if you surrendered focus, opened your soul to the void, you could begin to sense the spin, the vortex, the whole thing funneling, whirlpooling, the stars slipping and twisting and skidding and blurring, the moon a fatter stripe of white, the whole cosmic works corkscrewing through time, drawing to a center and picking up speed, and it occurred to Harley that this was the proverbial bright light and there was Billy pausing to grin with a beer at his lips, and Dad kneeling with his Sunday-go-to-meeting shoe polish rag, and now Ma and a fresh-frosted birthday cake held toward him in red-checked oven gloves and now throughout it all rising and stitching through the stars like a green, glowing asp an infinite ivy tattoo, and the ivy turning red and knotting itself into a barbed-wire burr, and then came a whooshing in his ears, and yet the greater the velocity, the more kinetic the feeling, the more peace, the more stillness, the soft surrender, and right near the end he was pretty sure he was given the answer: it came in the form of a question and it issued from a calf curled upon straw of gold and beside it a beautiful bald-headed child; he reached out his hand and he felt the warmth just beyond his fingertips, then everything went dark and was quite simply nothing at all.

CHAPTER 33

Later, Billy told him how it had all played out.

Intent in her tuck, Mindy hadn't noticed the lovelorn drunkard Harley gazing wobbily from the mist upon the opposite shoulder, but Yonni had, and when they passed the abandoned truck he put two and two together and when they dismounted outside the granary, he convinced Mindy to call Billy.

Billy arrived to find the truck but no Harley. Then he saw the Bible case and bottles. When he did a U-turn to head back for town, his headlights illuminated the crushed weeds where Harley had done his initial face-plant in the ditch. Billy, fearing Harley had wandered off drunk into the swamp—which indeed he had— summoned the fire department.

It was Boober Johnson—using the thermal imager to scan the swamp for stray muskrats while everyone milled around the abandoned truck—who spotted Harley's body glowing phosphorescent white on the screen like a passed-out ghost. The chief said it was "ironical" that were it not for Harley buying the thermal imager in the first place, they might never have found him. The chief was also pleased that in dragging Harley from the swamp, he was able to exercise all the amphibious abilities of the Argo.

HARLEY WAS UNRESPONSIVE but breathing when they reached him, swollen and mosquito bitten beyond recognition. He spent a week recovering in the Clearwater hospital. During this time Harley refused all visitors save Billy. He felt the swamp incident was the final act requiring a community apology, and was overcome with embarrassment when he thought of actually returning to town or setting foot in the Kwik Pump or showing his face at the fire department.

Upon his discharge he learned Mary Magdalene Jankowski had visited the hospital chapel every day to light a candle and offer a prayer on his behalf.

WHEN HE WAS back home, one of his first visitors was Sloan.

"Best news first: Lloyd's of London will pay up."

"But I thought—"

"Turns out Vance Hansen failed to have the paperwork notarized. As a result, the tower was still technically village property—you'll receive your payout.

"Regarding Tina Turner's ova, harvesting was—er—*interrupted*, but for those we did obtain, we have reached an agreement we think you will find most gratifying." He showed Harley a number, and Harley figured *gratifying* would be one word, yes.

"Regarding the remains of the calf—which amounted to some

scorched leather wrapped around a fireproof ceramic tracking chip—we have reached an agreement with the Vatican we think you will find even more gratifying." He showed Harley another number. "The remains will be preserved in the Vatican Museums. They are already winging their way to the pope.

"The reality show ratings have skyrocketed, and the exploding water tower actually triggered a bidding war over the film and book rights. That woman storing all that oil up there was the best thing that ever happened to you. If this thing had wound down of its own accord, you'd be looking at a fraction of the profit."

Harley didn't know how to feel about this.

So he decided to feel okay about it.

EPILOGUE

T hanks to good fortune arising from bad, Harley was able to fund the replacement of the sewer, the repaving of Main Street, and the rebuilding of the food pantry. He completed the buy-out of Klute Sorensen, hired a fleet of bulldozers, and converted half of Clover Blossom Estates to a land trust, a park, and community gardens. The other half he kept for himself, rebuilding the old fence lines so soon they were filled with mice and songbirds as before, and so that he could once again bale his own hay with his father's baler.

He furthermore sowed the renewed fields with a helluva bunch of clover.

CAROLYN AND KLUTE eloped to a small town in Central America. Carolyn pretty much had to, as the EPA, ATF, and several other acronymic branches of government were very eager to speak to her about the record number of environmental infractions she'd racked up. Klute, feeling freed from the burden of his ancestors, accompanied Carolyn to a weekly pottery class and took up surfing.

SLOAN OFFERED BILLY a job with International Talent Management, and he accepted, moving with his cats to L.A.

Six months later Harley's phone rang. It was Billy.

"I'm getting married."

"Whoa!"

"I'd like you to be the best man."

"Why, Billy—I'd be honored."

"Yah, me too."

"So who's the lucky girl?"

"It's not a girl, son," said Billy. "It's Sloan."

THE BEEFERS SURVIVED the fire, and one day when Harley was unloading hay for them, he heard a sound. He turned, and there before him was a little girl with her head full of curls. She looked familiar, but he couldn't place her. Then he looked up the driveway and saw her mother, waving and smiling.

"I'm all better," said the girl.

"Cured," said her mother, and now Harley knew: it was the girl who had come to hug the Jesus Cow that very first day.

"It was the Jesus Cow," said the girl, and her mother nodded.

"Well . . . and maybe the doctors? And the radiation? And the chemotherapy?"

Harley said it gently.

The girl smiled. Harley thought back to the day he drove drunk to stare in the window of the meeting house. How as a little boy he sat in that straight-backed chair, solid in his faith.

He looked back at the little girl, but she and her mother were climbing into a car, and Reverend Gary was driving.

I don't have it, thought Harley, *but I'm happy they do.*

YONNI DIDN'T LAST, but Mindy's metalworking business thrived, boosted in the early days by online sales of "Jesus Cow R.I.P." crosses and calf silhouettes fashioned from water tower remains, of which the village was pleased to be rid. In time Mindy and Harley would again cross paths at the Kwik Pump and resume neighborly discourse, but neither was in a rush. Driving past Mindy's place in late August, Harley spied a square of freshly fenced pasture, and, grazing within, a trio of beefers.

OF ALL THE checks Harley wrote in the wake of Swivel's grand conflagration, none was sweeter than the one that paid off the mortgage of the Boomler Catholic Church, the cascade effect being that Bishop Burkle took his deconsecrating eye off of St. Jude's, a move which ensured its existence in perpetuity and allowed for a ceremony to be held there one year later, in which Harley Jackson and Margaret Magdalene Jankowski were married by Father Carl. Billy Tripp and Carolyn Sawchuck served as best man and maid of honor, although Carolyn rejected the specific appellation on principle and was forced to attend the ceremony via Skype due to outstanding legal issues.

During the dance that evening, Father Carl got a bit deeper into the champagne than the bishop might have wished, and took Harley aside to remind him that as he was unbaptized, the Catholic church classified his marriage to Meg as a "disparity of cult." Overhearing this, Billy gave Father Carl a high five, and asked when he could join.

Following a brief honeymoon touring the shrines and grottoes of Wisconsin (Harley splurged on a used camper for the Silverado), the newlyweds returned to Swivel and set up housekeeping at Harley's place, with Meg's scrap yard being converted to strictly commercial purposes.

There were those who said Harley and Meg were silly to stay in Swivel, what with their riches, but in this they were of one mind: here they were at home, and here they would remain. Harley rejoined the fire department and doubled the size of his beef herd, but with Billy and his cats gone to California, he saw no reason to get another milk cow. He learned to run the car crusher and tow truck, but when he and Meg went out in the junk truck to winch some rusted beater from the blackberry canes, she always did the driving.

And so it came to pass that on a Christmas Eve not so very long ago Harley Jackson found himself rumbling off to midnight mass in the passenger seat of a Ford straight truck stacked with two squashed minivans and a flattened dump rake. As Meg worked the split shifter, Harley considered her profile in the glow of the dash and felt a fullness in his heart. Then he slid low in his seat so he might press his cheek against the chill window and look up to all the stars above.

Low overhead, he thought.

Glory Hallelujah, low overhead.

ACKNOWLEDGMENTS

FIRST AND FOREMOST, to my parents—anything decent is because of them; anything else is not their fault.

Lisa for keeping me in deadlines, Jennifer for enforcing them, and a special thanks to the assistants who maintain the chain. Alissa and Blakeley for worry-free management. Dave for webwork. Matt B. for math. Scranton. Dan and Lisa and staff for artful solitude. Dean Bakopoulos for an early (and humane) insight. Dan Schaefer, professor and chair of Animal Sciences, University of Wisconsin, Madison, for calf facts. Neighbor Ginny for faithful fact-checking. Racy's and Mister Happy, still grinding after all these years. Matt Marion for ongoing typing assignments. Ben in Ohio. Colorado blended and extendeds. McDowell family. Mi familia de Panamá. TFD and Emergicare for allowing me to carry one of their pagers when I'm home. Frank, Mags, the Joynt and Taylor's kitchen table crew (and from high school, Mrs. R.).

Vern and Kyle, because Kids These Days.

Anneliese, Amy, and Jane. For real life.

And a special gratitude salute for my nonfictional hometown of "Nobbern," always and forever framing my narrative.

ABOUT THE AUTHOR

MICHAEL PERRY is a humorist, radio host, songwriter, and the *New York Times* bestselling author of several nonfiction books, including *Visiting Tom* and *Population: 485*. He lives in rural Wisconsin with his family and can be found online at www.sneezingcow.com.